THE INVERANNAN ASSIGNMENT

David Clark Keachie

ISBN: 9781983223594

Published by Amazon KDP

Copyright @ David Clark Keachie 2018

For Jacqueline, Neve and Adam, always

With great thanks to Aileen Sherry and John Young

Chapter One

Homecoming

It takes me over fifteen minutes in the changing cubicle to get my blood-encrusted shirt off. The multiple wounds on my back – taped up quickly and apparently badly, had opened on the journey; the clumsily attached bandages having also either already fallen off or been removed by me when I foolishly thought the stitches had held. I remove the offending garment inch by inch, progressively detaching each caked and agonising laceration, pouring mineral water from my bottle over my back to try and release the scabs and to momentarily feel the numbness of icy water on my skin.

That done, my body beaded with sweat and shivering from the pain, I wearily mop myself with the cleaner parts of the bloodied shirt and put on the new, plain long sleeved black t-shirt. Leaving the store and avoiding the gaze of the changing room assistant, I head back to Queen Street Station to await my train back north to Mharisaig. I had bought the black t-shirt figuring that if it was warm in the train carriage, I could take off my jacket without anyone noticing the blood seepage.

As I enter the briefly delayed train, I realise that this may have been wishful thinking as the carriage is as cold as the outside, nearly. Barely into autumn and Scotland has already lost the feeling of summer, the leaves on the trees just about still there but the cold air putting them on notice.

The train rolls out of Glasgow, its meandering rail clatter diminishing as we leave the crossed tracks of the urban sprawl and onto the northern straight towards Fort William. I'm planning to get a bus home from there; there's bound to be a few running on a Saturday, even if they are hours apart. Arrangements have been made with both sets of employers I now seem to temporarily have, for me to recuperate for a week or two.

The carriage has a few fellow travellers, none of them on their own; a combination of holidaymakers and a couple of families with tablets and bags of food and drinks for the kids for the long trip. I'd decided to go this way home to just get there without fuss; it might not be the best or quickest from where I started or even the cheapest, but I needed a low-stress way and this fitted the bill.

1

I find my earbuds in my rucksack and start to listen to a playlist with some random calming indie stuff, Bon Iver, Birdie; a few others I selected a month or so ago when in a chilled mood. It's reassuring and I try to sleep with my head on the window, cushioned by my rucksack; this doesn't work well and I can't get comfortable so I lie forward on the pull-down table but it's not robust enough to be leant on. Right now, I think, I'd kill for a bed; a tiny pang of irony hits me but I repress it immediately; no point on dwelling on things.

It takes the best part of two hours to get to the half-way point, Crianlarich, having passed a few road-edged lochs and travelled through the more scenic western hills and valleys, dropping off and picking up as it flowed mellifluously into the higher ground, up to Tyndrum where it inexplicably stops for five minutes after picking up a group of what seems to be Spanish or French student backpackers; I can barely hear their voices over the music and they head forward to the first carriage to, I suppose, try and get seats together.

Realising I'm hungry after the trip south and having had only a sandwich and a KitKat since I left, I wonder if there's anything to buy on the train. It's not a long train so I guess they don't have a café; maybe a trolley will come round sometime. I hunt in my rucksack side compartment and find my mints, stuck together and altogether unhygienic so they go back in and I suck my fingers to get the sticky residue off. The swelling in my hands hasn't gone down much either, so I get the painkillers from my jacket and swill three down with my water, the last of my cheap meal-deal from earlier.

I hold my rucksack into my chest and lean onto it, my head now on the back of the vacant seat in front of me; I suppose I sleep then until the train lurches me to life. I turn and try to see if we're there but it's just a halt; the other platform has a station which looks like it's a restaurant now. I turn back to see the sign and it says Spean Bridge, so thankfully not far now. Another half-hour and I can get a bus home.

The train goes rapidly through the last stretch and we're there; we get in as the tourist train pulls away on the north-west route, half filled with Harry Potter fans as it goes to the famous viaduct. I'd wanted to visit there a few years ago but my parents hadn't got around to arranging it; doesn't matter now, I think to myself.

Leaving the station, I look for a signpost but instead see a supermarket and a bus stop to the side. I check the timetable and my shoulders slump; the bus has come here from Glasgow so I could just have got that. It's fifteen minutes till it arrives and I tell myself that I prefer trains anyway; I head into the supermarket to grab another meal deal and I've eaten it by the time the bus arrives and I'm on it, heading for Mharisaig for some rest and deep thought.

The bus takes the best part of an hour, back north but then forking westwards, eventually to a fold in the valley between two anonymous lines of Munros; Mharisaig is a village which everyone has heard of and thinks they might have visited, but haven't. Workers live there, the coast and forestry close enough to employ them but not close enough to make the place attractive, not for tourists, at least. It's the living definition of the one the highland clearances missed, we used to half-joke. There are some nicer houses there, mines included and some for those who like their boltholes devoid of day-trippers, but mostly just a few cul-de-sacs filled with council three-bedrooms, built for the families who made their living in manual labour. My parents were originally from Mharisaig, having been away working in various places across the UK until having me and returning to let me grow in rural idyll, or what their rose-tinted intentions were.

My journey almost over, I'm off and standing on the grass embankment as the bus rolls away to scenery better; I take a breath and lift my rucksack onto one shoulder, avoiding direct contact with the cuts but sore as hell anyway. I walk determinedly along the pathway, past the quick-running burn which then disappears underground to a gully beneath the disused train tracks from the long-closed Mharisaig train station. There's the short stretch of similar, mostly well-kept single-storey cottages, a few now holiday homes but mostly locals still there from way back; I try to think who stays here that I might know when a voice startles the hell out of me.

'Hope you're not back to start trouble.'

Still jangling from the fright, I look over to my side and see an old neighbour, Bobby Ghillies, standing with his rough Collie dog. He waves a hello and walks towards me.

'How are you Bobby, hope the wife's OK?' I ask him, shaking his hand and getting a sharp, jagging pain in my bruised knuckles.

3

He notices me wince and glances at my swollen hand, then up to me.

'Hmm - she's not any better tempered anyway' he shakes his head and looks down at the dog. 'She gets some Homecare now, so I can get out for a walk without feeling guilty.' I'm not sure what to say, so I nod and ruffle the dog's fur at the neck.

'Have you been away working - you look at bit rough?' He asks, leaning back and looking at the cut on my cheek and the light swelling at my eyes.

'Yep, been away working after I finished uni; ran into trouble and out of clothes on the way.' I tell him, shifting my rucksack to try and get less pain. 'All sorted now though Bobby; I'll get home and cleaned up then I'll be A1.'

Bobby looks dubious about my assurances of being fine but changes the subject tactfully. 'Are your mum and dad still enjoying the sun?' I think for a moment about what to say and Bobby now looks uncomfortable, like he wished he hadn't asked. 'They're doing great Bobby, living the dream and the Vida loca.' I smile to reassure him all was well.

His face moved back from concerned to cheery again. 'Aye, good to see you though, even looking like that. Away and get cleaned up, your stinking the whole place up.' He laughs and steers the dog away towards the T-junction which leads to the park and my old primary school.

I don't look back or respond, just walk as quickly as my aches allow, along Station Road and onto the side of the road. There isn't a pavement between here and my house, just a grass verge which in spring lights up with daffodils and tulips. Even though it isn't raining now, the ground is boggy, and my trainers aren't watertight, so, too late, I feel the cold water seep in and move onto the tarmac road.

The trees across the road are occasionally split by the larger private houses at the edge of the village, each hidden by wall or greenery. I used to know all the people who lived there, when I had the paper round in the village, cycling or walking to do my deliveries before school; trying to raise money for some concert or whatever my impoverished state required help with. There is a distant sound of a power saw, probably the Forestry guys taking down a cut of trees at the last section of the pine plantation. They do this regularly and with the village being beside a farmed forest environment; it's a familiar sound to me.

Five minutes later, I stand at the gate of my house and look at the garden and front door; I exhale wearily as I realise how unkempt it has become since me and my parents left. I had promised my mum and dad that I'd try to maintain the building - or at the least keep it half-decent; in an idle moment, I even had drawn plans, with best intentions to formalise them and convert one of the outbuildings into an office. That was as far as I got before reality bit that I hadn't the funds to make it happen and I had to find a real job; my dreams of working from home were just that. I see there's a broken window upstairs in the dormer, just one pane; hopefully an accident and not thrown stones, especially if it was someone with a propensity for breaking and entering.

I start through the gate and use the Yale key, pushing open the old, slatted wooden door which leaks when the rain drives into its face. It's swollen more than usual, so takes a jarring shove to get it moving; behind the door is a small pile of damp mail, which I ignore and head towards the kitchen.

'Aahhhh!!' I scream, as a wood pigeon cracks its wings and goes berserk inside the long hallway. Flailing my arms at it, I slip back on the mail, fall back onto the heavy hall radiator and, with a ringing skelp on the back on my head, lose consciousness.

Chapter Two

The Insider

The first time I came to The Insider offices, I had felt unsettled when I realised that although more modern than I expected, they were in no way inspirational. In my mind, the interior would have been a literary labyrinth, lined with cabinets of old editions, folders and the flotsam of Fleet Street gone past. In reality, it was a fairly typical rundown example of London office space, showing all the signs of underinvestment and shabby maintenance. Filing cabinets were used instead of dividers, leaving the place an odd combination of open plan and self-constructed fortress offices.

The Insider is an independent and moderately respected news agency, operating by the grace of private owners and feeding mainly the broadsheets with fillers and articles to draw upon when their own resources were stretched. After starting there as a summer intern while I'd been at university, I then did some freelance work for them, but after singularly failing to provide them with enough quality work from Scotland to justify my employment, I had had to face the unfortunate truth, that I needed to temporarily live and work in London. Thankfully, the few articles I did manage to submit had been well received and after some extensive editing, been published or sold to their satisfaction.

So, here I am, returning to receive - hopefully - a series of assignments which will keep me going financially and start to make a name for myself.

After a few attempts, I had finally managed to convince a group of house-sharers to admit me to their over-occupied property in an estate in Southwark, nowhere near where I wanted to be and with a damn sight more police sirens at night than I would have liked. That, and the mind-boggling rent for one room had launched me into London living - I had been there two days and felt vaguely itchy all the time thanks largely to the mattress, despite my addition of two layers of undersheet, which was my best efforts at getting some lining between me and the offending item.

I had left the flat earlier and went to Starbucks for a coffee and some overpriced cake, delicious though it was. Using my brand new pass, I head into the offices of The Insider and along the corridor; taking my seat at the less than generous workstation I'd been allocated.

'Hullo young man' says George Adams, leaning over his edge cubicle. George is in his late fifties, heavy but fit looking despite a recent heart scare. He's one those people who present a cheery demeanour when you first meet him which unfortunately but quickly disperses to reveal a truly dull personality. I had spent a few days with him when I first visited The Insider as an intern and initially wondered why other colleagues were scattering when he neared their desks. It didn't take me long to figure out that he was both boring and hugely long-winded, so as soon as he hove into view I profess my lateness, get up with my notepad and quicken past him. 'Sorry George, I'm late for Billie - give you a shout when I'm finished.' I try to sound friendly and look sympathetic as I give a backwards wave and turn the corner to the meeting rooms. I hear an invite being called behind me but already plan to leave by the other stairway to avoid George after the meeting.

I knock and go into the meeting room - I am indeed accidentally late and the assignments are already been discussed and allocated. It's really animated, seems to be some jostling for the best work, so I can't even apologise. I don't see anyone I really know except Emma, a staff photographer and Billie, who commissions the assignments and does most of the final edits before the work goes out. Billie waves me into a seat with only a momentary glance in my direction. The assignment they have been arguing about goes to a slim guy with a nervy, shrill voice. Billie is telling him that it's not necessary for him to take one of these jobs as they are close together, or close enough anyway. Emma looks like she's ready to burst with annoyance at someone and I'm happy to sit at the back and watch.

'That's mine then' he says, kicking up from his seat and leaving the room immediately after grabbing the file from Billie.

'Simon!' Billie shouts after him. 'We need to discuss this!' She takes a deep, calming breath and lifts the next file.

'Adam and Emma, looks you're going North too unless I can get Simon to do what he's fucking told and do both.' She leans over and hands me the file which I open and read through the précis. It's an interview piece with a colourful character, part former military man, part attempted highland laird. He's apparently transformed the fortunes of a rundown shooting estate over the past couple of years, lots of new jobs and innovations - a happy story for a Sunday broadsheet supplement or a magazine. The immediate drawback is that the shooting estate is in Wester Ross, even further north than Mharisaig.

It means me travelling back to the highlands of Scotland, despite spending a small fortune - in my terms anyway - getting to London, renting a flat and all the other expenses, not to mention psychologically cutting the cord with Scotland. 'No problem' I nevertheless say, as positively as possible, standing and heading for the door after a nod from Billie, who was moving onto the next allocation. Emma, the photojournalist who I had met first when I did my internship here, left with me. As I closed the door quietly, the meeting continued without anyone saying goodbye or acknowledging me.

'Is everyone normally this charming' I ask Emma as we stand outside, the chatter resuming without us. 'God', she exhaled, 'At least you missed Simon's tantrum about being underpaid and never getting the jobs he wants. He took that one even though it was just beside ours, Billie was going to give them both to us, but he was like a dog with a bone about it.' Emma was good company, she'd met me briefly in Glasgow when doing an assignment with another journo last year, I'd helped her with a couple of points of local knowledge and some of the spadework and we'd got on well. I'd thought about asking her to stay overnight at that time, but I guess she'd read the clumsy signals and as a result mentioned a boyfriend in London. Even with my record for misreading situations, I'd understood enough to back off and keep things on a friendly professional level.

Emma started to walk back through the main office. 'Erm, hold on' I say, 'I'm going to head down this way. I'll be back, later on, to see about our journey to the ever-sunny Highlands. I've got a few errands to run.' Emma gives me a brief nod as her mobile rings and she answers it. I try not to gaze at her - an effort on my part - and go back along the corridor to take the fire stairs down to the road. Outside, I make for the main road back to the tube station. I need to get something to clean the room and I'm undecided about hiring some kind of steam cleaner or just buying something from the supermarket. I get to the tube and head out on the Jubilee line without waiting too long. I'd never understood why Londoners complain about the tube system, they need to try getting home from Edinburgh or Glasgow after midnight, it's either an expensive taxi or taking a chance at a bus station that looks like a scene from Blade Runner.

Especially now that I had been assigned a few days away, I decide on the cheap option for cleaning my room, so I go and buy some sprays, foams and a sponge from the supermarket, then walk back to the house. I spend the rest of the morning cleaning the disgusting room and wishing that I'd bought gloves. By 1 o'clock the room at least smells cleaner and I've made myself feel slightly better by using all the limited supply of hot water produced by the ancient boiler, so no showers for the rest of House Beautiful. I leave the window open to try and let the carpets and curtains dry a little and head back to the office. As I go to leave, I realise that one of my flatmates is in the kitchen. Looking in, I see that he is sitting with headphones in, reading a red-top paper and eating toast. I think about speaking to him, but having nothing in particular to say, I leave without interrupting.

Back at the office, I meet Emma and find a cubicle as far away from George as I can. We spend some time planning the assignment - what type of interviews we might want, ideally who we should speak to get them, types of photo and agree on an estimate of word count. If we leave early the next day, we estimate that we could have the piece researched and the content built in two to three days. I could write it up before Friday and be ready for the next one on Monday again. Pleased with our planning work and content in our ignorance of any pitfalls or delays, we walk along to Billie's office for the OK.

'Hi Billie' She looks up and welcomes us into the chairs beside her desk. 'How are you getting on with the Scotland job then - sorry I didn't get a chance to talk earlier? That little shit Simon Conner had wound everyone up again.' Billie looked a fair bit calmer than this morning, her normally peaceful nature reasserted.

'We're doing fine, got a schedule for you to look over.' I tell her, passing over the file. I notice her head move back slightly and for the first time I realise that I must smell strongly of cleaning fluids.

'Sorry about the disinfectant smell' I apologise, 'my penthouse apartment on the river isn't quite ready yet, so I've had to move into a small cupboard in Southwark. The butler still hasn't turned up either, so I've had to pitch in with the housework.'

Billie and Emma both look bemused, my Scottish deadpan humour missing the mark yet again.

'Well, we're very glad to have you here, even if you have to slum it.'

We sit and run through the plan, Billie just adds a few pointers on what to ask about; she always seems to have time to know the assignments intimately despite running dozens at a time.

'Well, you kids have a good time, hope you are staying somewhere nice and cheap?' Billie asks us.

'I'll take my cleaning stuff just in case' I say as we head back to the cubicle.

Emma takes the lead on booking our accommodation, asking for two single rooms, not that I had any other preconceptions on that front. She gets us a decent price - we get an allowance but it doesn't cover much so we make sure that costs are kept down to maximise our profit on the assignment. I take a couple of sideways glances at Emma while she calls around the hotels. She's in her mid-twenties and has dyed her short hair slightly reddish since we last worked together. I know that she runs a lot, she had her Asics trainers and kit with her and has the lean look of an athlete. I force myself to think about the interviews and start to flesh out the outline from before, adding in Billie's comments which were, to be honest, a bit better than what I was going to do. Its dark outside when we have the schedule complete, Emma has booked a train at 8.45am the next morning from Kings Cross to Glasgow, then onto Inverness, where we'll get a hire car near the train station. We've booked the smallest car they had - a Chevrolet Matiz, which I'd never even heard of. I'd left my driving license at home in Mharisaig, thinking I wouldn't need it in London, so thankfully Emma will drive. We called and booked into what looked like the only B&B in the village where the assignment was, a place called Inverannan.

The phone at the desk rings. I reach over and lift the receiver. 'Hello, Adam speaking'

'Who? Never mind - put me through to Billie Lawrence.' I try her number, but after ringing for a while, no answer, I guess she's at a meeting or left.

I reconnect the call to me and apologise, offer to take a number and get her to call back. I can hear the caller exhale, impatience filling the air.

'It's Simon Conner here. I need an advance of some cash to let me get to this fucking job - who else is there?' I look round, but most cubicles are now vacant and I can't see anyone except for Emma, another one or two journos I don't know and George Adams, who I've again spent my time avoiding.

'Em, I can transfer you to George if that's okay?' I ask, already a feeling of amusement coming over me.

'Holy fuck, no - is there anyone more competent than George in the office?'

'Well, no-one I've met yet.'

There was a slight delay, a more resigned sigh this time. 'OK, put him on.'

'I'm putting you through now', I tell him cheerily.

I'm starting to enjoy this now, so I quickly check the directory for George's number and then put the call through without introduction.

'What was that about?' Emma had heard the call and seen my reaction. 'It was the guy, Conner, looking for someone to dip into the petty cash for him.' She looked away, avoiding speaking about the call. This seems a little strange to me, Simon Conner may have done something to annoy her I suppose, and he seems to have that type of self-superiority and arrogance which can't help seeping out in every conversation.

George comes over, his expression now less friendly than before and showing signs of a person recently disabused. 'Adam, did I hear that you are getting the train to Scotland tomorrow?' He says with a hopeful tone.

A feeling of trepidation strayed through my senses. 'Yes, but we've already booked the hotel, I don't think they had any other rooms.' I was making excuses without knowing the problem.

'No, no, it's not a hotel thing - I need you to give Simon some money, he's getting that train too.' I can sense Emma listening; she's stopped flicking through the notes on her desk. With no excuses coming to mind, I tell him 'No problem - do you have his mobile number, I'll call him at the station and give him the money?'

Emma is still listening to us and a glance towards her confirms that she looks far from happy. I start to think that there's some real antipathy between them, maybe I'd find out more.

'Or have you got his number?' I ask Emma. Immediately, Emma says no and goes back to her schedule. George says that he'll find it and wanders off to his cubicle. I spend some time looking around the office, waiting to see if George can rummage successfully and find the mobile number. It's clear that the workstations are mainly temporary or for hot desks, as most have hardly any family pictures or personal things around the cubicles. There are a few offices around the outside for the senior staff or for meetings, all empty as everyone except the late few remain. I take a walk to the water cooler and notice that the door to the HR Office has been left open. I take a step in and have a look at the files in one of the desks before I see that the tall cabinet for Personnel files is also open. I can't resist opening mine - just a few pages from my interview land a letter about my eagerness to join their esteemed organization and a couple of bland references from the university.

Checking behind me first, I pull Simon Conner's file, which was visibly the fullest on the rack and looked like it might be informative.

His had indeed been far more interesting in a relatively short time, including a couple of letters of censure - each similar in content about following the Insider Code of Conduct and the last one ending with a note that future behaviour of this kind may lead to disciplinary action. I have a quick look through at some contract documents in his file. He's on a monthly retainer but seems to get paid roughly the same scale as I do. Noticing that his address is in Chiswick, far more upmarket than my hovel, I close the file and turn to see George looking at me.

'I can't find Simons number here, unfortunately. Did you have any luck, George?' I ask before he can fumble his way to tell me I shouldn't be searching the HR files.

'Yes, here you go', he said, handing me a post-it and an envelope containing notes. 'You're not supposed to look at those...'

'Sorry, thanks, I've got to dash', I slip past him and towards my cubicle to pack up before George can try and start another one-sided discussion.

Emma has left me a post-it note in the middle of my screen, she'll call me about 7.30am tomorrow morning to meet up for a coffee before the train. As George looms back into view, I repeat my waving and running routine, files under my arm and jacket in hand. Heading towards the main door of the Inquirer offices, I stuff my copy of the files for the Wester Ross job into my rucksack, check my slightly dishevelled reflection in the mirrored walls in reception and walk out into the driving rain.

☐

Chapter Three

The Wood Pigeon and Me

I sit up in the hallway, I guess a few minutes later, alone in the cold and unnerving silence; to my back the door still half open. Standing unsteadily; I walk into the kitchen, which thankfully looks like it has been evacuated by the wood pigeon. It must have flown out of the open door while I was lying there.

The room is tastefully decorated in crockery, bird crap and assorted scraps of newspaper, possibly digested by the bird while it waited for me to return and painfully set it free. I start to fix up the kitchen, finding some cleaning things under the sink, which then reminds me of my London room. Seems all I've done recently is have misadventures with intermittent spells of cleaning. I run the water in the tap for a few minutes to get rid of a brown opaque colouring and take a long drink of cold water. 'What a state to get into' I hear loudly behind me.

I literally shake with the scare I get.

'For the love of god can you not knock before you come into a man's house?' I shout at the smiling idiot in front of me.

Niall McRae has been my friend since time started and in true Scottish fashion, he takes the piss out of everything I do or say. 'Well, I thought you were away living the dream and now I find you in here, looking like an oversized junkie and surrounded by Mharisaig's largest bird crap farm.'

'Get a cloth and give me a hand then.'

'No chance – Bobby just told me you were back from the smoke, looking like a down and out; I'm going for a beer later, meet you there at seven?. I nod, trying to remember if I have money left as Niall walks out. 'Get yourself tidied up as well, you manky bastard' he shouts back at me.

It takes me half an hour of hard work to clean the kitchen and hallway, my head pounding from my collision with the radiator and the cuts and bruises on my back and side holding me back. I find some strong painkillers in a cupboard, which blunts things long enough to finish the cleaning and take all the crockery and papers to the bin outside. Finally, I make a black coffee and sit in the musty but reassuringly familiar living room. I had left the coal fire to burn itself out the last time I used it, so without having a means of heating the room, I find and pull my old sleeping bag around me and try to relax, focus on the things I have to do. I feel myself falling asleep amidst churning dreams and for now, forgetting the hazy worries of reality, slip off to rest.

I wake up feeling better than I was before, despite my ever-increasing list of aches. I head upstairs and take a long, hot shower; washing my hair twice to make sure it's free from dust and to generally get back to a more socially acceptable level of hygiene. I even find clean jeans and a shirt, which although a shade too formal to fit my normal style at Mharisaig, has the benefit of smelling okay and not being torn and splattered with mud. After all this, I have no option but to go to the pub, there is literally no food in the house and with the only shop closing at 5, bar food is my only choice. I baulk at the thought of a drinking session and pledge to myself that I'll have something to eat, a couple of drinks with Niall and then back to the house. With my stomach grumbling for food, I lock the door and start for the pub at a determined pace.

When I reach the pub, it is fairly quiet, just a few old faces near the bar and Niall sitting near the fire with a drink, eating crisps. I take the crisp packet from the table and start eating. 'Pint please' I give him a quick smile to egg him on his way. Niall shakes his head but stands and walks to the bar, muttering something about spongers, cheapskates and my birth status. When he sits down and looks at his empty crisp packet, he hands me the drink with little camaraderie.

'So where did you get to? Must be somewhere nice to get into that state' he starts, leaning back and folding his arms.

'You have no idea mate. I just got back before you came round.' I take a long drink to wash down the salty snack.

'Well, do tell.'

'Later - just now I need food and more beer. What's been happening back here in Sleepy fucking Hollow in the past fortnight?'

'Hmm, let me see - just the usual round of dafties getting pregnant, some of them female. The local lads have started to get massively into fighting since then went back to school, so Tommy McGill's boys and their pals have been in and out of the polis station the last two weekends. The wee arseholes even set fire to our cottage near the Estate Gates; it's more just a pile of stones now.'

My mind flashes back to the cottage, derelict when I was a teenager but frequently used for secretive drinking sessions and kept in decent condition while it served this purpose. We even fixed the roof a little once in summer; all the better to hang out there when Scotland's almost omnipresent rainfall caused discomfort to our prodigious weekend alcohol input. We would use the old open fire; burning logs, sticks or once when things deteriorated, the old sections from the detritus of the kitchen cabinets.

'That's a pity; we always wanted to fix the old place up a bit when we had time.'

Niall looked at me quizzically 'Yes, that would be perfect, what with our joinery & electrical skills, plentiful finances and fantastic work ethic.'

'You are one sarcastic bastard sometimes.'

'I am one accurate bastard all the time.'

'Fair enough; I suppose we'd have done it already if we were going to. It's just a shame, that's all.'

I sank the remaining quarter of my beer and waggled the glass at my friend, who muttered something about London parasites and returned to the bar to resupply. When he came back, Niall looked at me with, for the first time since I came back, a look of something approaching concern.

'So how did you get in that state? Been sleeping rough? Or even worse, sleeping with someone rough?' He sat back and folded his arms, waiting for an explanation.

I considered how much or indeed whether to tell him. It was the first time I had to reflect on the past week or so from both a reasonable distance and in a place where I felt relaxed.

'I got into some trouble on an assignment. I've just bailed out just now for a wee break. I've done all I can do and to be honest, I need a rest.'

'You only left a couple of weeks ago, how the fuck did you get into trouble in that time? Was it in London?'

So, I told him as much of the events as I could, in order but editing out the illegal parts. It was, helped by the beer and the warmth of the pub, as cathartic as any conversation I'd had recently. Strangely, I felt more dispassionate than I had before, perhaps my naturally journalistic tendencies allowing me to be more spectator than participant after all was ended. Over the next half-hour, I spoke and Niall asked until my thoughts were clearer thanks to his atypically erudite support and queries. The narrative of my first assignment took a far clearer picture now we had discussed the rationale, motivations and even the psychological state of those involved. The names were kept off limits, for Niall wouldn't be told what was going to happen next, that was for sure.

So, after we had exhausted my heavily redacted story, we finished quietly with a couple of Oban malts from the bar.

'You've had an interesting first assignment, I'll give you that' he shook his head.

'Yeah, but I prefer if my interesting assignments didn't involve me getting bruised from ankle to hair.' I told him, finishing the last sip of my malt and tipping a drop into my remaining half pint of dark beer.

We head outside, saying cheerio to the barman and a couple of guys we know at the other end of the room. I wonder if they had overheard any parts of our hushed conversation, but I'm sure the low music and their own chat would have kept them out of hearing range; I have enough to deal with without rumours starting here at home.

'So what do you think?'

'Well it makes for a good story once you write it up, I guess.'

'Soon as my fingers stop hurting, I'll start typing.'

'I'll drop in tomorrow for a coffee, see how you're doing?'

'No probs; see you then. Mind and not crack a light about this.'

Niall turned slightly and smiled. 'You're a journalist; you know you need to tell me it's off the record before blabbing.' He cackled as he lurched along the side of the road home.

I watched him walk for a while; then under my breath, mutter 'Arsehole' before making my way back for hopefully a full night's uninterrupted sleep.

Chapter Four

Travelling to Inverannan

We meet at a small independent coffee shop near Kings Cross, Emma carrying a larger rucksack than mine; it appears superbly organised and gives the impression of being both expensive and a brand which mortals like me have never heard of. Most of the photo journos keep their cameras and lenses well hidden and not on display when travelling, probably a reasonable tactic when you look at the often nefarious types in railway stations and in transit. Walking around with six grand of visible and easily stolen photographic gear is not advisable, whether in London or not. When we get settled in the quietest table in the cafe, we talk through the assignment, most of which I had read the previous day so it didn't take me long to get my head around the details, or so it seemed.

'So what's up? You don't seem inspired to be heading for the delights of a few days in rustic Scotland.'

Emma went on 'I find these places can be quite...insular?'

'I guess so. It's probably just like my village - everyone knows everyone and you stand out if you're not local, particularly in the tourist off-season. If you watch your manners, you will rarely be eaten by the inhabitants though. The Wicker Man wasn't a documentary.'

Emma nods and then got the joke with a small smile. She files away the notes and we finish our coffees, the train due to leave in less than ten minutes.

I realise that, since I had been late for the meeting with Billie, I had missed the purpose of Simon Conner's assignment.

'So what is Simon going north for - he seemed awful keen to head to Scotland?' I ask, thinking that normally an ambitious Essex boy like him would only go to Scotland to shoot grouse with the boss or to go on a Stag Weekend to Edinburgh.

Emma looks at me thoughtfully 'I know. I wondered about that too. His assignment is to meet and interview yet another former civil service bod who's retired and written a moderately controversial autobiography. Apparently, he criticises the handling of the Iraq and Afghanistan conflicts and names some names that aren't already connected through Chilcot. Simon would never normally be interested in anything as political and dry as that. It's practically around the corner from where we are staying so we could have done it without too much travelling; Christ knows why he wants to go there. Billie even tried to give him our assignment and get him to do both, but he just wanted that one, for whatever reason.'

I think about this but can't come up with any reasons why Simon would want to do one of the two assignments unless he was trying to get away somewhere with Emma, but in that case, he'd have taken both assignments. Maybe he's a fucking idiot and just wanted a holiday in Wester Ross, who knows.

Emma goes on, not demonstrating any affinity with Simon whatsoever. 'He's spent all his time here trying to get something major under his belt to get himself onto the books of a red-top. He's not really into leaving London, I don't think I've ever seen him show much interest in travelling anywhere, so goodness knows why he's so keen to go to the other end of the country.'

From what Emma goes onto tell me about a few escapades Simon has been involved in, I'd agree that in normal circumstances Simon Conner would have to be dragged like a cow to a slaughterhouse to end up in an unglamorous part of Scotland, talking to some dull fossil about the detailed rights and wrongs of a political and military campaign which had already been analysed to death in every form of media and enquiry. If Simon had indeed found something worthwhile to advance his journalistic career without telling us, maybe I would be best to keep a weather eye on him. The only way to make your name known quickly in London is either to do something yourself, which might get you jail time or to stay within the realms of journalism and get a hold of something really juicy. There's no news in misbehaving priests anymore and even the tabloid buyers are getting fed up reading about celebrity paedos. That only leaves parliamentary orgies and alien invasions. Neither of which would typically be found in Wester Ross.

'Maybe Simon has heard that aliens have landed in the highlands.' I gulp down the last of my coffee and look at her.

Emma smiles back 'Well, let's hope Assynt is the new Area 51 then.' With that, she lifts her rucksack and I follow her to the platform, quickly grabbing my bag and phone from the table.

We take five minutes to figure out which platform we need and double check the boards. Emma is superbly well organised, making absolutely sure that we are heading for the right train.

The train is due to leave in less than 5 minutes so I call Simon Conner's number, which I had punched into my contacts list the previous night. He answers quickly and agrees to meet at the platform. I had thought about calling him earlier but didn't want him with me and Emma at the coffee shop, so I risked pissing him off by calling him just before the train was due to leave. I wonder how annoyed he'll be and, given he seemed desperate for funds if he has bought his ticket without the cash I have for him. If I have him judged correctly, a guy like that would wonder if I was deliberately screwing with him. He might be that type, but today his paranoia is fully justified, I wasn't going to let this go, especially if there was a top story hiding in the assignment. Being a good Scotsman, it was my duty to claim the home advantage for any work over the border.

Simon, however, does not seem to be too fazed by my attempt at Machiavellian tactics to annoy him, appearing more distracted than panicking at missing the train. He shakes my hand, says a perfunctory hi to Emma and takes the envelope which George had entrusted to me. With a damn site more nonchalance than I could have mustered, he strolls over to the ticket kiosks and walks back to the train to the same carriage as us just a moment before the doors close and it starts off from the station.

Emma and I had booked table seats but Simon packs his small case in an overhead compartment two seats along and on the other side. He walks over, checking his phone while talking to us.

'I don't mean to be antisocial, I'm going to sit over there and get some work done. I'll catch up with you before we stop, yeah?'

With that and a slight motion of his hand - perhaps meant to be friendly - he sits down and opens his laptop at the flip-down table. He types quickly but it is too far - and the screen too small - to see what he is doing from where I sit.

'Shall we try and get this into order then?' I smile at Emma, opening the assignment folder.

She had not given me any indication that she actually liked me, but after confiding her concerns about the unclear reason for Simon travelling to Scotland, I suppose that we now had something more in common. My naturally degenerate mind has started to move into optimistic mode about the trip and I subconsciously ignore that fact that Emma might well be out of my league; also being a couple of years older and considerably more urbane than me, I can't help but feel rather gauche in her company.

We read the papers in no particular order, Emma passing them across the table and them quickly accumulating in front of me; she is a real speed reader. We both take notes in silence at first but start reviewing and making comments, at a low tone to avoid anyone overhearing.

'This guy has had a life less ordinary.' I say to her while reading the wiki in the file. 'He's made some job of turning this business around.'

His two and a half years at Inverannan Estate had apparently transformed a highland package of some 17,000 acres from a loss-making downward spiral to a business employing dozens of locals and having a turnover far, far higher than before. After purchasing the estate from a rather ineffective consortium which was quite possibly a failed tax dodge, he had invested in grouse shooting facilities, fishing, deer stalking and even had plans for a 9-hole golf course in a valley near Inverannan village. In a relatively short space of time, Galloglas had brought new prosperity and made one hell of an investment in, what would generally be thought of as one of the farthest and least accessible backwaters of Highland Scotland.

Emma passes me a few photos of him from his active military years, presumably sent by him as part of this preparation portfolio. They show a wirily built man of medium height in military or sporting attire, certainly a character that looked every bit the British army man, through and through. From the earlier couple of pictures where he was younger and fresh-faced through to the obviously later, more senior ranks, where a slightly broader build had developed and his hair receded until only a buzz-cut remained, helping to portray his strength and, if my judgement were to be relied upon, a sense of a man who would be as confident in other aspects of his life as much he was as in his military career.

In the file, his army timeline showed that he'd been posted in just about every British garrison from Belize to the Baltics, seen active duty in Northern Ireland and the Falklands in his early career as well as a few commendations for UN-related postings, mainly training and advisory roles in a number of countries, even eastern

Africa for periods on and off for seven years. I guess that he provided all the information to The Insider as I doubt very much that the general public was allowed to know about such specific information on military careers.

Although the details are comprehensive to a point in time, the information in the file is, however, lighter on a period in his post-military life, despite being highly and unexpectedly detailed in his previous career. I take note that there are three years of almost no information between him leaving the army and taking over the estate at Inverannan. Another point I make a note of is that there is no mention in the file about other investors. Although this might not always be a typical piece of information to be in the public domain, I would have expected to see an indication of an investor or even a holding company with a Panamanian shell involved somewhere. I add this to my notes, with another addendum to perhaps not ask the question directly. In my studies and limited experience of journalistic life, I had picked up on the principle that the financial side of a business is often the one least popular to ask about, certainly to someone who may have something to hide.

Chapter Five

Mharisaig Cottage #1

We had spent lots of time over the summers and weekends at the fields near the Estate cottage; the river was great for trout and grayling, although like most adolescent fishing in Scotland it progressively relied on booze to make it interesting and indeed tolerable. Niall's older brother was a reliable source of lager and vodka, albeit taking a hefty surcharge per visit to the local shop.

Looking back, I wondered what the couple who owned the shop thought about a skinny 18-year-old buying industrial quantities of strong lager every second evening between June and August. I guess that cash is king even in rural Scotland.

There were often times where we had parties at the cottage with an open invite to anyone needing a slice of drunken excitement and company to relieve the crushing ennui of being young in the countryside; which meant everyone we knew, unless their parents had a close grip on them - a problem which I certainly didn't have. My parents were always hands-off in my upbringing, loving me but sure as hell not going to be doing anything resembling helicopter parenting; possibly satellite parenting, but nothing closer.

One of these nights I met the first love of my life. Tess was an older cousin of my classmate, Anna Berkmann. She smiled at me when I hugged Anna as she arrived at the Estate Cottage and I had one of those rare moments when I could think of nothing to say and nothing to do. I had to force myself not to stare and to present a reasonably sane and hopefully sociable front, although I had the familiar thought that she was not only out of my league. I sat with Anna and Tess for a while, listening with some detachment to their update on all things school and social until she informed Anna that she had split up her boyfriend, a boy she had met in Brisbane; she didn't want a long distance relationship at her age and they would stay in touch as friends.

This was exactly what I wanted to hear. Suppressing my initial urge to grin like a love-struck moron, I nervously asked her about where she was staying. Not exactly dazzling conversation from me, but I was still struggling with awe from the smile. Tess told me about her family, they had moved to Australia but her mother couldn't settle, so she and her two brothers had returned, leaving their father over there until he could get a job back in Scotland. They were staying with Anna's family until her mother could start another nursing job and get a house organized wherever her new job would be.

'So, what was Australia like?' My conversation still hadn't moved away from basic; however, the smile had indeed unnerved me badly.

'It was OK. We stayed outside Brisbane and my dad worked in the city at the Bank. Not that much to do but the school was fine and the weather was better. My mum couldn't handle the bugs and stuff. That didn't bother me and my brothers - except the spiders. Massive things compared to here.'

Tess told us stories about insects and lizards, snakes and something called an Echidna which we'd never heard of. This gave me the opportunity to occasionally gaze at her, which was exactly what I wanted to do most. At 10pm, Anna and Tess had to go, so in a moment of what I can only think of as panic-induced desperation, I asked them if they wanted to come round to my house for lunch the next day. Probably more through surprise and politeness than anything else, they both said yes before saying their goodbyes.

After they had gone, while we were still sitting at the fire, Niall turned to me with a genuinely cynical expression.

'Lunch; since when do you do fucking lunch?'

I exhaled. 'I couldn't think of anything else.'

'Could you actually make lunch? I've literally never seen you eat anything that needed heating up.'

It was a fair comment. I didn't know if my parents had thought that they were teaching me to be independent by leaving me to feed myself, but my inherent teenage laziness meant that that - other than the odd dinner they made me, I existed on sandwiches, biscuits, apples and chocolate. This may also have contributed to my current complexion but notwithstanding; I had no previous experience of making lunch, or indeed any other meal, for attractive visitors.

'And your house is manky.' Niall opined as he walked away to find more wood for the fire.

He was, as so often the case, quite correct and worryingly so about my home situation. We weren't a particularly house-proud family, to say the least. It tended to be left to an occasional bout of energy from either of my parents to remove the piles of mugs, plates, Guardians and Observers from surfaces and to be honest; we must only have vacuumed on a quarterly basis. At one point a couple of years ago, we had a dog which arbitrarily and entirely of its own volition went to live with another family in the village, as they were feeding him and giving him attention. The father of their house came round to discuss it, but since we were collectively aware of our lack of emphasis on the mundane acts of shopping, cleaning, feeding and general welfare, we were happy to see the dog have a better life with the children of his household rather than me and my parents. When he left, I looked out the back of our cottage to his kennel and felt a slight pang of sadness. This however dissipated quickly as I looked at the minefield of dog crap in our back garden and realised that I never once walked the dog when it was raining, snowing or when I was too tired to bother. He's gone to a better place, said my father at the time, and he wasn't wrong.

As I thought about my lunch preparation the next day, I heard my parents leave for work as normal, leaving the house in its default setting - shambolic. Normally, I would be the last person to bother with this; it was just how things were. That day though, it was a problem.

So, for just about the first time in my life, I had to unilaterally clean the cottage. The kitchen itself took me an hour to wash dishes - many of which were covered in solidified food from meals I was fairly sure we had eaten several days before. I cleaned the floors, units and found a place for every item, leaving it in a condition I had rarely witnessed in all my sixteen years.

From then, the living room and bathroom took me until 11.30, at which point I realised that I had 30 minutes until Anna and Tess arrived, no food and no ability to cook. I shoved my shoes and coat on, raced down the front path gathering my bike from the ground where I'd left it and cycled at Olympic speed down to the village store. After 5 minutes, I had selected a carton of fresh orange, a macaroni cheese kit in a box and a sponge cake. This was as idiot-proof as the limited stock of the shop could provide.

Getting back home, I put the macaroni on to cook and went upstairs to get a shower and make ready. Not having read the instructions properly or adjusted the heat after it started boiling, when I got back downstairs, the water had burgeoned over the hob of the cooker and onto the floor, the kitchen smelled revoltingly of burning water and the pasta was almost disintegrated.

'I am fucking useless.' I told myself.

I cleaned up as well as I could, put the lot in the bin and sat in the living room. My nervous pre-date type feeling had passed and I was now in the land of fuck-it, so I put on the TV and lay back on the now-clean sofa.

A few minutes afterwards, the doorbell went and, with my carefree moment dented by the realisation that I had destroyed lunch, I went to answer the door.

Tess stood there herself.

'Hi, how's things?'

Tess gave me the smile and everything was fine with the world again. 'I'm on my own – Anna had to go with her mum to visit her gran.'

This was good news but made me feel nervous again as I thought Anna being there at least would keep any gaps in the conversation to a minimum. 'Umm…good. Well. Hi. I…hope you're not hungry or have really low expectations when it comes to lunch.' I beckoned and we walked into the kitchen. The smell of burning water was still overpowering and she looked at the mass of overcooked pasta now cooling in the bin.

I explained 'I tried to make simple macaroni cheese, which turns out to be a lot less simple than I expected.'

Tess went into a fit of giggles, which sent me the same way.

She dried her eyes of the laughter tears and moved to me. We kissed, rather unexpectedly, and so began my first love.

Chapter Six

Simon's Cunning Plan

Simon has no money in his accounts, quite the opposite. His several credit cards are all at their limit and his two current account overdrafts have also been exhausted, the price of a lifestyle which he knows he can't afford and a monthly salary which his peers make in half a day in the City. Simon would have followed them into their lucrative old school-access-only financial world but even his father's contacts couldn't help someone with a complete lack of arithmetic and mathematic skills. He knew this himself so didn't try, thinking that his mediocre business skills would be better placed to make him a famous London writer, critic or journalist. Unfortunately for Simon, London was chock-full of equally well-connected aspirational writers who had, in general, far greater abilities than he turned out to have. So, he languished in The Insider while he spent his inheritance from his parents and his last remaining lately-deceased uncle, eventually finding himself with neither familial nor pecuniary support to satisfy his spending.

He had not yet sold his flat, as he was acutely aware that his outgoings would only increase if monies became available and, after if he used the equity to pay off the various encumbrances he had already run up, Simon would only have about two years before even the funds from the sale of his flat would too run out, leaving him not only broke but homeless. Plus, his favourite thing in the world was hosting parties there, the only time when he could act as equal to his friends, with excellent wine, food and a smorgasbord of cocaine to enjoy in the company of the stellar cast now in London from his schooldays and their newer acquaintances. Simon found this also to be the best way to gain a reciprocal reward, mainly the invites to country parties, France and skiing, which he often had to refuse once he examined the costs involved. This cut him deeply, having to pretend that The Insider had given him a critical piece which no-one else could do and all that, you all enjoy yourselves in Biarritz, break a leg and tally-ho.

Simon knew that he had to do something else, but with none of his financial inheritance left (thanks Columbia) and with a career which paid little more than a teacher, for god's sake, what were his options. It was with this in mind, that Simon became the middleman in a number of friends-only cocaine deals, even squeezing out a little more profit by cutting it himself, testing to check it was still adequate for his friends discerning palates. This helped for a while, but expenses are expenses and Simon would spend his profits within a day or so of making them, especially after a period of snide criticism of his wine choice at his parties, expensively resolved after a trip to one the more choice outlets in Knightsbridge. Here, a very pretty and helpful lady explained to Simon why certain years and terroir were the optimum for the necessary quality of grape production in their preferred vineyards; the talented wineries they supplied would then create the only bottles they could possibly recommend. Coincidentally these were eye-wateringly expensive, however since his friends also shopped here, he felt there was merit in having the staff know who he was and what he could afford, thereby activating the possibility that they would mention this to his chums at some point. At the end of this period, Simon was left with an even greater requirement to maintain standards and the commensurate urgency to generate regular, large sums of money.

The subject was raised after one of these parties, Simon and two of his more narcotically-minded friends sitting on sofas after all others had headed off home to sleep off the wine and coke if their pounding hearts allowed. Simon had told them that he wasn't challenged enough by the world of journalism and was looking for something both lucrative and not necessarily legal, which certainly described their jobs in the City, but in this instance was intended to steer them onto providing him with an entry to the deeper world of the narcotic trade in London. What Simon did not fully appreciate was that his friends were exactly as dispassionate and inwardly rotten as their professions suggested.

Since school, where Simon was neither clever nor sporty, he was perpetually the hanger-on to his group of friends, in their suburban idyll of wealthy parents and superiority. His parents were friends with their parents in their pseudo-social round of parent's evenings, fundraisers and holidays, making it appear that a community existed rather than a constructed production line of upper-middle-class families squeezing their children faecally towards their equally lucrative lives in the capital. Simon had no actual best friends along the way but seemed to always be there, tolerated by all but befriended by none. He was definitely and acutely aware however of an inequality of status that served to feed his frustration, to the point where he was now ready to take risks not countenanced before.

His friends, Miles and Terry, told him of their limited ability to help but gave him several anecdotes around where the good coke was coming from, new suppliers and acquaintances whose fortunes had been made in just a few months. Simon's eyes were fixed as they spoke and his mind, influenced by the chemical intake of the party, became set on joining this happy group of nouveau-riche whose only crimes were making money secretly and helping the busy professionals of the city to enjoy their well-earned leisure time. All well and good thought Simon, but who does one call to gain entry to this business? He certainly had no money to invest, but he had, thanks to his connections and maintained by his parties, access to some of the heaviest users of cocaine he could imagine.

One of his co-conspirators around the sofas, Miles Ullwin, told him that he knew of a supplier whom he, in turn, had known from university, recently passed away from too much product self-testing. This had created a very temporary gap in the market for high-quality merchandise, which was likely to close before too long. Simon quizzed him about gaining access to the wholesale market and was delighted to hear that an opportunity was available. Before his friends left, they had, in the manner of a group of drug-fettled fanciful males, settled on the best way for Simon to use these connections to meet a supplier and shake hands on a deal to place him in the end-point of the London scene. Simon didn't have the remotest idea of what he was trying to get into, apart from the imperative to make money. His insular upbringing and the lack of realization that his friends were taking the piss out of him were the final clinchers as Simon set out the plan in his mind to enter the drugs business.

The next afternoon, with Simon waking with a headache which blinded him, Miles phoned and told him that he'd called the contact on his behalf and that they were up for the proposal. He gave him an address, a name and a mobile number to call and arrange something, which made Simon bite like a hungry trout in a very small pond. He called after he'd had the last of his coffee and some aspirin to settle his head, speaking to the rough-sounding but

29

helpful Scottish bloke who agreed for him to come up and see if they could do business; Simon effusive in how much he could help, but told that it would be better not to talk business over the phone.

So it was that Simon, with no money to speak of, having arranged a meeting with this contact in the north of Scotland, and a very tight timescale to get it, decided to use The Insider to fund his trip. He went into work early on Monday morning; his last five pounds used to buy a Tesco sandwich and coffee and looked through Billie's assignment files before she arrived. There were two assignments in Scotland, both coincidentally just as far north as the address he'd been given. He would get the closest one, whatever it was and sort out an advance to pay his ticket and somewhere to stay. He'd thought about little else than the phone call yesterday and since these Scottish dealers seemed to know his friends, he was sure he could persuade them to supply him a few kilos and they would get paid back the agreed amount rate after he'd sold it. The profits, he'd keep. What Simon didn't know was that the mobile phone he'd called had been answered by a city colleague of his friend, primed with the story and feigning an accent Scottish and rough enough to convince Simon. This had been a euphoric moment for Simon; the dealer had confirmed that he knew his friend and had expected his call, agreeing in principle to the deal but all being subject to a meeting, where if he passed muster, he'd get some product. Simon didn't realise that the conversation on the other end of the line was taking place on the bar in the West End, with a number of partially inebriated posh boys writhing in hilarity while trying to stay silent as it unfolded on the speakerphone.

As the call closed, they fell about in helpless laughter at the thought of Simon heading for Highland Scotland to meet a non-existent drug dealer and convince him to hand him several thousand pounds of cocaine on approval. His naivety was legend in the group and their wider colleagues, but this was a prank worthy of their superior intelligence and standing, to which they were rightly proud. They made some calls to others but made sure not to tell the 'softer' types who may try to contact Simon out of general pity or to avert too much humiliation for him. The 'normal' types knew that he was a bit dim but a good egg and would take it all in his stride, he had money after all and this was just doing what boys did, pranks and all that.

The next morning, Simon packed his rucksack and hoped that the other journalist, some new guy he'd never heard of, was bringing him the expenses for the trip. He'd been so hyper at the thought of the deal and the expectation of real money that he wasn't thinking straight and had zoomed out of The Insider – hopefully for the last time – that he'd completely forgotten the money, typical he thought. That and he'd found the remnants of a small bag of product when he'd been tidying up after the party, snorting it before leaving his flat before the meeting to give him an energetic start to the day.

He had just got to the train in time, the new guy, a Scot, funnily enough, had given him the money and he was on the train he needed to get. There were plans to be made, so sat apart from the Scot and Emma, a photographer who he'd invited a couple of times to parties. He hadn't had any luck with her, so generally ignored her now, no point in doing anything else. Simon opened up his laptop and started to compile a spreadsheet of friends and their acquaintances that he may reasonably do business with. He also set out another column where he imagined the amount of product they would use and how much they would pay for it. Simon spent a long time on this during the train journey to London but spent most of his time on the Inverness leg of the journey veering between quiet contemplation of what to do with the wealth and suppressing panic attacks about the situation he was about to enter, alone. He wished that he'd asked his friends to come into the deal as partners, it would be great to have company in this, but the downside would be that he'd have to share the profits. In his mind, the profits issue far outweighed the discomfort of having to meet this supplier on his own

Arriving in Inverness, Simon chose his time to land the two others with the assignment he never intended to carry out; using some vague personal excuse after he'd made a call on the mobile to talk to Miles, again without any success. He thought that Emma might be pissed off at landing her with the assignment, so didn't hang around for any more small talk, just walking back to the station where he'd be able to hire a car for the next leg. He checked his wallet after a minor panic as he went through the door and hired a Volkswagen Golf. Simon didn't want to turn up in a really small car but the expenses wouldn't go any further than the VW. He drove out of Inverness and across the Kessock Bridge;

following a printed sheet of directions and map he'd Googled in the office, just before the meeting the day before. He put on the radio but the signal started to crackle after a while, so he settled in for a determined drive to his destination and the start of his fortune.

Simon drove quickly, in the manner of a London commuter. He attracted numerous honks of horns as he cut in front of slower travellers as he overtook but for fairly long stretches the traffic was thin and he enjoyed the novelty of quiet roads and the ability to throw the hire car into bends at high speed. He lost control a couple of times but with nothing coming the other way, his erratic driving went unnoticed and unpunished, with the possible exception of a speed camera which he had a distinct feeling that a flash behind his car may have been. He wasn't aware of it, but his journey took him in roughly the same direction as Emma and Adam, they going east to west too but farther south and on a more scenic route. He stopped a couple of times to check his map against the unexpectedly car-free intersections, although the road signs, in English and Gaelic, were clear and placed well, taking him through Dingwall, up past Bonar Bridge, Lairg and then hardly a house for the rest of the journey. He finally got to the part of the road where he expected the house to be, however, there was little there but a cottage, locked up and with no signs of current habitation. He got back in the car and drove a little farther until an unsealed track split away from the main road, appearing to be a private track, hopefully to the address he had been given.

The address that Simon had been given by his friend, Miles and confirmed on the first call by Simon to the mobile number was the most remarkably remote location. The city lads had decided, after much hilarity and a number of alternative options – including sending him to a random house, a police station, a fish factory and, if such a thing could be found, a brothel in Inverness - to settle on Miles' uncles highland retreat. This retirement pile was in the furthest and most inconvenient to reach part of the country that they could imagine, making it the hardest for Simon to get to and therefore the funniest option. Added to this, Miles and many of his other friends had been there years ago, without Simon, for one of his birthday bashes when at university and he thought it would be quite the chuckle to finally send him there, uninvited as he had been on that occasion. They also found it hilarious that, if he were a little smarter, he would check out the address and make the connection through the family name back to Miles, who had the middle name Allanton and had known Simon since they were at pre-school, as something of a test to see if he deserved an opportunity to see through their charade. Of course, Simon was not that observant and had believed his friend without a thought that he may just be sending him to the north of Scotland for his own brittle amusement.

So, Simon bumped the car along the track towards his pre-selected destination, the road built for a four-wheel drive rather than the tarmac-focused Golf. There in front of him was a square, rather fadingly grand Georgian mansion with an old Land Rover to the left-hand side, with a trailer beside it covered in blue tarpaulin. He parked beside it and looked upwards to the first-floor windows of the house, where a figure of an older man stood looking at him. Simon waved, but no response came, the man moving away and hopefully coming to welcome him at the door. He left the car and walked across the compressed gravel, pulling his jacket around him against the harsh breeze. He thumped the lions-head iron door knocker twice and waited for a response, reminding him of a Hammer horror film he'd seen a long time ago.

There followed a bi-puzzled conversation between Simon and the elderly man who came to the door. It became apparent to Simon, through the language barrier between his own drawling London accent and the man's heavy Gaelic brogue, that he worked there and no-one was currently in the property. Another few exchanges were required before Simon could make him understand that he was expected by Mr Allanton and that he would best come in.

'Naw.' Growled the elderly doorkeeper. 'Naebody telt me aboot ye.' He then closed the door with not an offer of help, which left Simon no option but to return to his vehicle. He sat, wondering what the hell to do next, as the man returned to his first-floor window for a glance at Simon, sitting in the car. He thought about trying again, but then accepted that if Allanton wasn't in, given the nature of his business, it was reasonable, if inconvenient, that his staff wouldn't let anyone in who they didn't know about. Safety first in this game, thought Simon. So, he put the engine back on, activated the heater and waited until someone arrived.

He dozed off for a while, wakening after an unknown time and blinking after the long journey. Still, no-one else had arrived at the house for the meeting and now it was 9pm and getting dark. Even though dusk was late in the north of Scotland, it was pitch dark two and a half hours later when a more modern four-wheel drive pulled up beside him. Simon got out of the car, heart thumping and shook the hand of the driver who stood beside his car, looking slightly perplexed. Simon thought that the man looked like someone who would be in this business, all dark clothes and muscular looking.

'Simon Conner.' He offered.

'How can I help you?' He had a polite but hardly Scottish accent and didn't sound entirely welcoming to Simon, whose nerves were screeching and his heart palpitations were inwardly audible.

'I'm expected by Mr Allanton. It's a business meeting. My friend, Miles, made the arrangements. I spoke with Mr Allanton just this afternoon.'

Allanton looked at him with a cold assessment. He saw a nervous looking, thin Londoner who appeared to be suffering from some delusion that he had spoken with him and had some pre-arranged business. Allanton knew that his father, who owned the house and was not the type of man to forget an appointment despite his advancing years, was away overnight on business and that he would have passed on any information about a meeting to him unless something had prevented him from doing so.

'Do you have any ID?' asked Allanton.

Simon was taken slightly aback by the request, having assumed that his introduction from his friend and the conversations on his mobile would cumulatively be enough. He was also aware for the first time of another two men who had quietly come out of the other side of the car and now watched him from the door as they lit cigarettes. He fumbled in his jacket for his wallet but had left it in his rucksack. Opening the rear door of the Golf, he found it in the front zip pocket where he always kept it. He took out his Press ID, turned back and handed it to John Allanton.

Allanton was not, unlike Simon, a trusting individual. He had been well schooled in the requisite privacy of his career as the right-hand man in his father's many and varied business interests, which had taken him from his twelve years in the army into full-time work with the highly lucrative and global organization which Sir Mathieson Allanton still oversaw, even in his current semi-retirement. Sir Mathieson now preferred to spend as many days of his week walking, shooting, resting and generally keeping away from all the excremental unpleasantness of his business, leaving the hard miles to his son and his other underlings but keeping a weather eye on all from a decent distance. So, John Allanton was now the man who people called to set up business dealings of a minor nature, not his father. This made John extremely dubious, especially when Simon's credentials for a business meeting were evidenced by a UK Press Identification card, which was hardly standard practice in the circles he moved in. He considered his options carefully and then decided to have a longer chat with Simon inside the house, before taking any impulsive decisions.

'Come inside.' He smiled broadly, and Simon smiled back.

They went inside, Allanton introducing himself as Peter Smith and the two men as his secretaries in the business and welcoming Simon into a pleasant, warm library which exuded wealth. He was left alone while Allanton fetched some coffee for them and took the opportunity to have a walk around the room. It was lined with books, with one wall filled with what appeared to be genuine and superior at that, art. Simon didn't know much about art but he thought one or two might be Gainsborough's, leaning in to try and read the signatures on each. There were no personal items on the desks or any indications that this was a place of business. Simon wondered what their reasons were for basing themselves so far north, but he assumed it had the advantage of having very few policemen here and no chance of being spotted doing anything wrong. Allanton dropped in with a coffee for him, but left again, saying that he had a quick call to make.

Allanton sat down at the kitchen table with his two colleagues, drinking coffee and waiting on some food heating under the grill, much needed after their long day. They had been out and about since 6am that morning fetching and delivering as they were required to do twice a week and this week, two days in a row to make up for delays the previous month. Usually, this was their time to wind down and have a couple of whiskies together, but today, Simon had dropped in rather unexpectedly. They had used this building for two years as a place to stay while they worked up here, no product ever allowed near it as it was his father's home, but useful to stay while they moved the gear from the coast to the estate, ready to be transferred to the estate vans and a few other anonymous vehicles used to take it to Glasgow, Manchester, Birmingham, Liverpool and London, the biggest drop of the week, every week. John Allanton was the coordinator, his two colleagues assisting with overseeing the exchanges and a number of estate workers doing the loading and driving. It was an operation as slick as Amazon and paying a similar amount of tax.

The three men knew the issues to deal with here. Firstly, he would never have been invited here, by Sir Mathieson or anyone; secondly, he wasn't known to them; thirdly, he was a journalist, for fuck's sake; and lastly, they had no idea why he was here. Allanton tried to call from the landline to his father's mobile with no success, then at the Estate in case he had arrived early, but he hadn't so he left a message to call back. In the meantime, Allanton would have a friendly initial chat with Simon to see what he wanted and then they could discuss the situation when things were clearer. They also knew that, as a journalist, he could not be trusted to discuss any business, and that options for dealing with him must be considered from the outset. Allanton took a breath outside the library door, smiled and entered.

They had an informative chat, prompted at each salient point by Allanton, about how Simon had reached the house and what his intentions were. Simon told all, about his friend Miles having the initial connection, giving him his name and blurting his proposal to take several kilos of cocaine off his hands on a sale and refund basis. Allanton listened with utter disbelief, hidden behind a sombre, nodding mask. He made the connection that his idiot cousin, Miles, may have set this up, but couldn't for the life of him figure out how he knew about the family business or why he sent this moron to meet him, especially without calling first. Simon continued to tell him about the exponential potential for selling directly to his friends, connections and their connections, London running on coke like a steam train on, well, coke.

Allanton wondered if Simon was either a complete idiot or was having a punt into some kind of investigative journalism at the expense of his cousin and the business. Miles had always been a liability to the family, kept out of the main part of business due to his lack of serious thinking, a buffoon whose parents recognized this as it developed and found him a safe job in the City where he couldn't do himself much harm and would make enough money to keep him out of everyone else's way. There were five other cousins variously involved in the business across several countries, two sons and three daughters to Sir Mathieson's two late siblings, his sister - Miles' mother and her husband being his only remaining relatives of that generation.

John preferred to stay in the UK with his wife and family, making a normal life away from his Monday to Thursday work, helping his father's retirement to gradually take place without breaking the ties of the business too early. In this business it is hard to retire when all your family and workers rely on the structure staying in place, for both their income and their personal safety, so John knew that he was the next fulcrum for the business, and he knew what he wanted to do to develop it over the next decade. His views were popular with his cousins, who were happy for him to inherit the role, but his father would still be required to nominate him formally as successor before he freed himself from the shackles of leadership. At present, however, his father was still in charge and would have to be contacted before any actions were taken on the Simon problem.

John Allanton finished their conversation as cordially as it began, Simon keen to get an OK on his proposal and he asking all he could think of to best inform decisions. It was very late, so Allanton told Simon to stay overnight and talk again in the morning. The older doorkeeper was called in by Allanton and told to take Simon to a guest room and make him some supper. They shook hands and, glad to be away from the jangling Simon, John Allanton went into the kitchen for a de-brief with his two colleagues.

They sat facing each other, the two men listening to Allanton relating the conversation. Neither of them could provide a satisfactory answer without speaking to Sir Mathieson, who was expected back tomorrow but hadn't returned his calls as yet. They decided to sleep on it, finished a malt whisky each and headed off, Simons fate left hanging.

Simon slept soundly, the effects of the coke from Sunday's party now completely out of his system and the nervous tension of the trip and the meeting having exhausted him to the point where he had no energy to worry about the next day. He rarely slept eight hours, but that night he did, not even put off by the slightly damp feel and the smell of the room, heated by an ancient iron radiator on the wall beside the window. When he woke, it was to the unusual silence of the highlands. No traffic, no noise at all except the occasional bird outside the flaking single-glazed windows. Simon wondered if his host was up and about and wanted to get a decision as quickly as possible, maybe even get back to Inverness with a handshake and an agreement to come back and pick up the gear, maybe even a sample to keep him going. He hadn't thought much about getting a heavy bag of cocaine back to London but assumed that he could just keep the hire car if they wanted to give him the coke straight away. He'd probably bring it back a week or so later for the next lot, so the company wouldn't have a problem if they were well paid for it. Money was always the solution to unexpected challenges, thought Simon.

Meanwhile, Sir Mathieson Allanton had indeed called his son back, puzzled at the situation but as ever, cutting to the chase. This involved asking John to take forward two basic actions, firstly to call Miles in London to determine his involvement in the situation and secondly, depending on how Miles conversation played out, to either send Simon back home with the commensurate threats to prevent his further involvement or for John to end Simon's days in a manner which could not readily be connected to Clan Allanton. He also, more worryingly, told his son that Galloglas was entertaining two journalists at Inverannan, ostensibly for the purposes of a promotional article on the Estate. Neither of them could fathom what possessed Galloglas to do such a thing without consultation, but they agreed that it fitted his increasingly rogue behaviour and would require further discussion, which they scheduled in with other tasks they planned for the week ahead. John closed the call and joined his erstwhile companions in the kitchen, McGowan having just lurched off for household duties elsewhere.

As John and the two colleagues discussed their preferences for the latter option, Simon was unwittingly dressing for breakfast in the most drug-dealery clothes he had with him, which served to make him appear somehow even more ridiculous when he entered the drawing room for coffee and toast with John Allanton. John looked up at Simon as he entered, trying not to smile at the slim figure, dressed like a reservoir dog and now seeming to affect a pronounced swagger for some unknown reason. Simon shook his hand with a rather slanted approach, as he and his friends had been known to do with their local dealer, a colleague of one his friends who affected an almost entirely new persona to adapt better to his sideline, all glottal stops and Detroit clothes, despite having been brought up just outside Braintree.

They had a pleasant conversation over breakfast, Allanton probing discreetly about his career in journalism and Simon vehemently decrying it as a waste of time and something he'd be glad never to have to go near ever again. Simon was desperate to keep the conversation on track and focused on them providing him with a large quantity of drugs, but he didn't want to appear too keen and was actually enjoying all the interest which Allanton showed him. Simon thought that he seemed a really nice bloke who was showing some real interest in him before they were to shake hands and become business partners. Allanton was increasingly keen to kill him the more he listened to Simon, but purely on a personal level. Instead, he invited him to pass the time in the library downstairs until he had completed some essential tasks at hand.

And so, John Allanton left to try and corroborate or disprove Simon's ramblings, making calls to Miles' office, which at least had the benefit of being unlikely to be part of any activities against the family business. Miles was too busy to take his call, he was told, being in the middle of his trading activities at that point in the morning. They promised John that his cousin would be passed the message and would be told indeed that it was urgent. He made some other calls, including to his wife to gain a few minutes of sanity and affection away from the business. She told him of their girls sports day, of skinned knees and teas in the garden, of bright smiles and new dresses and they, in turn, made John Allanton shed a momentary tear for missing his children and for having to stay away, up here, with clowns like Simon and with the work he did. He placed the receiver down and wiped his eye, inhaling and wiping the emotions back like rain from his car windscreen, letting him get back into character. He was, to all who met him, a strong man. Tall, dark of face and hair and with the bearing of a military man, he knew that he was exactly the man his father needed to take over the business. John Allanton, however, would make some changes as soon as he took the reins. Firstly, if Galloglas wasn't already dealt with, he would make it his first priority to do so. He knew that Galloglas was a venal type from his work with Sir Mathieson; however, this can sometimes be a useful trait in an operative and can thusly be tolerated. No, John knew that the problem with Galloglas was that he had mutated into a bullshitter with delusions of higher places in the business, developed a taste for the management side which he was ill-suited to, despite his newly-released talent for talking shite for hours. Allanton had been surprised when his father had appointed his Rottweiler assistant as head of the cover business on this project, however at the time he didn't appreciate that this was the catalyst for Galloglas developing ambitions, or perhaps even more worryingly, Galloglas manipulating the situation to place himself where his longer-standing goals were intended to be realised. John Allanton involuntarily hit the base of his fist on his desk in frustration at the situation, Galloglas lording it up in a mansion while his masters unobtrusively – and riskily – took the role of moving the product through the estate. John swore to reverse this when his father left him in charge, he'd be back with his family and Galloglas would be driving the fucking car to fetch the drugs, at best. The actual best would be for an unexpected trip with the two loyal men now sitting down in his kitchen to take Galloglas somewhere high and quiet, and throw him off it.

Calming himself down again, John opened his laptop and despite the lack of internet access, started to reply to emails he had ignored for the past few days. He'd take his laptop with him tomorrow morning, plumbing into the Inverannan secure satellite connection to send his responses, both confidential and social. He had to reply to his cousins, a great, close bunch who without exception deferred to him as the heir apparent, supporting him and the continuity of profit he represented. He did this, each carefully written in an oblique, indirect manner, referring to his children as an allusive contrivance for the business, telling each relative a version of the same thing; the success of their exams, homework completed on time, birthday parties arranged as a cover for the upcoming latest of their bi-annual group meetings. He set the timer on each email to send simultaneously at 0800 hours the next morning, just after he arrived at Inverannan House, regular as an army drill. That complete, he went to the kitchen and spent an hour having lunch with McGowan and the two operatives who seemed relaxed, although they were also keen to understand the position with Simon, the unexpected visitor. As ex-army men, they never over-stepped the mark, which Allanton appreciated greatly although it did remind him that Galloglas had, conversely, got right under his skin by doing the exact opposite.

He left them and dropped in on Simon, forcing a smile back to his face on his behalf, apologising for the delay and telling him to continue to be patient, all would be well, just a few things come up he had to deal with first. McGowan had already brought Simon some lunch and coffee and when Allanton left him; he seemed reasonably content to sit in the library in the autumn sun to await confirmation of his proposal and his deal to be completed. Allanton went back to his office and sat down, this time spending half an hour replying to his former comrades, many of whom kept in touch regularly, bound together by their experiences and their desire to keep their group together through friendship and regimental honour. Some of them were training for the Invictus Games, a terrific source of motivation and camaraderie for those friends of his who had suffered greatly but survived to make the most of their new life. He smiled at the humour in the emails, laughing out loud as he read them taking the piss out of each other even more now than they did before Helmand and all that, all the dust and hospitals and waiting and shooting and dying, for some.

☐

Chapter Seven

Go Jump off a Cliff

I had been seeing Tess for about six weeks when she gave me the crushing news that her family were going back to Brisbane for at least another year. Her father had been unable to get a job back here and the Scottish weather and the distance from her husband had caused Tess's mother to rethink her plans and give the sunshine another try. Our relationship had easily been the best part of my adolescence until that point and the sadness I felt when she left had sent me into a kind of solitary mourning for the next few weeks. I had moped around the house as only teenagers can, during that latter part of July and into August, then back to school for my fifth year. The distraction of the daily structure of travelling by bus to the school and getting back to my studies actually helped, the weather taking a turn for the better and Scotland having an Indian Summer which let me reintegrate with my friends at least at the weekends.

On the second weekend after school restarted, we were in the rundown and partially derelict play park on the outskirts of the village, a group of eight of us, deciding whether it was possible to relieve the crushing boredom of being fourth and fifth-year teenagers in a highland village. We reviewed the choices - cinema, baths, shopping, restaurant, bowling, museum or the shopping mall. Since none of those things was actually anywhere near where we lived, we were left with the traditional rural pursuits of either procuring alcohol - which required money and means, neither of which we had access to at that point; or to do something so dangerous that only a teenager brought up in this rural idyll would consider viable. There were, of course, some choices on this front, falling into three main categories - height, speed or water based. Older friends had the option of introducing other entertainment which we were generally too young for, but accounted for the astonishing levels of both teenage pregnancies and drug misuse in the area.

Our popular choice that day was to head for the river and take a trip on 'inner tubes', which was the inflatable inner of tractor tyres. Most of us had access to these, so it only took an hour or so before we met up, having grabbed whatever towels and swimming costumes we needed. There were six of us, four boys and two girls; we were enjoying one of those early autumn days which are often warmer than summer, but of course, no-one had told the river that it was meant to be warm. It took us about 5 minutes to realise that water which flows down from a highland mountain is not going to be something you would spend much time in.

'It's painful that' said Ronny Thomson, getting out of the water and standing up to his knees in the fast running water in front of the stony plateau where I sat.

'Yep, that's not for me.' I looked at him. He generally looked fairly clean and tidy despite his family being completely skint. His father worked with a forestry contractor and he had four siblings younger than him. Today, however, the effect of icy water and the residue of some weird brown foam from the side of the river had lent his knees a certain pale, toxic look.

'We could go for a proper dive.' I smiled and pointed downriver to where the water deepened and the sides heightened to become a ravine.

'Hmmm. That's no deep enough.' He looked dubiously, squinting to see what height the water got to on the rocky bank.

'C'mon, this is boring.' I got up and started towards the higher banks. The others followed me a few minutes later, the swimming on inner tubes proving a short-term thing and as we'd already come this far, everyone seemed ok with a new challenge. We walked along a sheep track until the bracken cleared and then we gathered at the small grassy ledge above the river. The speed of water was stronger here, as the river narrowed and the misshapen sides rose higher to give a different feel to the river, one heck of a difference from the friendlier beach to a nerve-inducing drop to the rumbling water. I looked over and had to agree that although the river was about half the width here, it still might not be deep enough. Often after rain, it got another few feet deeper here, but the unseasonably dry spell over the past two weeks had dropped the levels to something as low as I'd seen at this part of the river.

'Just tuck your knees up when you jump, you won't go down as deep' I told them. There were underwater rocks to avoid too, so we found the best clear jump spot and settled to launch from there.

'There is absolutely no way I'm doing that' said Alex Nolan, looking down to the unsettlingly shallow water. 'You'd be lucky if it's three foot deep.'

'No way, it's because it's clear it just looks like that.' I was adamant that it was safe, well safe enough for our danger threshold.

'Shitbags!' I turned and told them. With that, I faced back to the river, took a short run and leapt with my knees up out into the air. A brief feeling of fear and then the juddering coldness of the highland water struck me like lightning borne electricity, every part of my skin feeling the suddenness of the shock until my head came back above water. My backside had just touched the rocks at the bottom but not enough to hurt me. I whooped at the rush of the jump and waded to the side, pulling myself up a small narrow tree growing at a ledge. There wasn't an obvious way back up the stony ravine at that section, but my main objective was to get out of the water and let the feeling return to my skin.

'C'mon, what are you waiting for?' I shouted up blindly to the others. As soon as those words left me, I felt that I had done the wrong thing; then I absolutely knew that I had done the wrong thing. I was unable to move or speak and looked up open-mouthed to the underside of the ledge.

Announcing himself with a yell, Alex plummeted past me from above, legs straight and with little thought to the shallow waters. I knew just by the microsecond glimpse I had, that he was going to hit the bottom of the river really hard. I jumped back into the water towards him before he even had time to surface and got a hold of his slippery, inert body as it floated, pulling him up and doing my best to direct him to the side. Either he had fainted or been knocked unconscious and kept going under when my grip loosened. I wasn't strong enough to pull him to the side so the best I could do was keep his head above water as we went downstream with the current. I knew that although it was quite far to the next stony beach, it was the best chance to head there, to where I could pull him somewhere we could get out. I leveraged him as high as I could, when I could, first holding him under his arms then pushing his back upwards from behind him. I scuffed my back on projecting rocks as we swept along but held on, the cold of the water helping to numb the bumping from the stones as I did my best to hold Alex up and get us out as quickly as I could.

After god knows how long, we were there, my body vibrating with cold and fear and the effort of trying to keep him from going under the water. The others ran to help and when they arrived they took over, pulling him fully out and onto the stones. I wasn't thinking too straight and all I heard was a hubbub of voices, someone going for help and finally Alex coming round a little. He looked utterly dazed and pale, not speaking but at least they got some dry towels on him and were taking care of him. His older sister, Michelle came over to me.

'You are an absolute arsehole, making him jump - he's broken his leg and could have been killed!' She was drying and furious and turned back to where Alex was lying, his lower leg oddly pointing in my direction, unlike the rest of him.

I had perhaps initially felt that I deserved some sympathy and attention, but instead, it looked like Michelle had, probably correctly, cut through the situation to the truth of the matter. I looked down at myself and couldn't believe the number of cuts on my legs, body and arms. As the numbness receded, the pain started gradually to increase. I stood up and walked back along the ravine path to get my towel from where I jumped. No-one noticed me go; they were concentrating on getting Alex warmer and propping up his head. I limped to where we had jumped and towelled my cuts and grazes gingerly and sitting for a while, unsure what to do. I heard a noise and turned to see some people, thankfully followed by Ambulance staff, running along the path behind me; one of my pals must have run back straight away to the nearest house to get someone to call them. I looked along the path after them and wondered whether to go back and see how he was - and face the reality and consequences of my actions - or to head back home and get myself cleaned up. Remembering the anger in Michelle's face, my natural impetus to avoid blame took over and I turned right towards home. It took about twenty minutes to walk back, first passing the waiting ambulance at the road end, then across the fields and past the railway station, leaving the pavement and taking the verge for the last part to my house. There wouldn't be anyone in at this time, so I went straight upstairs to the bathroom and took off my wet shorts and threw them into the sink. Everything was stained with my blood but at that point, I just needed to get warm and try and see how bad my cuts were. I went into the shower, its jets weren't powerful but it hurt like hell and gradually I could see my cuts properly. There were dozens of small cuts and grazes, nipping like crazy under the warm water. I decided that shampoo wouldn't help at all and would probably make it more painful, so after a while, I got out, dabbed myself with the oldest towel I could see and looked in the cupboard for some antiseptic cream. It took me a while, but I eventually put the cream on each graze and cream and plasters on the cuts. I couldn't reach all of the cuts on my back, but a look in the mirror showed me it was mainly grazes, although it hurt really badly.

I put on a loose tracksuit and cleaned up the bathroom, despite my poor condition, put the bloody shorts and towels in the washing machine. I had only used the machine a couple of times and it took me a few efforts to remember what my mother had told me about heat, spins and the trickiest part, where the ON button was. Although my parents weren't exactly OCD about cleanliness, I still didn't want them coming back from work to a blood-stained house. I looked back into the bathroom, and with the exception of the shower curtain, it was mostly clean, or at least as clean as it had been before I arrived. I took a couple of Paracetamol and went to my bedroom. It was, as usual, untidy, but exhaustion just got the better of me and, closing the curtains and door, I crashed out completely on my single bed.

I stayed at home that day and the next; largely unaware of what had happened since the incident at the river. My parents spoke with me in my room and checked out my cuts; made sure I was OK and left me to it. They told me that they were going to see Alex and his family that evening that he had indeed broken his leg, although had got out of hospital quickly and with no other problems. I slept through this until my father awakened me the next day. His smile, especially rare, was welcome and my tears rolled easily when he held me.

'Ow,' I said, as his hug tightened.

'Oh sorry' - he moved back, just realising that extensive cuts and bruises aren't helped by squeezing.

'How are you?' he looked intently at me.

'Erm, I'm fine.' I was still unsure how much trouble I was in, the words of Michelle had been playing in my mind, so there was a worrying scenario where everyone was as furious with me and I could be in serious trouble for my part in the accident.

'You did really well at the river. Alex's dad says you saved his life.' For the first time in a long time, my dad looked like he was going to join me in my tears. I looked at him closely, his long face full of care for me, reminding me of my young childhood where I spent so much time with me. He had been at home a lot more then, before he got the job in Inverness and I got older, not needing my parents so much, partly through acceptance of necessity and partly as my independence naturally increased with my teenage years.

I didn't know whether to tell him that Alex wouldn't be there without my urging, my stupidity and my pathetic attempts at popularity. I struggled for words but wanted to find out if my father knew the full situation and if there was any resentment towards me from the others.

'We shouldn't have been there. It was...my fault we were. I jumped in first and then shouted on him to jump too.' I looked into his eyes to gauge whether his response was genuine or sugar-coated to make me feel better.

'Well, no, you shouldn't have been, but Alex told us that you said to tuck up his legs and he didn't.' I had wondered if this

46

would mitigate my blame and my body relaxed as I realised that at least Alex wasn't angry with me.

'How's his leg?' I asked, looking away.

'It's broken, but a clean break, so no problem after it heals. He was told that the shock caused him to black out when it happened.' My dad thought carefully about his next words pausing as if weighing up options of how to phrase his words, as was often his habit.

'His parents want to thank you for what you did, they are coming over later. His sister too asked us to thank you. Michelle thinks she said some wrong things to you when it happened, she was...upset when she spoke to us.' He paused and looked at me with his head slightly inclined. 'What did she say to you?'

'Not much, I suppose she was scared. We all were.'

'Well, she wanted you to know she is sorry, I'm sure she will be OK once everything settles back down.'

My dad left me to my rest, I felt incredibly relieved at hearing that I wasn't being considered the only cause of Alex's broken leg and near drowning. I reckoned that if Michelle wasn't pissed off with me, the others should be fine too. The thought of losing my friends as well as nearly killing Alex was definitely my underlying fear, so if it turns out that I get to be the hero here, it would just be wonderful.

I was kept off school that Monday and, since the pain in my back was not lifting, had to be taken to hospital for an x-ray. I had three cracked ribs, the unsurprising result of reversing down the river with Alex and colliding with multiple underwater rocks. I had actually hoped that some treatment was available, but unfortunately, it was just tough luck and painkillers for me. I spent the next two days lying about in the house on my own until I felt like going back to school, or at least felt so bored that this seemed the only way to move on.

My high school was about eight miles away in Inverloch, most pupils having to travel a fair distance every day, as is normal in our part of the world. I went to the bus stop on the Thursday morning, the autumn weather still cold but thankfully the rain staying away. Typically, the first person I see there is Michelle, talking to her aunt who lives in the house nearest mine. They both turn to me and her aunt beams a smile comes over and gives me a big, heartfelt hug.

'Ow' this is becoming a habit. I mean, it's nice they want to hug me, but come on.

'Oh, so sorry' - she jumps back slightly. 'You were very brave. We wondered how you were.'

'I've got three cracked ribs they say and I'm a bit of a patchwork quilt of wee cuts.' I smiled to make light of the agony inducing bear hug I had just endured.

'You should go see Alex after school; he'll be desperate to see you. There's the bus!'

With that, we said our cheerio's and got on the bus. The others were all there too and we quickly got talking about what had happened. In twenty minutes, the group was back to normal, my fears were allayed and Michelle was looking at me with what I could only assume was warmth, a long way from her fury at the river. I looked at her a couple of times and smiled, but we didn't speak together, just the two of us, not just yet.

Chapter Eight

Arriving at Inverannan

We change stations at Glasgow and take the northern train to Inverness where we plan to grab a meal before separating from Simon and ready ourselves to embark on the last leg of our epic journey, a trip in a very small car all the way to Inverannan. Simon sits beside us on the train now, seats at a premium and probably since he hadn't a decent excuse not to. Still, he hardly speaks to us, either in Glasgow, as we walk to Queen Street Station or really anytime on the journey. At different points along the way, he tries to make a call to someone called Miles, with an obvious lack of success and increasing frustration, made worse by my attempts to annoy him by pointing out landmarks as we travel. His voice becomes squeaky as he leaves another voice message, then glares at me with impotent fury as I ask if he's having problems contacting someone.

I am indeed enjoying being back in the north, albeit for the wrong reasons.

It seems like the train journey to Inverness will never get to its end, delayed by problems on the track and not helped by my inability to sleep. Finally, we get there and disembark to a cold, early evening in the busiest time of day, offices closing and shops still busy with tourists.

We leave the station as Simon gets a call through, immediately heading up a side alley away from us and covering his mouth. After the call closes, quite quickly and sounding to me like he was just leaving another message, he puts his mobile in his pocket and stands for a moment with his back to us, seeming lost in thought. He comes back to where we stood to wait and looks at Emma, not me. 'Sorry Emma, I need to go back to London. Personal thing, you know - a family thing.' He takes out the beige file which I assume contained his assignment and hands it to Emma. Emma tells him that she is sorry, but he seems just intent on leaving as quickly as possible with little chat.

'Can you do this one? It's not that far from where you're going. Sorry.' With that, he walks back along the street purposefully, as we watch him go without having had the chance to ask anything or to take it in.

I watch Emma's expression of disbelief as Simon jogs back into the train station.

'Fuck sake', says Emma, uncharacteristically, but with feeling.

Emma then turns away, shoving his file into her bag and says to me that we should look for somewhere decent to eat. We settle on Chinese food in a warm, rather functional restaurant but with a welcoming host who supplies us with a pre-theatre menu, ideal to keep our costs low. Refreshed by our hastily-eaten but delicious dinner, we head back to the station, find the rental office and pick up our hire car. We take the main road west, out of the town and past the Moray Firth looking immense and impressive, as it opens into the sea after flowing from Loch and then river Ness into the wider water. Away from the spread of Inverness, all traffic and bustle in the midst of the open highlands, we head for Ullapool; then keep north until we finally see signs for Inverannan. I'm not sure it's the quickest way, but then again I'm not sure if there is such a thing on the highland roads.

We travel in relative silence, the atmosphere made more awkward by the situation with Simon. It is clear from Emma's attitude that she has even less time for him now than before, a view which I now increasingly share. I wonder if my preconceptions of Simon were correct - he seems to present a very separate and un-engaging personality, like he doesn't need or want to have social interaction outwith perfunctory comments. Even when we were walking away from our train after arriving in Glasgow, when Emma and I were discussing photographic choices, he did join in slightly, however, his conversational approach seemed to be based on informing what he thinks about something, in this case, Emma's camera, apparently is not the best or newest model available and that a different type of lens is far superior to those she uses. I find it difficult to imagine Simon having a wide circle, or indeed a very small circle of friends. I certainly couldn't listen to him for long without developing, in our short time together, an inherent and unlikely to be reversed antipathy towards him. I also suspect that Emma thought that we'd been played by Simon and that he'd left us with his assignment for a reason not yet apparent.

After another two hours or so, having enjoyed being driven through the superb scenery, I catch sight of the signpost late and tell Emma to turn off the main road here. We approach Inverannan village from a well maintained single track road, lined closely at the start by pine forest, then opening to the more typical heather and granite moorland interspersed by the craggier lochan-strewn landscape to the more even land where grouse are, for part of the year, left unadulterated and more accurately, un-shot. There are signs marking what looks like the boundary of the estate, very professionally produced with high-quality graphics, only missing a 'by royal appointment' addendum to complete the majestic presentation.

We drive for about another three miles without seeing another vehicle, just "passing places" well marked and at regular intervals. The road appears to be, unlike most in the highlands, almost completely new and flawlessly maintained, a difficult task considering the severe conditions this part of Scotland endures each year, and that's just the summer. The going is slow, many of the bends are blind and have a very awkward camber and I think to myself that the road is a credit to the engineers, whoever they were. We reach the village as the first glimpses of evening light arrive, and I'm glad to stretch my legs and spine after their compressed time in the hire car.

I hold my phone up optimistically. 'Good old highlands, no danger of breaking the silence with the sound of a mobile phone ringing.' I circle and try to resolve the lack of signal to no avail.

'So what do you do to chat to your friends back home?' Emma asks with a slight smile.

'Well, we talk sometimes, and there's always the Post Office.' I smile cheerily and open the boot for me and Emma's bags. I lower them onto the pavement and hand her the camera bag. She smiles at me; she seems relieved that the journey is over too.

I smile back. 'Good driving Emma, thanks. Those roads are full on, never a straight bit to get a break.'

'Well, I wouldn't like to do that trip every day. Couldn't enjoy the scenery for concentrating on the road, my hands are sore gripping the steering wheel too tightly.'

She held her hands up and they were crinkled red from palm to fingertip. I hold back the urge to laugh and advised that getting her hands around a large glass of gin and tonic would be my cure. For the second time and by far the best, she smiles widely at me, which almost knocks me over with delight. Steady, I think, let's not make an arse of ones' self.

The Bed and Breakfast is pleasant and unexpectedly picturesque, an unusual arts and crafts house set back on a well-tended lawn and elevated up a set of stone steps from the parking bays at the road. We are welcomed in as night starts to come down and after a sandwich and some tea, head of to our rooms for an exhausted slumber.

When I wake the next morning, I have missed breakfast completely. Emma has apparently gone for a walk down to the loch and the jetty, which looks to be about half a mile in the distance. The sympathetic B&B landlady, Mrs MacEachen, makes me that wonderful Scottish quick cuisine, a roll and sausage. For the uninitiated, this is ideally a square, flat, meaty piece of steak sausage on a (for me anyway) crispy morning bread roll and with a dollop of tomato sauce. Join with a mug of hot strong tea and I'm ready to face the world. After this and quick shower and change, I walk out to meet Emma on her return from her recon to the loch. She waves as she sees me heading towards her. The morning is warmer than yesterday but as is essential for this part of Scotland, we are both wearing winter fleeces and a jacket even in spring, until perhaps the day warms up later. Emma looks wonderful, face coloured pink with the cold and the high-paced walk down to the waterside and back.

'It's lovely here' she says, slightly out of breath from the incline back.

'Yeah, sure is. Cold, though.' I zip up my jacket.

'That's because you were lazy and spent the whole morning sleeping.' She rebukes and looks at me with a mocking expression.

'I do my best work when I'm sleeping I'll have you know. I even dreamt all the interviews and done the assignment in my sleep. If I hadn't forgotten it all when I wakened up, I could have written it up and gone home.'

She laughs, I hope in amusement rather than pity at my attempt at humour.

'Well, given that you can't remember anything, maybe we just stick with the traditional approach and do the project awake and by speaking to people. Come on.' She walks past me, striding towards the B&B.

'It might come back to me!' I proffer, but Emma is giving my nonsense no further attention.

And so we call ahead from the landline at the B&B, to the number we had been given for the Estate to confirm our appointments with George Galloglas, as well as hopefully one with an Estate Manager. Ideally, we plan to speak to someone else locally to provide some information and a few paragraphs of Q&A to outline their perspective on the changes to the estate and where it was going now. I could envisage a fairly good piece coming out of this and wonder if The Insider already had an interested party to take this one for publication. Add in some high-quality photos courtesy of the talented Emma and we could have a nice 2,500-word piece, probably costing The Insider's owners under £3k and being sold to magazines in at least six countries for about £12k a time. Not a fortune, but stuff like this at least must at least keep the lights on back in London.

Emma's role in this - me being a rookie - is not only camera work, but also advising on the story and generally being the senior person here. Although part of me wants to say that I should be the assignment lead as the writer, a larger part of me is just happy to learn from her, how she coordinates and communicates better than I know how to and to see what methods she uses to manage the gig. Emma has worked on dozens of these and has no doubt been allocated to work with me to help me through my callow moments as a new journalist. I also wonder if I had made noticeable mistakes in my earlier couple of jobs as an intern and no-one had enlightened me, or whether this was a standard induction, working with an established professional as a buddy to help me learn.

Either way, I was deeply reassured and glad she is doing this, her positive manner on the phone helping to get an appointment, if we were lucky this morning, with Galloglas himself. If not, we are informed by the Office Manager, hopefully, sometime the next morning would be practically definite. The situation seems a little fluid for my liking but I'm keen to meet the main man after reading the intriguing yet incomplete retrospective of his career, so even if we have to wait, it will be fine.

Emma now makes a call to the contact for Simon's assignment, arranging this for after lunch, which seems to be received with polite approval at the other end. She then calls Billie and spends ten minutes telling her what happened with Simon and sorting out

53

our handling of his assignment. Emma places the handset down and looks at me with a pursed expression.

'What's up?' I ask with concern.

'Billie hasn't had any contact from Simon. He should have phoned her and let her know the situation.'

'Well, maybe it's something serious. Perhaps a bereavement or something?'

Emma shakes her head. 'He's not got any close relatives I know of. His parents are dead. I only know that because George told me that he only got the job at The Insider because one of the Directors had known his father years ago and they felt obliged to help him out when his dad passed away.'

We couldn't figure out anything else at this point, so we agree to focus on Inverannan and pick up Simons assignment later.

Chapter Nine

Mharisaig Cottage #2

The September weekend had arrived, along with the heavy rain and strong winds, as if released overdue after the sunshine of August and reverting the population of the village to their default position of staying indoors when not working or at school, wondering what to be up to. We had decided to head for the cottage again, its roof hopefully still giving rude shelter to half its footprint which still had a fireplace and some crappy broken chairs we had sourced from various parents' garages and back gardens. Not exactly an ideal situation, but the thought of getting together with friends for a few illicit cans of cider was a welcome relief from sitting at home watching the rain trickle incessantly down the single-glazed windows at home. My house was so draughty that I had a fair tolerance for cold and wasn't unduly bothered by sitting in a damp, ruined stone bothy as long as I had some good company and a bit of a fire to take the edge off the cold. We were lucky this evening, the wind direction drove the rain onto the best part of the roof, leaving us inside fairly dry. The last time we had been here, we had stacked up some branches and logs in the corner to keep them dry, which had worked well as everything outside was now well and truly sodden. Niall had brought half a bag of sugar, a rather oblique act which I now realized was ideal. He poured the sugar over the kindling and newspaper in the stone hearth and lit it with a long match, the fire immediately burned blue and orange and we were straight into a good fire and the pleasant smell of burning toffee.

We had collectively funded and brought a slab of 12 cans of cider and also someone had brought an almost half-full bottle of their fathers' whisky, the disappearance of which was likely to cause an issue later in that household. The talk was of the school football and shinty teams performances the previous day, neither of which concerned me greatly. I had been in the football team briefly before the coach realized that my reasonably impressive skills were not matched by physical effort. After a couple of months where he tried cajoling, shouting, praising and just about every other psychological approach to resolve the issue, he dropped me from the team, bemoaning my laziness and unwillingness to "track back" or "run". It was just my nature, I'd rather let others do the running while I, basically, don't. I didn't even try to play shinty as it looked even more effort than football with the added fun of losing your teeth to a wildly swung stick. We passed the whisky bottle around, but it was a dark island malt which tasted like medicine to me, so after one small swig, I demurred on the next passes.

We were gradually joined as the rain eased by a few others from the village. Word spreads fast around these parts, I thought to myself. More booze had arrived with the newcomers and music had been provided via an ancient boom box which had to have the volume control moved skilfully or a blast of crackling static would punish our ears. I fucking hated Techno but give it its' due, it gets a party going. There were about fifteen of us by nine o'clock when Michelle and her three friends from Inverloch arrived. They were staying at Michelle's' house for a sleepover so had some spare time to hang about with us Mharisaig rustic types, dazzling and urbane bunch that we were.

The rain had gone off and one of the guys had brought a tarpaulin, so everyone got to sit more or less inside and listen to the banter from the drunker and louder of the group. I hadn't really had much of the whisky and only a little of the cider, so was a good bit straighter than the rest of them, to the point where I couldn't really be arsed listening to them when they got to the loud and showing off stages, which was most certainly the point we'd reached. Jamie had just tried to backflip off of the rear wall of the cottage and almost broken his neck and I'd stopped one of the younger guys from S3 from pissing in the fireplace. Time for a quiet exit, I thought.

While everyone was stopping Jamie from repeating his unsuccessful attempt to become Mharisaig's land-based high dive champion, I surreptitiously wandered off outside and along the path to the small bridge over the burn and past the gate to the road. I heard a shout behind me and stopped, turned to see Michelle walking towards me.

'Are you escaping without telling anyone?' She mock-rebuked.

'Aye, it's time for me to head away; I've had enough of accidents and ambulances this year.' I had spoken without thinking and looked sharply up to see if I'd offended her.

Thankfully, she was fine and gave a little laugh. 'Yeah, you and me both. I wanted to say sorry for shouting at you at the river. I got a fright when Alex went into the water and was frantic by the time you dragged him out. I didn't know what I was saying.' She looked at me with the start of tears in her eyes.

'It's OK; my dad told me what you said. It was my fault anyway; I was showing off and...well you know I shouldn't have jumped in either.' We looked at each other quietly for a moment before Michelle broke the silence.

'I'd better get back to my pals.'

She stood, waiting for me to say something profound, but I drew a blank on the witty response front, so I moved towards her and kissed her. She reciprocated and we kissed long and hard for a minute or so before she pulled back and rested her forehead on mine.

'I really better get back to my pals before I do something silly.' She said softly.

'OK,' I managed to growl, dizzy from the kiss and the sweet haze of her perfume. 'Next time maybe we could both do something silly.'

'Look forward to it.' She whispered. She broke away, turned and walked back along the path towards the cottage. I looked at her as she receded into the distance and wondered why the hell I didn't stay until everyone was drunker or just follow her back. Maybe I do have principles, after all, I thought as I walked away from the now distantly faint Techno beats which had started off again at the cottage.

☐

Chapter Ten

The Laird and the Land

The meeting at Inverannan was arranged to start in an hour and the estate main building is only a fifteen-minute drive from the B&B. We have the outline questions we developed on the train, some nice easy stuff about changes over the past couple of years, where next and so on, but we spend the time we have going over them, making amendments and adding topics which may come up, as well as adding a couple of questions which I had previously kept separate, around the funding and ownership and perhaps even some personal or professional enquiries on Galloglas himself. Emma is slightly hesitant when I add these, she says they may be out of scope for the assignment, which is probably true but after all, I am meant to be a journalist.

After we had finish reacquainting ourselves with the blurb, we drive from the B&B to the estate, through what hardly deserves the title of village, again along a single track road until we arrive at the estate. New, stone pillars at the gate welcome us through and present an unexpectedly impressive view of the main building. A confection of Victorian architecture with three asymmetrical spired towers, joined by mock castellated walls, all in granite and looking every part of the centrepiece of a shooting estate.

'That's a wow from me', says Emma.

'Yeah and how' I reply softly. 'Looks like Walt Disney made a wee castle for Queen Victoria right here in Scotchland.'

We pull up around the back of the building; there is an unusually high and narrow black door in the left-hand side which looks the most likely entrance for us. Outside, a solid looking workman stands to have a cigarette and looking at a notebook. He looks over at us and comes over eventually. 'Good morning' he says, rather more loudly than was necessary.

I get out of the car and introduce myself and Emma.

'Are you expected?' he says again in his curiously sonorous voice.

'Yeah, we have an appointment with the Mr Galloglas. I tell him, looking over his tweedy and mud-spattered figure. He looks at me and lowered his head to see Emma in the car. With a bellow of 'follow me', he strides back to the house and opens the door, beckoning.

We grab our kit as quickly as possible and follow. He has sped off to somewhere else in the building; however, a small, friendly bunch of office staff were there to welcome us in. One of them, the office manager whom Emma had spoken with earlier, had a name badge Eilidh and a most dazzling smile.

'Really sorry about Ranald, he is deaf as a brick wall. He's under orders from the boss not to ignore visitors, but it annoys him that he can't hear well, so if he's not got his hearing aid in, he keeps it short and sweet.'

'He's fine' I smile back. 'We're from The Insider; I've got some ID somewhere.' After a less than dignified rummage through my jacket, bag and back pockets, I show my Press ID which has rather unfortunately got enmeshed with some soft mints in the side of my rucksack, obscuring part of my photo with congealed goo; Eilidh smiles, not fully suppressing a light snigger. Not for the first time this year, I wish I looked slightly less 'green' as I am fairly sure my youthful looks make me far too much like an apprentice rather than a qualified journalist.

'Well, you're in luck. Mr Galloglas has come back early and is ready for you in his office.' She turns and calls an internal line to what sounded like a secretary. 'I'll take you up.' Emma strikes up some chat about how lovely the area is and how lucky they are to live somewhere so beautiful.

We are lead up and through a side door and enter what appears to be a service corridor, then more stairs up to the second floor. After Eilidh knocks twice, we are ushered through to a far more imposing book-lined room with two men sitting at rather ornate desks. Eilidh introduces them as the Estate Secretaries, however, no names were given and the men barely nod to us despite our polite hellos. They clearly are not particularly interested in having any discussions, although I'm not sure if this is because they are busy, not interested in visitors or whether it is due to our profession. Eilidh shows us into the next room where Galloglas rises to meet us and proffer his hand. It is like shaking hands with the Terminator, I visibly wince at the thankfully brief compression.

'Very nice to meet you; how was your journey?' he asks.

'No problems at all, it's a lovely part of the world. Bit of a trip to get here, but it's worth it.' I tell him, stretching my fingers back into shape after the handshake.

He looks at me and nods. 'It is that, and from your accent, you're not from that far either?'

I admit that I am from Mharisaig and he tells me that he knows the place, thinks has been there a long time ago.

After asking permission and receiving a wave of his hand to proceed, Emma sets up her tripod and camera gear and asks if we could take some photos at his desk to start off. Galloglas says 'Just leave it for now, let's have a chat then we'll see.' Emma looks a little uncertain but leaves her camera where it is and sits down. She says 'of course, whatever suits' and looks at me, a slightly unnecessary prompt for me to get on with it.

I quickly appraise Galloglas. He looks a fair bit older than even the most recent photos we had in our file, hair greyer and his skin more weather-worn. Anyone could tell he was ex-military, his spine set straight in the manner of a man who spent time marching and standing on parade and his thickly muscled neck held back in a permanently rigid posture. He is dressed casually, looks like Ralph Lauren Polo. The short sleeved shirt show off tattoos on one arm, the other clear. It looks like a regimental badge on most of his muscular right forearm, with lots of names etched tightly on every inch of the remaining skin. He notices me looking at his tattoos and held out both arms for me to see.

'Regiment and fallen comrades, in case you're wondering' He looks at me with a half-serious, half taking-the-piss expression.

'I was wondering why one arm is full and the other arm clear.'

He smiles. 'That, my boy, is the right question. This arm is the one which I look at when I want to remember my old life and this one.' He held the clear arm out. 'I can look at and pretend I was never anything but a civilian.' He sits back slightly and seems happy with our nodding response to his trite explanation, although I think that this seems more like something a moronic professional footballer would do.

'I've got other tattoos, but nothing appropriate for this interview.' We laugh obligingly at his small joke, sure as hell it wasn't the first time he'd used that line. I think that is also his prompt for us to move on.

60

'Do you mind if we make a start?' I ask. 'We've prepared some questions but if you want to discuss anything else, please just go for it.'

'Then let's begin' he says with what I imagine is a hint of condescension.

For the next thirty minutes, Galloglas replies a series of my questions as if born to it. He tells me of his long-standing desire during his military career to end up somewhere in this area, his enthusiasm for the project and the quality of the people he worked with. He speaks of market opportunities, the popularity of sporting activities, his plans for expansion and, with little prompting from me, what his motivation is, outwith that of mere profit.

His passion for the project certainly appears to be both genuine and avid. 'You see, this area and most like it, have traditionally been owned by either old money, which is generally too self-satisfied to move forward commercially or by nouveau types who liked the idea of being a landowner but have no idea how to lead a team or how to build a solid business in co-ordination and co-operation with the community. The first option is stale and only serves at best - to stand still and the latter...well it can bring anything from chaos to clearances, neither of which is any damn good to anyone.'

I am making notes for follow up questions while recording the interview. I ask 'So how would you describe your approach compared to those?'

He lets me offer this welcome prompt with a glint of a smile. 'Have you ever been to New Lanark, Adam?'

I had been there on a day trip when I was at University, so I nod and say 'so you're the new Robert Owen? Isn't that a bit patriarchal?'

Galloglas bristles slightly at the allusion but his enthusiasm, I think, prevents him from rising to my negative point. 'You misunderstand. That approach was admirable in its time and place; my approach has the same altruism mixed with a commercial approach but not the same scenario. This place, like just about every other village in the highlands, has been through hundreds of years of the strangest twists. It was backwards and harsh when other parts of Britain were civilised, it was emptied of the best and the strongest during the clearances, the rest left in the industrial revolution, the closing of the railways choked it a bit more and now we look round and wonder at the pretty scenery and try to see what we can do to make a life here. Well, I haven't just made a living here, I've brought prosperity and profit and, this is just the start.'

'So you see yourself as a benevolent laird, with a commercial imperative?' I am intrigued by this unexpected rationale.

'No, not at all. It's a much more collective ideal than that. All our team here are committed to the project and they put their heart and soul into their work.' He seems about to start another pitch to us, but checks himself with visible effort, drawing back into himself and looking at his watch.

I am genuinely intrigued by his fervour for his work here and am rather disappointed when Galloglas rather abruptly apologises for going on too long, thanks us and asks us to arrange a follow up the next morning, saying he has a conference call to join. My general impression is that we had made an all but too brief but promising start to the assignment. Emma deconstructs her unused camera gear and we say our goodbyes to him, arranging with the office staff on the way out - not the secretaries - to come back at the same time the next day.

Emma packs her camera equipment in the boot and joins me in the car as some light rain starts. I look at her for some kind of feedback.

'Well, what do you think? Good start, bad start, come on, I can take it.'

She smiles slightly. 'Good - well, bland maybe, but good.'

'Bland? He stopped when I was getting into the interesting bits. Ten more minutes and he'd have told us his plan for world domination.'

Emma nods agreement. 'I know, we'll need to try something tomorrow to get his blood up again, that looked like it was going to be interesting when he slipped us the news that he had a social project on the go, rather than a hunting and fishing business. I didn't see that coming.'

We drive back through the gates and with rain flecking the windscreen and the highland sky turning to sinister grey, back to the B&B to prepare for our afternoon covering for the redoubtable Simon. We get there as the heavens open, rain bouncing off of the road and making us run up the path and stairs to the sanctuary of the house. I ask Mrs MacEachen for a map, which neither of us brought, forgetting that online provision was sparse here. Not only does she have a map, but she knows where we are going, giving me handwritten instructions of how to reach it, avoiding a road which looked viable on the map, but she describes as a "tyre-burster". It's about forty-five miles back along the way we came to Inverannan, then a fork almost straight north and eighteen miles or so onwards to the east, the property being the most prominent of the tiny village and a former manse, easily found I'm advised by our host.

We set out, after being supplied with sandwiches and tea and I'm now feeling good. Despite having only the length of the journey to prepare, we agree on some standard, open questions and decide to play it by ear otherwise. Emma agreed that any lack of preparation was down 100% to Simon, relieving us of any culpability if the article is rubbish due to lack of prep. That said; the blurb has got enough pointers to let us wing it without an in-depth knowledge of what is a rather convoluted and complex situation anyway. The place was a heck of a long way to drive, but easy to find, there being only one road going through the valley and besides what looked like a salmon river and an open, desolate loch. We eventually find, as expected, a prominent granite-built villa just outside of the tiny hamlet and get out of the car, backs stiff again; out into the cold highland air, we push through the wooden gate and up a wheelchair ramp to the door, where we are met by the man himself, no doubt notified by the unusual sound of a visitors car.

Forster is a game old bloke, hair receding to a horseshoe and thin as a stick. He has an accent which has definitely a hint of Highland background but with a very distinct southern English correctness keeping it in check. I suspect that when he worked in London it would have been less highland sounding and more London, making him no doubt indistinguishable as a Scot. He brings us in, walking slowly and introduces us to his wife, Ella, who seems to get around the house with a wheeled Zimmer frame. She wheels off to a room across the hall to give us privacy, as Forster makes tea and we do the rest of the introductions and small talk. Eventually, we sit down in the formal drawing room of the house, cold as winter but otherwise ideal for the interview.

As we run through the questions, making a contributory piece for a larger, post-Chilcot article which The Insider had been remitted to complete the UK interviews on behalf of an American publication, it occurs to me that Simon could have had absolutely no intention of making his name with this. James Forster, our subject here, is a retired civil servant who formed part of a group who participated in a post-Iraq War audit on spending. Following a gagging order, he and others were unable to speak of their findings; however, this had been recently lifted, triggering our sponsors request for an interview. Forster was, as far as this interview proved, a capable and knowledgeable procurement specialist who, uninvolved at the time, had been chosen to review where the public money had been spent after a chaotic period in Iraq and, to a lesser extent, Afghanistan. He was passionate about his work and fumed at the lax practices of the Americans, which had spread to the British elements they worked beside in both countries. There we no photos required here, so Emma helped with the questions, doing easily as well as me and probably better, showing a familiarity with the subject which I somewhat lacked. I had a broad awareness but some of the "lost" amounts of money were staggering and, according to Forster, ended up in the hands of corrupt organisations via unscrupulous military and civilians alike.

Emma asks with some pressure, 'Isn't this just typical of most government projects, spending far exceeding the original estimates?'

He looks up and shakes his head solemnly and superciliously, like a heron swallowing a fish. 'No, not at all, not at all. In the instances where over-runs occur on civic or central government projects, these are still reported to the appropriate channels and managed, despite their increase from estimates. As such, any over-spend is managed and can be audited at a later date.' This sounded like a load of government-management bollocks to me, but thankfully Emma is switched on here and maintains a more professional response.

'So, rather than the usual incompetence causing over-spend, what we have here is genuine fraud?'

Forster thinks for a moment; then beams at her. 'Not the words I would use, but in essence, yes.' He goes onto recount a number of audits he had been conscripted for in the past, a couple of IT projects which ended up stratospherically above their budget and one in London which a redoubtable former Mayor managed to bluff his way through a catalogue of idiocy and mismanagement, all in more detail than I can comprehend without feely woozy, Forster's voice a natural soporific.

The recording devices, both of which I use here, would be enough on this one, my notes sparse as the detail surpassed my ability to comprehend the vagaries of procurement procedures and best-practice contract management. What Forster did though, was to send me into a daze of daydreaming during which I thought I may have a rationale for Simon's selection of this job. If he needed to sod off and do something on his own up here, but didn't want to get into any more trouble at the Insider, he could have set this up so that we'd do his assignment – which Billie would be fine with – and leave him with the excuse of a personal tragedy to mitigate his withdrawal. He must be skint though, to go through that rigmarole to get a ticket to Inverness, for reasons I still don't get. Forcing myself to pay attention, I realise that Emma had been asking all the prompts and questions while I had been in a fug of boredom-induced daydreaming. After waiting for Emma to ask the next question, which tells me where we've got to, I ask the next one.

'I rather think we already covered that in a previous question' he sniffs, correctly intuiting that I'd not been paying full attention.

I move on to the next with a curt apology, this time Forster holds forth with more vehemence, but still choosing his words carefully in the manner of a consummate civil servant. He tells me of the audit in Iraq, the buildings not built but signed off and paid in full; phenomenal amounts paid to civilian security firms; heroin rumoured to have been impounded but re-routed by unscrupulous individuals for their own gain; and lastly, a suspicion that too much of the opium farms left intact to suit the same individuals who had longer-term need for these raw materials. A bit far-fetched, I thought, maybe Forster is seeing monsters everywhere, even in our side, which I find difficult to believe.

'So, how did this situation come about? I thought that our involvement in military-led campaigns was meticulously planned?' I query, actually starting to get engaged in the subject.

He looks at me and exhales with almost a snort. 'Incompetence; Greed; Possibly a combination of those factors and that of the American leadership making it impossible to have the degree of organisation required to carry out an organised plan, certainly during the post-conflict period at least. I don't believe that either country have anything like a clear understanding of where the money was spent, and it's now too uncomfortable for those in charge to admit the mistakes. By doing so, they would still be culpable, so it's being brushed under the carpet, so to speak.' He takes a bite of a biscuit and sits back, ruminating I assume. I stay quiet, assuming he had more to say.

'Plus, it is possible that some of their activities are ongoing. That is to say, many of the contracts were complete, however, I suspect that business relationships may have been formed between indigenous leaders and those unscrupulous forces from the western coalition.'

'What makes you believe that?' I follow.

He smiles at me. 'I spent some considerable time on the audit, travelling in the area and reviewing what meagre information had been retained, most of which were of poor quality. This travelling period, however, allowed me to listen to the frustrations of those honest but less influential figures in the service. Their strong views were that deals had been done behind closed doors to effectively share the loot of the country and the contributions of governments between the involved parties, in exchange for which a relative cohesion was agreed. This arrangement had the advantage of enabling the local warlords to move into the vacuum created and control the area with their own, western-friendly thugs who in turn ensured that towns and villages in specific areas would cause no trouble. The down-side being that the whole arrangement was officially unsanctioned and unethical, both in terms of the remit of the engagement and in the fraudulent use of funds allocated by both governments.'

This is heavy stuff, not exactly new as I had read earlier from the file, but from a former middle-ranking civil servant who has chosen to break ranks, definitely news-worthy if corroborated by evidence. It could be that there is information contained in other elements of the overall project, which would make the profile of this work extremely high. Emma asks a couple of follow-on questions, her greater knowledge of the subject helping her to manage the interview better than I can. It takes about another hour and a quarter to exhaust our repertoire of enquiries, and we pack up our kit again to set back out for Inverannan.

While I'm getting my jacket on and packing my rucksack, Forster asks Emma where we are staying. She tells him that we're at Inverannan, doing an article on the Estate. Forster nods at the mention on the estate. 'I've heard of the man Galloglas. Friends of ours sold him some land bordering the Estate; he paid a very fair price. A man with ambitions, it would appear.' He shook our hands. 'Good day to you and thank you again for visiting, I did enjoy our discussion and look forward to seeing the finished article.' We thank Forster for his time and agree to keep him informed of the progress of the piece.

After finally getting back the long road to the B&B at Inverannan, we spend some time in Emma's room at a window table writing up notes of the Galloglas interview into almost a legitimate draft. It's one of the least pleasant parts of this job, interminably transcribing recordings to a usable text. I am in the habit of making minor changes to the actual wording of answers, partly to make the piece more interesting and partly to reflect improvements which I should have made at the time, by having a differently framed question or having missed an opportunity to elaborate. I change the sequence of some answers too, moving part of Galloglas comments to appear that they were responses to slightly differently ordered questions.

Emma was aghast at my creative changes to the text. 'Who the hell taught you to behave like that?' She puts her head back in a motion which does not suggest approval.

I grin and, not for the first time since challenged on this approach by tutors and colleagues tell her, 'If Hemingway could do it then I don't think it can be considered a major issue. Let's get dinner; my stomach thinks my throat has been cut.' I stand, grab my jacket and open the door. 'Meet you downstairs.'

She burst into laughter and shouts after me 'No, he fucking didn't, you arse!'

Unfortunately, Mrs MacEachen is just outside the door about to knock as I open it. She looks at Emma with, in my estimation, a mix of extreme disapproval moving towards horror. Wordless, she turns and walks back down the stairs.

Emma is crimson and looks at me wide-eyed.

'If you get chucked out, there's a nice hotel 65 miles back down the road' I whisper, closing the door softly.

I go downstairs after standing in the hallway for a few minutes, trying to stop giggling. After composing myself, I knock lightly on the open kitchen door and see Mrs MacEachen. We have a chat for a few minutes and she seems to settle down and forgive Emma for her outburst. I go back out into the long hall and start to read some of the tourist leaflets which are on a white wooden stand by the door. Momentarily, Emma comes down the stairs, still slightly coloured and looking for Mrs MacEachen.

She comes out of the kitchen and gives Emma a hug. 'It's OK dear, don't you worry a bit. You enjoy your dinner and I'll see you in the morning.' She goes back to the kitchen without a further word and closes the door.

Emma is completely confused.

'It's OK.' I tell her. 'I had a wee chat with her and she's cool.' We close the B&B front door behind us and start off for the pub for lunch.

Emma now has an expression of puzzlement to replace embarrassment 'Thanks...what did she say?'

'Well, she's pretty old fashioned but understanding.'

'Understanding of what?' Emma looks at me, holding her hands open, annoyed at not comprehending what's happened.

'Your condition; I told her you had Tourette's.'

Like kids, Emma chases me until her anger turns to uncontrollable laughter. We are at the pub and can't go in until we stop hee-hawing and the tears stop running. Hitting me one last time on the back for fun, we go into the pub to see what they have on offer. Similar to Mharisaig, the pub is the absolute centre of the village, it has a small shop in the rear of the building and takes deliveries from online stores, as almost everyone who needs to, goes in there most days. The pub room itself is a long, narrow, mock timbered space with a well-stocked bar at one end and a small stage at the other. If they had bands playing in here, it looks like a tight venue. The ceiling is low and damaged at a number of places. The barman sees me looking at it.

'It's the aftermath of birthday parties, ceilidhs and especially last Hogmanay.' He waves at some of the worst holes in the plasterboard. 'We used to repair them, but after a while, it's easier to ignore them.' I nod my understanding and order us drinks. There are two other groups at tables although it is quite early in the evening. The barman gives us a menu, limited in terms of choices but certainly not on quantity when it arrives. We sit at the farthest table, near the unoccupied stage but close to an antiquated oil heater which is taking the chill off of the room. After some good

Scottish Lasagne and chips, we are ready to plan the next day. If we get to meet everyone at the Estate we need to, it would maybe even allow a spare day here to clean up both days work and write up the final content, ready to email to Billie at the Insider and edit as soon as we get back to London.

I have a pint of cider and Emma has a Guinness which looks enticing, so I have one too though I'm stuffed after dinner and we fall to easy chatting in the relaxed atmosphere. Emma tells me that she had been to school in Wiltshire and then university at Durham, also having done Italian there. She tells me about spending six months in Milan as part of the course where she did her portfolio of photography, which helped her get her first job in London before moving to the Insider for more money and travel opportunities.

'So, where have you travelled with The Insider?' I ask, taking a considerable swig of my drink.

'Well, I keep getting sent to Scotland to babysit new journos.' She smiles.

'Apart from that.'

Emma exhales and says, 'Well, France, Andorra, Switzerland and Italy. Italy is the best for me, so I've tried to get there at every chance, holiday or work.'

'So, you've manipulated Billie to send you to ski resorts while pretending to actually work?'

Emma laughs. 'Exactly; same as this trip, always a free week in the middle, spend our fabulous salaries mixing with the beautiful people.'

'I knew it.' I shake my head at her. 'Come across as professional and fabulous but it's really just all about free flights and hotels for skiing.'

She glances at me with a wry smile. 'So you think I'm fabulous?'

'Definitely' I grin. 'I especially like the way you tolerate my immature behaviour when it pops up?'

She nods 'that is a challenge.'

'And the way you cope with your condition.'

'Fuck off' she says.

'Sometimes' I smile back.

We leave the bar after finishing our drinks, at Emma's prompting. She may sense that for me, two drinks is exactly the number required for me to start on my next six. With our follow-up appointment with Galloglas hopefully at 10am, her guidance on this, as most others, is of great importance.

The B&B front doors are not locked when we got back and we go to our respective and solitary rooms as quietly as possible. I say goodnight to Emma but glance towards her as she goes into her room, for any signs of encouragement. There being none, I close the door to my room softly and, thanks to the beer and a half stone of Lasagne and chips, fall asleep within minutes.

☐

Chapter Eleven

Simons Plan may not Work

Back in London, Miles Allanton Ullwin was making the biggest decision of his business career. He was a very, very, clever trader in foreign bonds, helped massively by having the benefit of excellent contacts both in the UK and in various European, American and Asian banks which he provided reciprocal advice to when needed. He had it made, taking 90% of the profits on his trades so when he hit big, he won big. Like Simon, he spent big too, but he wasn't yet near where he wanted to be; not at the top yet, where the big sharks swim in a deep pool of easy money. He, like Simon, had a plan to reach greater heights and he was now at the point where he had to throw all his chips in.

He wanted a house in the Dordogne which cost money; he wanted a fleet of classic cars instead of just the Porsche 911 he drove; he wanted fine art at a level he couldn't afford now; he wanted to bid for them with the high rollers and make another fortune as they increased in value while hanging on his walls. He wanted to be able to afford a more expensive girlfriend than his current girlfriend, one who he could take to a ski-lodge he'd buy in Chamonix, then invite his family over to show them that he could become fabulously rich without just taking the family business route like his cousins.

He knew they were all working for their uncle, selling real estate globally on their individual franchises and all making an absolute bundle, but for whatever reason, they never invited him to join, not that he would have anyway. He wanted to be in the City, making his own way with other people's money and taking the cream off the top for himself, that was the perfect life for him. He'd even given up sport for this, no more rugby or lacrosse as he had a social life which made more contacts and therefore more money for him as he rose. Soon he planned to gradually ditch the friends from school and university he still saw, they were really becoming a bore and didn't really help him anymore, he'd reached past that point. He did miss the rugby though, the effort and the outlet for his tension had been terrific, but no time for that now. He had piled the weight on after giving it up, but had joined the gym and increased his use of coke which everyone knows is just the best for weight loss.

Today though, he knew was the day to make money. He told the receptionist to hold all his calls, even those from the investors he had attracted and cherished as the stock of his trade. The President of the European Central Bank was making a keynote speech at lunchtime, the content of which could potentially send the markets he knew intimately into a stratospheric climb. He had to prepare for this in the morning by buying the market in preparation for what he was sure would be an afternoon of great purport, his strategy to go long and sell at the right point to maximize profits, hoping that he alone would be clever enough to read the signals in the speech and ride the waves of money which would follow.

Miles, uncharacteristically, spent the morning quietly with no interaction with his chums on the floor, who put his lack of chat down to a comedown from his famously herculean coke benders. Miles was indeed heavily chemically enhanced that morning however he had focused his entire attention on trading the markets and then listening to every word the President said, translated instantly to every market across the globe. Miles sat, gazing at the broadcast on his screen, drenched in sweat despite the expensive air conditioning which cooled the office and ensured that the precious traders only breathed filtered and cleaned air into their valuable lungs. He waited for the moment when he would rise and punch the air, more passionately than he had before, so much riding on it that mere mortals could only seek to imagine how it feels to be so powerful. The speech came, the infuriating man taking his taciturn way to get to the critical points, where Miles would be the recipient of the prize he yearned. Everyone else in every bank expected a cautious, vigilant statement which would stabilize the contracts, but he knew better, knew the chap who worked for the President, knew that he would deserve his payment from Miles a while later as reward for leaking the information to him, knew that he too could buy a lodge in Chamonix with that kind of money. He thought of Simon, working for peanuts at The Insider, trying to find out something hidden too and smiled at the irony.

The speech reached its pinnacle, eventually, and Miles heard exactly what he wanted to hear, his heart pounding inside his chest and his shirt now thoroughly soaked. Someone asked if he was OK but he couldn't stop watching the speech to respond. As he jumped in delight at the announcement, he felt the pain in his chest like a knife but there was no knife there when he looked down, just his shirt, soaked with sweat and something stopping his breathing, the pain reaching his neck and then, for Miles, the trade was over.

They tried CPR on Miles in the floor of the office, then the Ambulance crew did their thing, then at the hospital, they tried again but Miles was gone; never having bought his lodge in Chamonix and never having had the opportunity to provide his cousin with a much-needed explanation of his prank on Simon. Unfortunately for Simon, as well as losing a friend and a formal confirmation of the reasons for his visit, Miles had also spent his last two days so focused on his trading that he had ignored the nagging reminder that he had intended to call his uncle and brief him on the prank. He had fully intended to make sure that Simon would have been accommodated for the evening, his uncle would have been fully informed of the situation to save him stress and then Simon would head back home to face the ridicule. His death of a cardiac arrest, at 1.47pm that day, due to being overweight, unfit and having abused narcotics and alcohol for several years, denied Simon and those subsequently interested in resolving his situation the full facts. Miles' colleagues on the trading floor would go back to their business as soon his body was removed and were keen to pick up on the trading success he'd been about to celebrate. They would drink in his honour in the bars and nightclubs later, partly a celebration in his memory, but mostly because of the vast increase in their bonuses gained as a result of the Miles plan, picked up on quickly and shared by his replacement traders.

So the City of London just kept rolling along and indeed some fortunes were made that day thanks to the President of the European Central Bank, just not one for Miles, although according to the terms of his will, the share of profits he would have enjoyed and the proceeds of the sale of his flat and car were awarded to his parents, to enable them to enjoy those additional monies and impart a small proportion to his old school for the purposes of supporting their rugby development and the institution of a Miles Ullwin trophy, to be awarded annually to the victors of competition between the four houses of that leafy institution. For Simon, unsurprisingly, there was no provision.

***▢

John Allanton looked up from his laptop and realised that it was almost four o'clock, he'd spent way too long faffing about with the cached emails but hey, what else can you do? He rang Miles' London office again, spent a few minutes on hold after asking for him, giving a thumbs-up to McGowan who had toddled in with a coffee for him before shuffling back outside. He was then connected, right as he took the first sip of his hotter than hot drink, rather expecting to have to stay on the line until someone fetched the idiot Miles.

'Mr Allanton?' the unrecognised voice came down the line.

'That's correct. Can you put me through to Miles Ullwin? I'm his cousin and I need to speak to him as a matter of urgency.' John wasn't sure who this guy was, but he thought for some reason that he sounded uncertain of himself.

'It's um…rather bad news I'm afraid. Miles was taken ill, earlier, we had to call an ambulance and well, sorry to have to tell you this - we've heard back from the hospital, his parents have been contacted. I'm afraid Miles passed away. A heart attack we've been told. I'm so sorry."

John listened to his sympathetic platitudes with a degree of disinterest, muttered something about thanking him, for some reason, said goodbye as he closed the call.

'Fuck Sake' he said, with disbelief.

John didn't need to speculate much what had brought on the heart attack, because in his mind, Miles was always an accident waiting to happen. At their cousin Fiona's wedding last year, Miles had spent more time in the toilets ingesting coke than he had in the party, ending up carried to his room semi-coherent and trembling yet still trying to keep going.

John also thought that, whether Simon was making it all up on not, there was no evidence to confirm his story, which moved the little Londoner into a Very High-Risk category for the security of the business. He called his father with the news about Miles. Sir Mathieson seemed genuinely saddened at the news of the passing of Miles, whom he remembered as a small, rotund boy with an easy

74

smile and a habit of falling over and skinning his knees more frequently than was usual. When he had composed himself, Sir Mathieson Allanton told his son that Galloglas' two journalists were from the same organization as Simon, albeit incomprehensively at his invite. Neither man knew exactly what this meant, however, it could not be mere coincidence that journalists from the same organisation turn up simultaneously at two of their organisation's three properties in the far north west of Scotland at the same time. Sir Mathieson advised that John and colleagues should use coercive force to determine the true facts about the purpose of Simon's venture to enable them to take a full, collective approach to the three subjects.

John placed the receiver down with a sigh like the last breath of a dying man. He preferred to get the mechanics of his profession handled with consummate efficiency, then fly south at the weekend to his family and the normal, idyllic life they lead, albeit funded by the family business. Saddened by the news of Miles and now with a loss of temper fuelled by a combination of frustration and a deep dislike towards Simon, he quickly briefed the two operatives on his father's orders and without delay entered the library, giving Simon, who sat trying to read a book while attempting to calm his increasing worry, quite a start.

Simon was wrenched from the chair by John, the strength of his hands and arm juxtaposed against Simon's scrawny arms as he was pulled up and out. He was dragged through the door outside and into the four-wheel drive car, into the back beside one of them. John Allanton, no longer the friendly companion to Simon, drove them the hundred or so yards silently, stopping at a rather neglected looking garage building. Allanton opened the door and Simon was pulled inside, with as much resistance as he could muster despite his physical disadvantages to these men. They grappled him into a wooden chair and bound him to the arms with what felt like plastic cable ties, cutting painfully into his wrists as they pulled them through.

'What's going on Peter?' he pleaded 'There's no need for this, please!'

Allanton looked at him with confusion; then remembered he'd given him a false name. He nodded to the two men.

He thought his wrists were just too painful and was about to complain, just as he found out what real pain was actually like. The first few punches came from the taller of the two secretaries, who stood over him and lashed five or six left-handed punches to his face and stomach. The second grouping came from the other man, this time his right side battered and again his stomach. Simon voided himself at the outset, the shock creating the involuntary, although understandable bodily response to the sudden violence. He looked up at John Allanton with blurry, painful eyes and tried to speak, which he couldn't do because of the trauma just received by his diaphragm. Allanton punched him directly in the face, harder than the others had hit him and Simon, his black drug-dealer jeans full of his own fluids, was given the short-term relief of unconsciousness.

'My names not Peter' he told him, with some vehemence.

John Allanton had not meant to hit Simon. His father had been quite specific about the need to get the information from him as quickly as possible to bring all the information to him timeously and to resolve the entire matter before any possible external and additional risks were created. That said, John Allanton really, really disliked Simon.

He and the two men drove back to the house to have a coffee and wait for Simon, if he wakened in between, to accept his situation and provide them with the facts, rather than the bollocks he'd tried to spin them about starting a cocaine franchise on their behalf with his now-deceased halfwit of a relative. John received a call from another of his operatives in London, confirming the employment status of the three journalists. He approved the London operative's suggestion to gain access to the offices of The Insider and gather as much intelligence as possible on the assignments, which he was not sure would convince him either way, however Sir Mathieson had always stressed to him that knowledge was power and that any possible source of information should be sought to better assess the situation and inform on a strategy. He had learned much from his father, had John Allanton.

The three men ate a silent dinner and an hour later, drove back the short distance to the garage, where Simon still sat, now awake but puffy of face and horrible of smell. John squeezed water from a plastic bottle over his head to clear away the blood and stood a few paces away from him, partly to get a good look at him and partly to put him a couple of yards away from the stench.

'So, Simon, what are you doing here?' Allanton stood squarely, looking to Simon as if he was poised to walk over and thump him again.

He started to try and talk, but only a croak came out. Allanton nodded to his colleagues and one of them, his mouth and nose covered by a hankie it appeared, walked to him and squeezed water from the nozzle of the bottle into his mouth.

'Have you heard of waterboarding Simon?' asked Allanton. Simon gazed at him, his bowels already empty or more would have arrived at his jeans.

'It's a most persuasive technique; my friends here have used it to great advantage since it became fashionable in their circles. Me, I don't like cold water splashing on me, so I'll leave it to them. For you, if you want to leave this garage alive and avoid an extended swimming lesson from these guys, it's time to cut out the bollocks and tell me the truth.'

The tears were blinding Simon as he begged that he had been telling the truth.

'Pleashe, pleashe, Milesh will tell you, we had a plan. It was after the party. Pleashe.' He sobbed.

'Unfortunately, Miles passed away earlier today. So, we have no way of proving the bollocks you told me now, even if I had the desire to do so, which I rather don't now.' Allanton fought the stench and walked closer to Simon. 'So fucking talk, or we'll lay into you.'

Simon wailed from the core of his very being until Allanton slapped him, it was like being hit by the oar of a boat, knocking his tears and saliva as far as the wall of the garage. Simon struggled for consciousness and sobbed through the agony of now what he felt was the loss of another tooth, hard to tell through the cuts and swelling of the inside of his mouth.

Simon started to blurt out a repeat of his story and a thought came to him as he told of the party and the beginning of the plan.

'Terry. You can call Terry, he wash there, he'll remember. Pleashe, I've got hish mobile number.' Simon bestowed a bloody grin and gestured with a nod to the phone in his jacket pocket, having thankfully thought of a joker to play at this most painful of games.

Allanton looked at him with a fury like he'd never thought possible of the previously affable man and Simon clenched himself as he jumped almost on top of him. 'Oh right, you fucker. You want me to call a mobile from my landline, activating some bastard you've got primed to call the cops and get a record of my number calling them. You little bastard, don't play games with me!' Allanton was right in his face, spitting with anger and then he turned away, pulling the phone from Simon's pocket, throwing it to one of the men. 'Get on with it.' He told the two men, as he left the garage and Simon to a period of interrogation at the hands of two very, very, menacing individuals. He wailed, not for the first or the last time that day as one grabbed him while the other looked at the phone, checking if he had a code or fingerprint set up to access, knowing that any piece of information about Simon may well be found there.

Two hours later, the two men walked wordlessly back the track to the house, smoking as they went. It took them half an hour to shower, change and place their wet and bloody clothes in the washing machine, set to the hottest temperature to best remove the stains. They sat down to a late supper with John Allanton, cooked by McGowan, who had been with his father for more years than John had been alive, yet learned never to cook well or even make a palatable coffee.

'So, what did you get?' he asked as he started eating. The two men he sat with were absolute professionals and he had no doubt that Simon would tell them what he knew. He also regretted slightly that he had been heavy-handed with Simon, that his own quickly-found but deep loathing of him had influenced his decision to give him a comprehensive appreciation of their questioning techniques.

'Fuck all. He's telling the truth. I think it's possible that your cousin sent him here for a laugh, or to wind you up, or both.' Allanton stopped eating and put down his knife and fork. 'But he wouldn't know I was here. Miles would only know his uncle was here, he wouldn't have a clue about me.'

The secretary went on in as he picked at his food. 'That's what we think. This guy seems to be just trying it on, get into the business because he's been told about a contact and needs the money. He doesn't know your family involvement, just thought it was some Scottish guy that Miles had contact with who is a supplier. Even has call logs to prove it he says, we're going check who he's called recently, but not from here or on that phone. We'll get a list off of it and get it checked at Inverannan, make some satellite calls and see who answers. He sounds like he's fucked financially, told us about trying to keep up with Miles and how he's got more debt than Greece.' He paused and looked directly at Allanton. 'He says this is nothing to do with his job and believe me, we worked on him. I think he's just a bystander, but we need to sort it out now we've done him over.' He sat back, his report complete.

Allanton agreed. Despite all the apparent nonsense which Simon spoke, no-one on the planet could go through what he just did and keep telling a set of lies as absurd as this. He looked from one to the other. 'So, we've just tortured a journalist who had no previous idea about our business?'

'Yes.' Was the response from both men, simultaneously.

The other man took a turn to report. 'We asked him about the 2 other journos, he told us that if they were up here at Galloglas, they must have been invited. Says he left the meeting and took the first job, but knew there were two jobs up here and he travelled as far as Inverness with them, made up some excuse to separate and make his way here. He doesn't have a pot to piss in, so needed to pretend he was doing one of the assignments to get the money for his train fare.'

Allanton had the impression that the two men, normally as reticent as men could be, were trying not to laugh.

'Fuck sake' Allanton put his hands over his forehead and leant forward, his supper forgotten as he realised just how pathetic yet problematic Simon could become.

'There's more. The two other journalists think he's returned to London with a personal problem, but he hired that car in Inverness and drove here, so we need to deal with that. We could deal with him but the boss doesn't like that option as you know, generally. They're journalists, they have a line of reporting, who are likely to try and trace him if they know he didn't go back on the train.' He stopped, leaving his report complete and for Allanton to take the lead.

'I need to speak to dad' said Allanton, to himself as much as to them, wearily.

Simon lay on the floor of the garage, his entire body shivering and bleeding. He had never thought that such agony and torture could be brought against a human body, especially not his. His wrists were in agony from the cuts made by the plastic ties, so he looked for something to free him from them. There was an ancient rusty saw in a pile of wood, so he struggled painfully over to it, inching his wrists onto the blade and gradually running its teeth along the binds; he nicked his skin twice, but kept going agonisingly until they fell open. Exhausted beyond himself by the effort, he saw a plastic tarpaulin in the corner, covered in dust and dirt, maybe a cover from a tractor or something but usable. He went to it and pulled it on top of his soaked, throbbing body and passed out, the pain gone for the moment.

The three men decided eventually to leave Simon there in the old garage for the night, mainly because getting him into the house involved some unpleasant work to clean him up, but also because they had other work to do. The drop into the loch was early the next day, so they had to get a few hours' sleep, wake about 5.30am, drive to the loch and meet the boat. Conditions were calm, so this was a good time to do it, unlike the two postponed drops they had to tolerate last month when the winds were unseasonably strong and smaller boats could not be risked, not the men and certainly not the product. So they woke, still clothed, met in the kitchen and then set off for the coast without much of a thought for Simon, comatose in his garage, a problem to be solved after their supply chain activities were complete.

Chapter Twelve

Mharisaig Parenting

I spent my fifth year at high school more or less knuckling down to studying, exams and trying to get in a position where university would be my next step. I spent a lot of my free time with either Michelle or with my pals, now a slightly different group as some had left school at the first chance, either leaving for work or staying and doing casual work on the estates nearby. I had earlier more or less settled on English and Journalism as my first choice for university, so dropped the science subjects and focused on more relevant topics. My mother's job had been relocated to an office in Peterhead, so now stayed away from Monday to Thursday, leaving me and my dad at home. It became even more of a bachelor feeling to the house, my father not at all applying any strict rules to my life and quite detached about my relationship with Michelle and all that went with that.

In a rather apposite manner, I had nagged my dad to start doing more housework, which he took on board only slightly and very occasionally. He seemed to find it vaguely amusing as he could not fundamentally see why I placed any importance on this. Michelle thought that he was operating on a higher intellectual plane and just didn't find that whole dishes/ironing/hoovering thing important, whereas I had the distinct impression that there was a solid streak of laziness running through the male side of our lineage, manifesting itself in our grubby household. I wondered if I should ask dad if our predecessors, my late grandfather and great-grandfather, were also lazy bastards.

I passed my prelim exams with flying colours in January of that year and only three months later appeared to ace my fifth-year exams. The plan was to get more qualifications, but I had, out of interest, put a couple of applications to universities at Edinburgh and Glasgow to see if I could get a conditional acceptance, which I really had no intention of taking up at this point, but was pleased to see that I actually got a conditional for Glasgow. This morning, I had got the SQA letter which told me that my five exam efforts had been rewarded with straight A's, which I had hoped for but as with most of my friends, had a pessimistic view of, to protect our hopes against failure.

We were celebrating and commiserating by turn on the evening when we had all received our exam results. Back at the now increasingly ruined cottage, I sat with Niall as he bemoaned his situation.

'One; one fucking pass, that's all I've got to show for a year trekking up and down to that fucking school.' He took a deep draught from his can of lager.

'Never mind mate, you've got sixth year to go, you know what to do now.' I reassured.

'Sixth year! Oh fuck no, I can't handle that. I need to get some money, get a car and get the fuck out of here.' He was not in the best of moods and at judging by the rate he was going through his cans of beer; he was soon going to be a very drunk, very poor scholar. I was in the sensitive position of having done well and wanting to celebrate, but having to keep quiet about it so I didn't piss my friend off further. To try and cheer him up, I told him that Michelle and her friends were meeting us here.

'Aye, fucking great.' I looked at him and he returned my stare.

'What?' I asked, genuinely not understanding him. Wondering where to go next on this one, I opened a can of lager and sought for the right, or at least passably least offensive words.

'Are none of them…your type?'

He shook his head and made an ironic sniggering noise. 'Don't be fucking naïve; you're just too self-obsessed to notice.'

'Are you gay?' I asked.

'No, I'm not gay, as if that would be any easier in this redneck fucking shitehole! I'm fucking useless with women. Have you never noticed that I actually haven't had a girlfriend yet?' He seemed fairly annoyed with me, verging on disbelief that I hadn't thought about it.

'Well, not really, I suppose I just thought that you weren't bothered just now about that side of things. I could ask Michelle if one of her pals fancied you.' I tried to be helpful but my heart wasn't in it.

'Oh, fuck that, another embarrassment in-waiting for me. I must be the only seventeen-year-old virgin in a twenty-mile radius of Mharisaig.' He sank a fair portion of his beer to wash the thought down, highly inaccurate though it was.

I pondered on what the hell to do next and we settled between us, that I would speak to Michelle later and see if any of her friends had shown an interest in him. I assured him that it would be completely confidential and I'd not do anything without checking back with him first. Still red in the face, he seemed OK with that, muttering something about me not making an arse of him, which I interpreted as his version of thanks for helping.

Just as dusk was settling, Michelle and a larger than usual group of friends arrived at the cottage, followed intermittently afterwards by almost every kid between 15 and 17 from the area. Everyone seemed to have a sense of relief at the exam results, either satisfied or just glad for the stress of waiting to be over. Although not everyone had brought booze, Niall had managed to get a bottle of tequila or Sambuca from someone and was leading the way on a version of slammers, using slices of orange from god knows where and crisps instead of salt. He seemed to have temporarily resolved his shyness thanks to copious amounts of alcohol, which I had suspected might happen after all his moaning. We spent one of the funniest and best nights ever at the cottage; it must have been 2am when we finally laughed our way back to the village. The last hour or so of it, I had been sitting with Michelle and a few others and only caught up with Niall after they had left me to go their own way and stay at her house. Niall hove into view, grinning widely and being held up by one of our girl friends from the year above.

'You going to manage home alright mate?' I checked.

'Fuckyeh' he slurred, both hands in the air. 'You know that thing?'

'What thing?'

'The THING'

'OK...what about it?'

'It's been sorted. No need to ask anything else.' He tapped the side of his nose and smiled. The two lovers departed, swaying from side to side like a trawler leaving a harbour in high winds. I watched them as they headed their own way, happy for my friend and his new partner and fairly confident that neither of them will have a particularly clear memory of the events of the previous evening when they waken. Which may or not be for the best, I thought.

I headed home and opened the seldom-locked door at the back of our house, leading into the kitchen. My parents' room was above the front door so I had, a long time ago, realised that the quietest way to get in was the back, although they weren't bothered about the odd late night, I didn't want to annoy them. The front door also squeaked like a trodden mouse and needed a serious bit of a shove if it had been raining, the ancient timbers expanding and just about sealing it to the door frame. I looked around at the mess of newspapers on the coffee table and sat on the sofa, moving some jackets and a hoodie or something to make space. I opened up the Education supplement of The Guardian and started to read an article about the costs of higher education, loans and the time taken to pay them off, a disconcertingly long number of years for a seventeen year old to countenance, especially one who had little money during their Spartan upbringing in a highland village. I started to think about what I should do, take on a small fortune in loans and go to university, stay here and try and get a job, well bollocks to that completely, I thought. With these and other confusing challenges rattling around in my slightly drunk head, I fell asleep soundly in a mass of jackets and crumpled newspapers.

I woke to the sound of my dad making coffee and toast before heading to work. He hummed a tune lowly as he did this, could have been Greensleeves I thought but settled on Song of the Clyde as it became clearer after the kettle finished boiling. He used to sing that to me when I was small, I remembered with a distinctly maudlin feeling, a happy memory rendered sad by the passing of time and made worse by the depressing morning hangover I nursed. Changed days indeed, I thought to myself. He sat down across from me and asked how I was.

'We went to the old cottage last night, had a couple of beers and a good laugh.' I told him.

'Well, if you can't enjoy yourself when you're young, when can you?' He sipped his tea and picked up a part of the newspaper to read while he munched at his toast and marmalade. He always wore either checked or khaki shirts to work, I suspect his rural upbringing meant that he couldn't see himself in anything more office-like even though he was seldom outdoors for work now. I could see that something was on his mind as he wasn't scoffing his toast at the usual pace.

'Did your mum tell you that she's getting her early retirement from work?' He asked casually.

I looked at him, but he was still apparently gazing at the newspaper despite having addressed me.

'Not really. Well, she might have mentioned a while ago that they were restructuring or something.'

'Well' he exhaled, 'She's getting to leave work and now it looks like I'm in a similar situation.'

I knew we didn't have much money, not that I'd ever asked their salaries or anything. We hadn't really gone on holiday much during my childhood and always had old cars, so along with the general frugality of my upbringing, I wondered if a reduction in income would be a serious problem. My concern immediately leapt to my university situation, if the costs I'd looked at last night were indicative, I'd be completely fucked without some help from my parents.

'So, what are we going to do?' I asked, as calmly as I could.

'It's OK, don't worry yourself' he told me, thankfully putting down the sodding newspaper. 'We have both saved enough to pay for your accommodation at university when the time comes, plus a monthly amount which should help with food and expenses. We think that you might need to take a bit of a student loan if you don't work part-time, but it'll work out fine.' He smiled a little, waiting for me to reply.

'So what are you and mum going to do? Get other jobs?'

'Well, we've been saving up pretty much constantly for twenty years, so we're finally going to go and live in Spain. Once we've got our works pensions sorted, we'll buy a flat somewhere near Malaga, we used to go there before you were born. We'll keep this place here for you of course, so it'll be fine, you're old enough to stay here for a while yourself until you leave for uni next year, so don't worry.' He smiled at me as benignly as only he could.

You utter bastards, I thought.

Chapter Thirteen

The Bountiful Laird

Emma wakens me early with a few sharp raps on the solid wooden door of my bedroom. 'I'm on my way!' I tell her and hear her footsteps as she descends the oak staircase to the front hallway of the B&B. I get up and wash quickly, my deodorant covering until I can get a quick shower after breakfast. Going downstairs and looking around uncertainly, I see Emma at the table in the breakfast room and join her at a chilly table by the window. A real fire has recently been lit in the hearth, not yet enough warmth coming from it to take the cold air from the room. The room itself is oddly decorated in predominantly royal blue with a dark mahogany fireplace. The walls are covered with gilt-framed prints of biscuit-tin Scottish Highland art, all stags, mountains and doughty shepherds. I wonder if Mrs MacEachen actually likes these or whether they were part of the show for tourists. Other than Inverannan House, catering for their wealthier customers, this is the only advertised accommodation on the estate, so this was the only show in town for hill walkers, holidaymakers and genealogy tourists.

Mrs MacEachen brings coffee and toast immediately, asking how we are and having a chat with Emma about our work today and suggesting some places to take photos. I wonder if she was just pleased that Emma hadn't sworn again, as there were two other, very quiet tourists in the room now. I grin at Emma while they were talking, however, she didn't seem uncomfortable and they both seemed perfectly friendly after last night's practical joke. Mrs MacEachen gives me a glance as she walks away which suggests that she has figured out that Emma does not have Tourette's and that I might just be a complete arsehole.

Our main breakfast arrives, scrambled eggs for Emma and bacon and pancakes for me, a wonderful way to start the day.

I tell Emma, 'I think she knows that you don't have Tourette's.'

She smiles back. 'Yes, I came down this morning and we had a chat. She does indeed now know that I don't have Tourette's, which incidentally you shouldn't joke about, and that you are immature, which I can joke about.'

Oh well, I think, probably a fair reflection of the situation. We finish our breakfast in relative quietness, however, there was a mutual understanding that Emma has confidently outflanked me and that our B&B host now believes me to be the arsehole which I can often be.

After breakfast, we decide to head up to the Estate Office slightly early to get an impromptu look around. Given that it is a shooting estate, we agree that it would be unwise to stray further than the immediate area of the building and its grounds. Since we didn't get a chance to see much the day before - and Emma tells me that it helps to get a few more specific questions if you look round the workplace of the subject - we would try and view as much as possible without trespassing on the projectile-based entertainment. I am starting to become accustomed to deferring to Emma's greater knowledge on some, or maybe all matters journalistic. After we finish breakfast and I get a shower and change into what I realise is my last clean set of clothes, having misjudged the number of days we were away when packing back in London. I make a mental note to wash and rinse some of my used clothes when we got back from the interview, intending to dry the clothes on the metal radiator which is so hot I can't touch it. Emma knocks and comes into the room fully prepared with her camera and kit bags organised, so we head for the car and drive along the pine-lined single track road to Inverannan Estate and through the gates again to the main house. We pull up at the same spot from the previous day but this time walk left towards a broad lawn at the side of the gravelled parking area. I am again impressed by the neatness of the entire estate. From the lawn, we have a view of what looks like a parterre surrounded by a low stone wall with spring blooming rowan trees planted at regular intervals outside its perimeter. We walk to the stone wall which has been either reinstated or is brand new, but either way had had some serious time and effort spent on its construction.

'Do you notice something' ask Emma, as I point out past the garden and to the woodland.

'What? It's very open and has lots of nice trees.' She looks at me with a degree of puzzlement.

'There's no Scandinavian pine trees left here. After we came through the gates and out of the Forestry Commission plantation, there wasn't one non-native tree on the land. There's been a major clearing here to remove every one of those. Look at the ground, stumps everywhere.'

For probably two to three miles from our elevated position, we can see hundreds of pine stumps from recently cut trees, leaving mainly birch, elder, rowan and some Scots pine. Probably for Emma, this wasn't as impressive as it was for me, but it was a lesson in how to return a forest to its pre-pine industry condition. Not only that, but it tells me that Galloglas is indeed a smart businessman, I didn't know the going rate for two hundred or so hectares of pine, but it would be a fair profit as a one-off for him. I tell Emma about this and we agree to find out more about his culling of the woodland in this morning's questions, I jot it down in my notepad as we got back to the car.

As we start back to the house, it is with some surprise that we saw Galloglas himself walking towards us with hand held out in welcome. We walk over and shook his hand in turn, exchanging pleasantries as we did.

'So, I noticed you were admiring my soon-to-be ancient forest' He smiles, eagerly and takes us back to the view to better explain his plans. 'I started to plan it as soon as I got here, then bought as much surrounding ground as I could and set to. It took until last month but for the first time in sixty years, you can see along the valley and over to the hills. If I get the next parcel of land from its current owners, it will be planted right up to the high ground, which is the edge of where they would grow anyway. I kept another three parcels to the south-east cleared as moorland for shooting, but this is the biggest land project by far since we started the project.'

He is clearly proud of his achievement so other than telling him how impressive it was and that he should be congratulated on it, I don't ask anything at that point, preferring to think it through a little more and reframe my questions after that. Perhaps he senses that I was holding back, or maybe he was just busy, but Galloglas turns smartly and invites us into the building for a coffee and to restart our interview. We follow him, saying a friendly hi as we passed by the office team and into his domain, his two secretaries aren't in, not that they had shown us any interest before anyway.

This time, he is more helpful to Emma and she spends ten busy minutes taking some really good shots of him at his desk, at the window and standing at a landscape portrait of Inverannan House, in all its Victorian splendour, now restored by this powerful man and his ambitious venture. As they do the shoot, I look around his wood-lined office, as impressive a working space as I'd ever had the pleasure to visit. Apart from a portrait of the man himself, there is a tapestry in the centre of the far wall, enclosed in glass. There are two other paintings on the wall and I smile at the thought of the tacky prints back at the B&B. I take a closer look and each and am impressed to see that they were both by William York McGregor, a renowned Scottish landscape artist and one of the famous Glasgow Boys. When I was university and skint, I had spent some time as a hobby on them, living as I did then close to the Kelvingrove Art Gallery. Either Galloglas has an excellent eye for art or he has a competent financial advisor as these are not only superb to look at but also an investment which, in these dark days of banker's bonuses, would be much in demand.

Emma is completely efficient at her work. Putting Galloglas at ease with her positivity and tangibly professional ability to make the subject look somehow more and better than reality, she completes the shoot in an amazingly short time. After the shoot, she shows Galloglas the images on her Macbook, discarding those where the light was imperfect or his posture hadn't been of the required standard. Clearly motivated by the attention and perhaps by the thought of prospective customers seeing these high-quality photos in the piece, he is on a high when we sit down to our coffees at his teak desk and make a start on the second part of our interview.

I place my papers on the desk, along with my voice recorder but this time also my phone as a backup. I had forgotten this the day before, but I'm trying to get myself into the habit of having a safety net in case something goes wrong with the main recorder. A lecturer I had at uni had completed an in-depth interview with an Old Firm manager at an off-season training camp in Portugal, only to accidentally drop the device into the bath at his hotel afterwards. It was funny as hell when he recounted the experience of spending five hours during the night remembering as much as possible and transcribing it, however less funny for him when the manager in question threatened to knock his head off at the next opportunity for printing a lot of nonsense. Not wanting to place myself in that situation, I now have an excellent app on my phone and an impact and water-resistant voice recorder as the two main devices when interviewing.

After reassuring myself that my journalistic basics had been fulfilled, I ask Galloglas about the regeneration of the plantations we had seen outside, particularly how the finances of the Estate are affected by the project.

Galloglas nods as I speak, opens up and takes an ultra slim laptop from his desk drawer. He turns it round to show me a spreadsheet and graphs, fairly familiar to me from my highland student days; it is an analysis of the previous and current silviculture estimates for natural regeneration compared with the statistical predictions of an intervention. I look over it for a couple of minutes before responding.

'So, you've given up a regular income and it's going to be replanted with no future farming. You have a commercial approach to every other part of the business. Why spend a small fortune on something which won't give you a penny back?'

He smiles at my question, one which no doubt he had anticipated. He sits forward and entwines his fingers as he replied. 'Ancient forest; that's what was here before the people, the sheep, the lairds and before the deer predators died out. We've cleared out everything that shouldn't be there, fenced the perimeter and this year, we start to plant. We have just under 250 hectares of land to be planted with saplings, a combination of my team and volunteers from two charities. We put the volunteers up for free in a couple of bothies and they have a holiday here, free room and board.'

He clicks on the second page of the spreadsheet and both I and Emma lean forward to try to quickly interpret the financial figures across four columns.

Emma looks at him with more than a hint of admiration. 'So, you've used the income from the pine extraction to fund the regeneration?'

'Most of it' he replies. 'We have some external funding to make up the difference but most of it was covered by selling the pine commercially. The bothies were ruined crofts, so we had to rebuild them first. We actually have a small village now, albeit no-one lives there permanently. The charity organises the bookings, cleaning and costs and food, we refund the food costs and a few bottles of whisky to thank them at the end of the day.'

Emma and I are suitably impressed but, despite his effusive and enthusiastic description of the project we sit and listen to, I have a deeply unsettling feeling which I don't want to speak about, not yet anyway. The figures for the income for the pine were massively inflated, to which end I could not imagine. I wasn't up to date on the exact market prices but I don't think they had multiplied by a factor of about 6 to 8 since a couple of years ago. I had enough mates back at home whose relatives work in forestry and weren't short to bleat about how hard it was to make money in that game, to know that Mr Galloglas is much more full of crap than we had thought. I listen to him describe the deforestation project with his now-familiar fervour and make some minor questions, jotting down some notes while he pontificates about the optimum method of accessing sloping land and how to build temporary vehicle access. It is clear that he didn't have any time pressures today and is using this to enjoy the sound of his own voice.

After he has exhausted the deforestation subject, with his discussion at least 80% directed at Emma, I finally get to ask my second question.

'So', I exhale slightly, hoping to prompt a more concise reply this time. 'The shooting side of things, can you tell me how this fits into the project and how you have dealt with critics of particularly the deer and bird shooting on the estate. There have been some voluble critics of this side of the business I understand.' It's verbatim stuff from my question set, predictable stuff, but my recordings and notes are filling up with content from the interview, especially given Galloglas plentiful replies.

'Indeed there has been a fair bit of criticism. Let me tell you why they are misguided on all fronts' Galloglas is not going to stay quiet and launches again into a motivated reply.

'If you had seen the land to the north-west before, it was either compressed by non-native pine or indeed the small older parts were dying since all the seedlings and young trees were damaged by deer. To make this a success, the deer and indeed the sheep from outside my property, had to be prevented from accessing the land, hence the perimeter fence.'

'We found that it was difficult in the short term to do anything about the deer other than culling them, so the business part of the project fitted perfectly with our primary ecological imperative. We set up the front of Inverannan House as a boutique hotel and restaurant, with these offices as you know, at the rear. Each year we plan to welcome between 300 and 500 hunters, each paying generously to do the job of culling the problematic levels of deer. Of course, managed by our highly trained and qualified staff and adhering to the regulatory requirements of the Scottish Rural Affairs Committee, including a comprehensive Deer Management Plan which takes into account not only the welfare of the deer herds but also the ecological impact on the forest in that area.'

Galloglas goes on yet again at great detail, giving us plenty of content on the awards he planned to win for this side of the business and how he is revolutionising the commercial synergy between tourism and land management. He shows me another spreadsheet which gives the income and a separate table with profit from the hunting part of the business. At this point, I realise that his enthusiasm and salesman-like demeanour masks at best a chancer and at worst a crook. Critically, the figures are again insanely inflated for the income from shooting. Not even the wealthiest customers would pay these amounts, far higher than even the most expensive near where I lived. Also, bizarrely, this over-inflated income is matched by the expenditure figures such as staff costs - ghillies, beaters and drivers along with others had a cost which, unless they were paid a hell of a lot more than anyone I knew in those professions, were a fantasy. The restaurant and boutique hotel is also exorbitant, although I had no work experience in this sector; it certainly looks like an expensive operation for this part of the world.

The question going around my head while he speaks is why have these ridiculous figures in a business? Perhaps Galloglas is a financial incompetent and it will all come crashing down any time. I need to get through the interview and regroup after talking all this through with Emma.

I have heard more than enough content about the admirable Inverannan project and the Galloglas fantasy finances, so I move on to his previous career in the military.

'You spoke yesterday about your motivation for your work here. Can you tell me at what point in your army career you first thought about moving into this type of business?'

Galloglas is again his element, starting by telling us the places he's been, which matched our bio files but added a couple we didn't know about. I suppose that these were shorter postings or even training sessions he'd carried out. Finally, he gets the point, choosing his words more carefully than before.

'I managed to save some money during my career and had inherited a sum from a relative, so at that point, probably after my second tour in Iraq, was when I first thought about it. I had some mates who had went into business after they left the regiment and done well, so I stayed I touch with them. They had invested in property and flourished, but I felt that if I had the chance, I'd do something in Scotland and make it not only an investment but also a working business. I monitored the sales of estates in Scotland and took advice on the pros and cons of running an estate. To be honest, I was generally told to avoid it, unless I was shoving up dozens of wind turbines, but I didn't want to go that way.'

I want him to elaborate on this, as it doesn't ring true to me, but I am also aware that this isn't meant to be an interrogation on my part, so I try to keep it light in tone.

'That's admirable on your part. Too many landowners making a fortune on wind farms doesn't do the area much good either. Can you tell me, are any of your former army comrades involved here at Inverannan?'

He answers tersely. 'No, not at all. I don't keep in touch with anyone from the old days now other than the occasional regimental reunion.' He looks at his watch and I know that we have to move back to the positive publicity side of the interview if I wanted to keep him going.

'So, other than the plans we've covered already, can you tell me the next steps in the project in more detail – it would be great for the piece if we could give the readers a taste of what's to come?'

Galloglas switches straight back to what I now thought of as salesman mode.

'Well, one additional investment we have planned with a partner organization is a facility at Loch Baxford. It has a jetty just now, but there is far deeper water about half a mile farther down from the existing single track, so we have a road extension project underway and when that's complete, we'll build a harbour and moorings there, potentially along with some tourist accommodation and so forth for visitors. This coast, albeit further south, has a lot of summer yachting interest and if we had something here, it could open a significant market for us. Did you know that there are over four thousand sailing boats on the west coast alone? Not to mention the potential from international tourism in the peak months.' He goes on to tell us the synergies between the sailing and the shooting/fishing market, in his opinion potentially the same customers at different points in the year.

I make a note to check who the partner was for the jetty project; if it's reached the stage he described there will be planning information available. The only issue with the check is that there is absolutely no internet connection available here, so that will have to wait until I could reach somewhere more connected. I am sure that Inverannan House will have its own satellite connection, as most of these places do. Small remote villages are however still a different matter, particularly like here, with a range of mountains between here and the world of broadband and a rugged coast on the other side. Back in Mharisaig, we got connected a year or so ago, although mobile signals are still patchy at best. Most people still rely on the good old BT phone which at least works during the worst of weather, even when the power goes out.

'So', I ask, adjusting the position of my voice recorder on the desk to help catch his occasional backwards lean on the high leather chair. 'What did you do in the run-up to buying Inverannan? Was there a period where you had a rest before all this hard work?'

He is visibly annoyed in this question, dodging it skilfully but briskly, 'I wanted a challenge after I left, and when this came on the market, it more or less fell into place. I planned most of the projects after reconnoitring the estate at the start and then, well, I've hardly thought about taking a break– keep busy dusk till dawn here.'

'So, how long was the period between you leaving the army and buying Inverannan?' I continue to try and probe, for whatever reason I don't know.

He answers, perhaps again with a pre-prepared story. 'About three years. I did some consulting work at that time and when that finished, I bought the estate.' He then gives me a look which tells me that he wasn't happy about this type of question, so I switch back to the positive line of questions. I had it in my head from the outset to switch question tone, trying to push his buttons with the friendly questions then rotate some which might invite him to reveal some facts, other than those he intended.

'You mentioned the shooting and fishing part of the Estate and how popular that is, can you tell provide me with the details of the numbers of stag, salmon, trout and so forth? It would be good to have this in the piece, to show the scale of the operation.'

Galloglas agrees enthusiastically again, probably thinking it a positive point for a promotional aspect and after finishing a couple more, he rather unexpectedly asks us to drop back in tomorrow lunchtime for a coffee before we leave, he'll have his estate manager provide some updated figures for us, as well as giving us the opportunity for another "brief" chat with him and perhaps a tour of the estate in a Land Rover. This is fine but we hoped to leave as early as possible, assuming we had the interview content complete – albeit only an anodyne version without whatever financial shenanigans he is up to. The falsely inflated financial figures and the three year gap in his CV at the end of his military career are strongly pulling me towards a deeper dig here, but there was an obvious issue that he would have no reason to co-operate and also, we had, as far as we knew, been sent here to do a piece which was completely vanilla. I help Emma pack up and shake Galloglas hand again as we leave. We head back the way we came, through the office without stopping for a chat with the busy team there and out to the car.

'What's eating you then?' Emma asks when we sit in the car.

'Couple of things; one, his financial spreadsheet is a load of bollocks.'

'How so?'

'Well, the amount of money he's spending on everything is insane. Wages, restaurant, projects, it's like money is no object and he's paying over the odds for everything. I don't know much about the running of hotels and estates, but what I do know is that it's hard to make a profit, so the owners squeeze every penny they can to keep costs down. This guy, he's acting like a billionaire, throwing money into speculative stuff like a harbour in the middle of nowhere? No chance that will make money, especially putting a road across to it, that can't be cheap.'

Emma shakes her head. 'He's probably just investing heavily for a big return. If he's got customers who are wealthy, they won't expect a highland café for their dinner, they would want luxury.

Even the harbour, it sounds reasonable that if there are no competitors up here, he might make a fortune on that after he sets it up.'

I'm not sure at all but keep the rest of my thoughts to myself on the way back to the village. If what Emma said was true – and I didn't think it was by a stretch – the amount of investment, on top of the purchase price for the estate, would mean that Galloglas would have to have invested maybe half a million in capital and a couple of hundreds of thousands in revenue costs already. If he's been there for two years; that means his income would have to be stratospheric to cover the costs, never mind give the impression of sustainability or some dream of a far-off profit. I know I have some thinking to do, whether to dig into this or disappoint myself by keeping everyone happy by writing up a nice promotional piece with glossy photos. After all, the premise of this article is that everyone gets what they want. The subject gets free publicity, their name in magazines far and wide and their ego massaged if the piece is written in that way. What I am toying with now is writing two pieces. There would be one for my employers to sell to their glossy partners and one with the facts examined. I might never sell that one, but it would be unconscionable to know that Galloglas was up to something and not to investigate further. I might even blog it anonymously if the mood took me, although my access to these details would always give a clue that I was the source.

These thoughts are percolating as we reach the B&B, Emma pulling the car into the space to the right of the house. We head upstairs and agree to go for a walk, Emma having seen a lot more of the village surroundings than me and clearly wanting some exercise. I would have preferred to chill out in my room, but know that a walk was probably the better option to stave off the boredom before I persuaded Emma to go to the pub again. We have the option to eat in the B&B but I didn't fancy the faux atmosphere and more importantly, the lack of a drink afterwards.

After an hours walk to clear our heads and get some exercise, we go with enthusiasm into the pub for lunch, something of both a tradition in these parts and a habit which I could absolutely identify with. Once inside, having exchanged pleasantries with the barman and ordered some pizza, hopefully, lighter than the previous evening's dish, we sit at the same seat and begin to warm up from the highland chill to the pleasantly ambient warmth of the bar.

Emma asks me about how I feel we had done on the assignment and I think it is now the time to express my deep mistrust of Galloglas and my now fairly certain opinion that we were being used by a charlatan – at best – to promote a business which either wasn't legal or had something in the background which might make us look really bad as journalists at some later point.

She is almost entirely dubious but I try to elucidate my reasoning on Galloglas.

'OK, here's my list.' I take out my notepad and start a new page, jotting down my points in no real order. I look round and see that the barman has headed off to sort out our dinner, so nobody to overhear us.

'Firstly, he has a CV gap of three years. Nobody has that. Nobody.' I stress.

'During those three years, he has given vague and contradictory replies about what he was up to, but 'consulting' appears to be the main story. Ex-military guys who do this, well, I'm not sure but doesn't that mean they are mercenaries or advisors to dictators or something? Let's be honest, it's a major question mark over someone who turns up with a fortune to spend.'

'His financial spending is bollocks, no matter what you might try to explain away. If he's spending that kind of money, there's no way he's recouping costs – the income must be nowhere near that. We didn't see one visitor in our two visits and yes, I know it's off-season for whatever shooting or sailing they get up to, but all I'm saying is he's got all those expensive staff and restaurant costs ongoing with nobody staying there. I mean, he's acting like a millionaire philanthropist, but he's not that, is he?'

Emma nods, which rather surprises me. I wasn't normally that persuasive.

'Yes, I had been thinking about that. We've seen about eight staff at the Inverannan, nor including the restaurant and whoever actually works the estate. He never mentioned any current income, just seemed to want to promote the business. OK, that's three things. What else have you got?'

Emma takes a sip of Guinness and sits back, awaiting my response. I flick back through my notepad.

'OK. He said he inherited money but didn't mention from whom, or how much.'

Emma looks dubious at this one. 'Who would, it's his private business; no-one would tell a journalist about their personal finances in a meeting. That's a no on point four Adam.'

'I'm just saying - it's unsubstantiated information which we're taking as truth. If he's dodgy, we've swallowed the lie and are giving a crook publicity.' I check around again for the barman, who now appears to be re-stocking the gantry and occasionally coming in and out with what sounded like small bottles of mixer.

'Number five.' I flick back and then jot it down on the page. 'He employs two so-called secretaries who look like retired bodybuilders. Not exactly Miss Moneypennies were they?'

'So what do you think they were?' Emma asks with more than a hint of dubiety.

I think for a moment. 'Hard men, Bodyguards, Henchmen or something like that. Goodness knows their job here, but they aren't doing anything remotely secretarial.' It is useful for me to speak about the situation; I'd not been able to formulate my opinion properly until we'd gone through each point. This punt is slightly reined in by Emma.

'So, on the basis of no evidence and – let's be honest – a leap of imagination on each of your points, you would suggest what? That we amend our actual job here, instead of writing up the piece our employer asked us to do, we do a hatchet job which nobody wants? Then, do we turn up back in London and ask Billie to market a piece she didn't ask for and would end up in court as soon as it's published?' Emma drains her glass and I realise I have only sipped my pint while I had been talking.

'Maybe there's a way to do our job and also see if I'm paranoid. I'll get you another of these.' I smile at Emma and stroll to the bar, timing it well as the barman returned.

I order a Guinness for Emma and a Talisker for me. I don't actually like whisky that much, but having been told that it was an acquired taste, am determined to stick with it until I did. The barman tells me that the food would be about another ten minutes as the oven hadn't been heated up. I guess it must be an Aga or something, but I tell him that as long as we have something to drink, it's not a problem.

I go back to Emma and started on my notebook again. 'OK, here's another one; there are no customers, but the staff in the office are working as if it's the floor of the Tokyo Stock Exchange. What are they doing?'

She thinks for a moment. 'Selling and taking bookings; marketing; arranging work with contractors; budgetary control.' She takes a drink and looks at me in a manner which I think may be described as askance.

'No way; my mates mum worked in an estate office and she did sod all, all day. And that was busier than this place.' I refuse to see the excuses Emma put forward on this one, but I am aware that I am being belligerent rather than persuasive now.

'OK, last one. The harbour and road' Emma starts to interrupt, but I ask her to let me finish.

'I obviously can't check this, but I think – including the road and a couple of houses he mentioned, he'll be spending the thick end of £700,000 on that project alone. My issue is that it's completely speculative, there's no comparable business as he said, so any income is a guess. That means that financing the work didn't come from a bank or other lender. No-one would touch that investment; it's a complete white elephant in the making.'

I take another long drink of my pint and keep going. 'I'm not from around here, but I do know a little about the sailing in Scotland. It's a short season and most of them potter around the south part of the West coast, Largs up to north of Oban and maybe the islands, weekend sailors usually. There's very few of the total that would be out for a proper fortnight around the islands and this, although it might attract a few, isn't going to be a major port of call. So, how do you get back your investment and the running costs for facilities, which are only used from May to August… and by only a tiny proportion of what I imagine may be an already saturated market?'

Emma is playing devil's advocate again. 'Yes, but Galloglas is a speculator. What if it's a success, you know, the only deep-water mooring in this part of the coast. It could even be a tourist novelty.'

'Have you seen the coast up here? My mum used to say, there's nothing there but hoose and heather.'

'What?' asks Emma.

I realise that my accent, normally well navigated by Emma, had been less than clear. 'It means there's nothing here. Heather, water, rocks and that's it. To top it all, it's not even that spectacular as the mountains are too far away. It's basically not that scenic, just rugged and not worth visiting. Sailors want scenery, a good mooring, islands and ideally a nice old village pub to drink in after all the hard work. Not an eight-mile drive in a car they don't have with them to an expensive Michelin starred or whatever boutique bistro in Inverannan.' I hit the button with this one, now Emma looked like she agrees with me, despite all my reasoning being based on surmise rather than anything tangible.

'OK.' She says, 'What do you suggest we do?'

'I have a cunning plan' I smile.

As we devour our lunches, we are interrupted by an unexpected visitor. Ranald, the rather hard-of-hearing chap who met us initially at Inverannan comes in, sees us and sits beside us, slumping on the chair beside me and grabbing chips from the side of my plate. He is dishevelled and appears that he had been on a long walk with a tall bottle of whisky, his boots and gaiters coated in mud as well as giving off a generally unwashed and booze-soaked vibe.

'You're in a good mood' I offer.

'Aye, that's because I'm happy, son.' He slurs, helps himself to rest of my chips and takes a drink of my pint.

The barman comes over before I can ask him where he's going and hoists him from the chair by his arm. 'Time for you to get home for a sleep Ranald' he warns him as he escorts him efficiently out of the door, giving me the impression he'd done this a few times before. Ranald leaves unsteadily, staggering out and down the stairs, clearly delighted with something, but that something manifested itself as being a complete pain in the arse.

'I'll replace your food and drink', says the barman, lifting both. 'Sorry about Ranald, he occasionally gets a bit much down his neck.' He leans towards me and confides that the estate guys come in for a half-bottle of whisky at breakfast time to get rid of their hangover and see them through their shift. 'Old habits up here, right enough', he says.

'And I thought Fleet Street had a bad reputation' smiles Emma as we wait for my replacement chips.

At this point, the bar starts to fill up. More locals are coming into the bar at intervals and I realise that this must be a busy afternoon for the pub, maybe the drinking weekend starts in earnest on a Thursday afternoon here.

'So, when will we get a chance to write up Forster's interestingly loquacious responses from yesterday?' I ask Emma as the tables fill.

'I think, Adam, that this is this afternoon's task.' I need this like a stag needs a well-armed hunter, but there's no denying that Emma is right and that our time would better be spent doing that than sitting here enjoying ourselves. I feel a rush of annoyance with Simon for landing us with this job, but it might work out OK for me and Emma; I'm the new guy, helping out the more experienced but unreliable Simon. We finish our drinks and head out of the heaving bar towards an afternoon of transcription and amendments. It's probably not ideal work after drinks and pizza, but we fight the urge to be lazy and once ensconced in Emma's room again, we plough unremittingly through Forster's loquaciousness.

I look at the bedside clock and its' 6pm, my boredom threshold was breached a long while ago and I couldn't care less if I ever heard anything else about audits and inefficiencies in the civil service.

'I can't do any more; I am bored shitless with this.' I lean back in the chair and yawn from the core of my being.

'Yeah, I think we're done; we can tidy it up on the train back.' Emma is frazzled too, her professionalism blunted by the minutiae of Forster's replies. We pack up the laptops and I save a copy to a pen drive I keep in my wallet in case someone nicks my laptop. Agreeing to get cleaned up and go to the pub again; I head into my room and fall asleep on the bed almost instantly, a testament to the civil service. Around half an hour later, I'm woken by a car revving as it passes outside the B&B and I lurch into the shower to get ready for another evening in Inverannan's top venue. I shove my clothes back on, spraying deodorant to freshen things up a little and using some gel try to make my hair stay where it's meant to be.

I check my mobile wistfully, feeling a little cut off from the world and wondering what's happening with my friends while I've been out of contact. Emma knocks my door and comes in to wait for me to finish up.

'I've been thinking.' She seems to have come over all serious again. 'You might have something about the Estate. I mean, if the financial stuff is a scam and we're doing an advert for his business, it's fine, he's just trying to drum up income; but if it's to attract investors or something, we could be playing along with a fraud, couldn't we.' I sit facing her, wondering where she is going here. 'I think we should go and have coffee with him tomorrow but you should ask what he wants from the article, see if he's trying to attract investors.'

I nod 'OK, let's do that. I can say that it's to help with the tone of the article or something. What if he says it's for customers but he's just kidding us – how would we know?'

Emma shrugged. 'I think you could give him some praise, fake a bit of enthusiasm for where the Estate would grow to and that might get him on another roll.' I agree with this, it could use his sales manner to make a mistake while he's off on a flight of fancy about Inverannan.

'Done' I say, picking up my jacket. 'So long as you buy me a beer.'

Emma shakes her head 'Costs must be kept to a minimum, no big nights when working.'

'Spoilsport' I tell her, my ready wit failing on anything better.

☐

Chapter Fourteen

Early off

When my dad had left for work, happy as a horses shit, I fell to thinking about my abandoned situation. After my thoughts had vacillated across a spectrum of emotions, I found myself becoming happy for them, but it's not every day your parents abandon you for a place in the sun, especially having saved up all their money to make it happen. I gradually accepted that they had taken a very deliberate decision to live like we were on the breadline to make their retirement dream come true, depriving us of creature comforts, holidays and in my case, any trace of designer clothes during my lifetime so far. I had accepted that while my pals often showed off some Ralph Lauren or Hilfiger clothing, I had to stay on the sideline with my sale items from whatever shops in Inverness happened to be closing down or from second-hand stores. At the time I survived each feeling of embarrassment, but it was certainly bubbling to the top of my psyche now. I kicked the living room door so hard that the lower panel came straight out and yelled at the top of my voice with frustration and anger, thankfully our isolation suited this type of blow-out. After this, my head hurt like blazes and I went to my bed to sleep off the last of my hangover and settle into self-pitying weeping for a time.

As I lay in bed for a while, possibly not in the soundest of minds, I decided to take up the offer of university at Glasgow and forget about sixth year. If my parents wanted to leave and I was in the way, well, I'd get out of the way and let them be remote and disinterested in me from afar, instead of me hanging on here in Nowhere, Scotland on my own. Wallowing in this bog of unhappiness and anger, I ignored the phone when it rang, probably Michelle but I didn't want to speak to anyone. I fell asleep and didn't wake up till 3pm, remembering what had happened and still internally adamant that I'd had it with school. I rummaged in my bedside cabinet and found the conditional acceptance from Glasgow University, reading it with a more serious effort than I had when it arrived. It looked like the course suited me, as I had thought, so just now to accept it and start to make arrangements.

Michelle. How would she react to me when I tell her? I lay back on my bed and felt tears coming again, the thought of leaving on my own, a martyr to my parent's lack of interest in me. After five minutes I had composed myself and even felt a certain hardness settling on my demeanour, thankfully and perhaps surprisingly, I didn't seem to feel a great deal of sympathy for anyone else except myself. With Michelle, I told myself that we weren't at the stage in our lives where we could be together forever, I thought; it would be fine. I knew within me though, that we really wouldn't.

I went downstairs and called the university number on my letter, spending half an hour confirming the situation, explaining my limited access to the internet and registering for student accommodation, which I'd have to wait for confirmation on. As I placed the handset down, I knew that my next priority was to speak to Michelle and talk about what had just happened. I called her and she answered almost straight away.

'I tried to call you earlier to see what you were up to', she laughed 'got a sore head? I think everyone has a hangover today, your mate Niall must be suffering, he was mangled!'

'Aye…I need to tell you something.' I knew that the best way to do this was face to face, and it was cowardly to do it over the phone. So, I thought, I'll do it over the phone.

I told her what had transpired with my parents, overegging the part where they wanted to be rid of me to help justify my decision to go straight to uni rather than continue sixth year at school. She was silent while I spoke and when I asked if she was OK, the line went quietly dead. Shit, I thought, that was ripping the plaster off and no mistake.

Michelle called back about an hour later, calm and detached, sensible and even supportive. This made me feel that she was more mature and that she was helping me now as a capable friend while I was being reactionary, self-pitying and possibly childish. I was vaguely aware that she could feel badly and unfairly treated but was being far more mature than I in handling the exigencies of the situation. We spoke for the longest time, eventually making a pact, real or wishful, that we would meet in Glasgow together at weekends and whenever we could and that everything would just be a new joint adventure, the distance would not be a problem. I think we both used this to bridge the emotional reality between our time together at Mharisaig and the separation to come. We finished talking when my dad came in from work, followed by my mum who'd been shopping in Inverness or something; I had forgotten that it was Friday and she'd be off.

That evening, we had a frank and to be honest, very helpful discussion in the living room, where we spoke about what their plans were; how they would support me at university and, as I now began to understand, their situation as parents having had their only child when they were both in their late thirties. It wasn't odd to have older parents, lots of my friends were born of second marriages or big families, so I had never been self-conscious about it but now I understood much more about where they were in life. I accepted that they had to live their own lives too, so by the time midnight came round, our respective plans had been collectively agreed; our reservations put to the side and a familial concord to make these things happen in place.

In the weeks after that, my parents received notifications of early retirement and the dates when they would be leaving their jobs, dad in October and my mum the month before. They were checking out properties and the healthcare requirements of going to Spain and this would be their project over the rest of summer and autumn, while I embarked on my unexpectedly early sortie into further education. In the middle of September we had travelled early to Glasgow by car, then train to sort out my accommodation, having decided to rent a room after being too late to apply for the six months university accommodation. Luckily, Robbie Sinclair, a son of a friend of my dad had a small single room to let in the West End, where I couldn't have afforded to live unless it was, like this, a price reduction for someone they knew and a favour for dad. I'd met Robbie a couple of times before, he and his dad had stayed an overnight with us once and we'd hung out at the ruined cottage. He was two years older than me, going into his second year, was really smart and a good laugh, and had got on well with my mates back in Mharisaig.

We viewed the room and the flat with Robbie and then arranged to bring my belongings down the following fortnight, giving me a week to get used to things before starting classes. In possibly the first spending spree I had witnessed my parents making, they bought me an iPhone and a MacBook, as well as some new clothes, albeit we did pick some of them up in charity shops, old habits die hard and all that. They were doing their best to set me up for university and I was genuinely thankful for that. We had a pre-theatre meal in a Thai restaurant on Great Western Road and took the last train to Fort William from where my dad drove us home. I knew this would be one of our last trips together, but the excitement of my unexpected start to university pushed my sadness at our imminent parting down, for the moment at least.

My last couple of weeks in Mharisaig were spent catching up and saying au revoir to my friends, their amazement at my departure tempered by their collective understanding that I and Michelle were the most affected by my decision. Everyone was also surprised at my parents leaving, which increased their sympathy for my own position, it being hard to imagine leaving me in a cottage in Mharisaig on my own and trying to keep on the straight and narrow. I spent the last two days with Michelle, doing what we did and being, I thought, ignorantly positive about times ahead. We said our goodbyes the night before I left, by way of helping avoid a tearful start to my journey. I walked Michelle home and returned with all the heaviness of parting burdening my mind along with the nervousness of travelling on my own the next day. I thought that Michelle, despite our promises to call and plans to visit, knew inside that we were over as a couple, which didn't help my increasing feeling of impending solitude.

When the time came, my parents took me to Fort William for the train, after realising that we didn't need to go by car as my belongings did not actually take up that much room and a large rucksack and one shoulder bag could easily hold my worldly goods. I had left behind the well-worn detritus of my wardrobe and took more or less the clothes we had bought in Glasgow. We shared our tearful hugs as I set off, wondering to myself how I got into this situation and, although past the point where I could reasonably change my mind, wishing I could jump back into the car with them. I got a grip of my emotions and, wiping away my tears, told them I'd call when I got there and not to worry; my mum, not normally one to show a great deal of emotion was red-faced and seemed not to want let go of me.

I got onto the train as it waited at the generically dull and grey platform, checking my phone for text messages, social media and emails before we left and my signal went with it. There were loads from my pals in Mharisaig, predominantly encouraging messages from my female friends and an amusingly abusive set from those eejit laddies who I spent my childhood with, typically outlining the opportunities in Glasgow to expand my sexual experiences. There were, however, two which required deeper reading.

The first, from Tess in Brisbane, was brief but wrenchingly awful. She told me, in terms which made it apparent that she had written the email in a tearful mood, that she had been told by Anna that I'd been seeing someone else; that she was hurt and disappointed and after that, to wish me good luck at university, and finally that I was a bastard, which in this instance, I had no qualms in agreeing with. I sat back, my embarrassment at myself causing a reddening and an all over wave of heat. I sat with my head in my hands until I fought back the tears and sent an apologetic email back, telling Tess that I didn't mean it to happen and not to be angry with me. I hoped that not blaming it on the pointlessness of a long-distance teenage relationship would indicate to her that I was being genuine and, with more than half my intentions being based on the possibility that we may meet again, I shouldered the whole thing as manfully and as profusely as I could. I sent it as the train started to move and then opened the last message, from Michelle.

Michelle, perhaps knowing intuitively what was likely to happen, or perhaps from knowing that I had already had a short but poor record on long-distance relationships, told me that we'd just spilt for now and see what happened if we met again sometime. For fuck's sake, I thought to myself, this is beyond a joke now. I realised that I had lost signal and wouldn't be able to respond for god knows how long, so composed a series of versions of my reply while the train variously slowed and sped in what I felt was a seriously annoying manner southwards. I settled on a mature, loving version of a reply which had the benefit of being closest to the truth and would come across as less self-pitying and juvenile than the other efforts. As we came through Crianlarich, I briefly got a signal and off my reply went. That done, I watched the scenery go past for the rest of the journey, feeling slightly numbed and depressed over the ending of two relationships on my Scotrail journey.

I had got into Glasgow with no delays and headed to the West End, albeit getting slightly lost and ending up in Partick, which I decided I wouldn't need to visit again. After a ten minute walk back uphill, I found my bearings and got to the flat, a key having been provided on my previous visit. The flat was unoccupied, my room vacant and as clean as it was when I'd seen it. There was, however, a different smell, of cannabis and stale lager, which I had suspected may have been the case when I had met Robbie before, he had the look of a stoner albeit with more than a dash of IT geek thrown in. I didn't want to get in company too much with him, for one he was in second year and I was still seventeen, well warned by my mum to behave and still callow enough to at least try and stick to parental advice. I sorted out my clothes into the wardrobe and had a rest after the early rise and long journey down, although there were too many worryingly guilty emotions jumping around my adolescent brain for me to sleep.

My separation from Mharisaig complete in both the physical and emotional senses, I settled extremely well into life in Glasgow over the following weeks. I got a job in an Indian restaurant, taking orders over the phone, running delivery orders from the kitchen to the drivers and when they were absolutely stuck, waiting tables despite a complete lack of ability to carry plates without dropping cutlery and leftover food. The manager only permitted me to carry two plates at a time maximum, even though the more talented waiters seemed to effortlessly balance four plates along their arms. Despite my calamitous efforts, they kept me on and paid very well considering the difficulties I caused, a credit to their patience and their willingness to persevere with someone who to all appearances would never have the manner or the dexterity to actually do the job properly. The main point for me; was that it allowed me to fund a decent social life which my allowance from my parents was unlikely to enable.

During those early weeks, it also became apparent why Robbie was keen for me to take up the last remaining room in his impressive West End apartment. Robbie was a relatively high-volume drug dealer to university students and basically needed someone my age to gain entry to first-year customers for all their cannabis and various tab-based requirements. We came to an uneasy agreement in the third week of my university term, when after my initial refusal to participate personally, I had introduced Robbie to one of my classmates who was more than willing to embark on a lucrative point of sale role on his behalf. Robbie was happier after that, his business needs fully met and me quite happy to keep quiet about the real reason why a second-year student with limited resources and mild body odour managed to have a stream of attractive girlfriends and fund a playboy lifestyle while spending twelve hours a day sleeping. Those arrangements in place, my first year at Glasgow carried forward impressively as I worked, studied, submitted papers, passed exams and celebrated my eighteenth birthday without significant problems, although this urban idyll was not long to endure.

Chapter Fifteen

The Drop

They usually took about 65-70 minutes to get there and away, after unloading the boat with the local men, whose job it was to transfer the gear from the island; they packed it into a number of compartments under the seats and boot of the reliable Range Rover and the equally adapted Nissan van which met them there. That complete, they then drove both vehicles to their destination in the grounds of Inverannan House. That day, Allanton drove quickly and quietly, annoyed by Simon and at the similarly unexpected arrival of the journalists arriving at Inverannan, not exactly a threat, but perhaps a catalyst for change. John Allanton had been involved in similar activities elsewhere in the UK for his father, but he always felt that they were riskier; more likely to be noticed by the Authorities or even be interrupted by rivals, the ever-possible threat of Albanian or Russian muscle having a go at them if they knew where they operated. That was the beauty of his father's empire – no-one at the lower levels or their competition knew how they controlled things, not really, not how it all fitted together or how they infiltrated the market with goods wherever they went or even how they stayed so far out of it that they could hide in plain sight, their representatives controlling the local levels.

Despite his misgivings at being so close to the front line, John liked some aspects of this set-up; mainly that it let him keep his work a physical distance from his family, in a place where they controlled the situation almost completely and where they had the capacity to move product around with relatively minimal risk. His father treated this as his pre-retirement project, supported by John and others, despite being in a position where he could and possibly should, have moved abroad for better weather and lower proximity to risk. John knew though that his father's real purpose here was to impart the remaining knowledge and acumen from those many years' experience to him before he moved out of active participation in the day-to-day of the business. John knew the mechanics as well he needed to, but he knew that his fathers' culture was still slightly beyond his grasp, a grey area to the son who preferred greater clarity, a man whose wife half-joked of his

OCD but they both knew that he didn't have the inherent perception to comprehend the nuances of situations, particularly those he had no experience of. It was this last enlightenment which John Allanton sought to achieve before he strode across his father's empire; before he took primacy over his cousin's franchises abroad and before he could place his mark on the organisation which had tentacles in every westernised country across the globe.

John grimaced unintentionally as the thought of Galloglas came into his mind, his father's protégé who was possibly moving from plain sight to another more high-profile place, by inviting journalists into a location where they might well find out more than he wanted them to. John knew that he had grand plans too and would, if the family were not so embedded in the business, be the one who could stage a coup when his father did pass the mantle to him. It may not be altogether a vexatious problem he started to think; the issue of Galloglas' judgement in bringing the journalists into play, if John could turn this to his advantage. If Galloglas were replaced by someone more typical of his role in the business, someone malleable and just happy to earn money and stay anonymous for their tenure, this project here could continue with less hassle and risk and perhaps even for the franchise here in the UK, more profitable. Allanton was sure that Galloglas financial outlay on the Estate was becoming more than they paid him, generous though it was. That left the possibility that he was either skimming the profits, cutting the gear somehow to increase the volume or charging the distributors more than he was instructed to do. He'd shared these concerns with his father, which was why they were meeting with Galloglas the next day and why he now sent the secretaries there for part of the week to monitor his supply chain; albeit they reported that all was above board, well as above board as a hugely illegal narcotics business could be.

They had arrived at the jetty at the start of the rising half-light of morning, the northern skies taking on the sallow grey hue like they were still not quite awake but trying to give illumination enough for them to convey their product without slip or fall. John had watched, his face obscured by unrequired sunglasses, snood and cap as his men did the work, not three minutes in the moving and packing; he liked to think and describe it as a Formula One pit-stop, the delays meaning problems, so the work had to be done with maximum efficiency by a practised and professional team.

Today they were proficient as ever, the plastic-wrapped white product sealed in larger black heat-shrunk parcels which were precisely uniform to fit into the cavities in the car and van. He watched as they placed the seats and boot cover back in place and got into his car without any discussion with the underlings. They knew not to look at him, to converse with him or to try to engage in any way. The natural cautiousness and reticence of these islanders were ideal for this type of work; they were well rewarded for their part-time efforts, efforts which helped them to make a good living up here, where work can be scarce and a decent income hard to find even for hard-working men. Half of these men were also ex-military; an attribute which his father continued to value and one which had proven invaluable in the past, their rigid adherence to instructions as well as the capacity to not only organise well but also hold a certain menace to others being their key attributes. He sat back in the car and removed his headgear, driving smoothly along the single track road to Inverannan, starting the riskiest part of his current duties. It was in this leg of the supply chain where he was in possession of exactly 78 bricks of cocaine, totalling 85.8kilos of the highest grade product on the planet. Even after the chemists did their work later, adding almost 30% in quantity before being moved to the next stage, it was still considered to be some of the best coke the sellers had ever had, attracting a cost slightly higher than that of their typical competitors. John was always subject to a clenching in his stomach during this short drive, uncomfortable in the risk which he thought unnecessary for someone of his standing in the business. He focused on the road, his two companions silent as usual as they gradually made their way to Inverannan and the Estate of Galloglas. It was there that his father had converted a small stone barn into a drive-in / drive-out workshop, a method he'd used a number of times before. From the front, after a long drive along a forestry track and after a metal security barrier was negotiated, they pulled up at the gate, opened by an estate worker, who also opened the main doors and beckoned their vehicle to driven inside, closing the two doors behind them. John Allanton looked out of his window at three Inverannan Estate vans and a couple of other vehicles with their tailgates open, boot cavities ready to take a proportion of the product in each. To the side, cartons of chilled venison waited to be loaded on top and packed on top of the boot, along with other goods from the estate, to be delivered to the restaurants we owned in each of the cities we dealt with. Allanton left the car to let the workers get in, putting his sunglasses and cap back on and walking to the house, dropping into the office to say hello and then, after using the toilet, back to the car and onto the next drop.

Galloglas watched John Allanton cross the lawn and enter the front door of Inverannan House, his powerful frame and gait as ever a reminder that he was indeed, physically anyway, a suitable potential replacement for his father at the head of the organisation. Galloglas ached to be in control of the organisation, from the core of his psyche to the clenched fingers of his hands, gripping the back of a chair like he was strangling Allanton. Galloglas hadn't been born into the family, hadn't been born into any family that would have helped his career, not in the army and not in the outside world. He'd rose through the ranks by dint of his own ability; a feat well achieved while working part-time, at least for the best part of his military career, for Sir Mathieson Allanton, who was then, of course, Lieutenant-Colonel Allanton. Galloglas had been promoted to a senior non-commissioned officer first in Belfast; then steeped in the mire of conflict and knowing no glory was to be made, became desperate to get anywhere else his regiment would be willing to send him. When he came to the attention of Allanton; that was when his fortunes really changed, his new mentor needing men with muscle, determination and just enough intelligence; and him needing to get away from a place where the dangers weren't in front of you to fight, but round every corner in a car or at a window. Thanks to Lieutenant-Colonel Allanton, as well connected as anyone in the army could have been and with more old school tie contacts from Fettes, Oxford and Sandhurst as Galloglas could imagine, they were both able to take up roles of a more global nature, with training and advisory roles being their preferred headlines to cover their special forces roles. Galloglas knew that, although he had many skills, he was selected as a subordinate who was able to provide his absolute loyalty and discretion, while having little or no compulsion over eradicating a series of threats as deemed fit by his paymasters. Allanton too was in his, albeit more elevated role, known and utilised as an officer who could get the dirty work done and in the 1970s and 1980s particularly, there was a lot of dirty work for them to do. Under

113

the cover of their remit and protected by the Official Secrets Act from disclosure by any of their colleagues or civil servants in each location, they were comfortably unidentified to all but those at the top of the decision-making chain.

Galloglas leaned back from his standing position and flexed his arms, thinking back to those days and smiling. When he had a quiet moment, he sometimes mentally ran through the chronological list of those he'd terminated, feeling no post-traumatic stress whatsoever, in fact it often helped to settle down to sleep as he tried to remember all the events he'd personally operated on or trained some locals to do while doing their best not to blow themselves up first. Galloglas had been good at his job, that was for sure, and now he wanted to be outstanding at this, his first command, Inverannan Estate. He looked down at John Allanton driving away from the house and reddened slightly, knowing that he was ignoring Galloglas and avoiding showing him respect by coming into the building without meeting him, a fact which would not be unnoticed by the staff. Bristling, he sat down at his desk to convert his irritation into hard work, the work of building the estate.

Chapter Sixteen

Glasgow Bites Back

I spent the summer holiday after the end of first year lazing in Glasgow, only visiting Mharisaig briefly to check on my parents now-vacant cottage and enjoying the peace, Robbie and others having decanted to Ibiza for a whole season of debauchery; it was all too soon time to start my second year at Glasgow, this time the work harder and requiring more effort than before. I kept my contact with an increasingly frazzled Robbie to a minimum, always remaining friendly as I absolutely required the flat to be kept on for the present and ideally to the end of my course. This was looking hopeful as Robbie professed a desire to expand his mind with post-graduate courses, while contracting his mind with an ever more exotic combination of new tabs from his Ibiza friends. When I first met, him, he gave the impression of a somewhat nerdy but genuinely funny bloke. He now looked increasingly like someone who would not be living a long and happy life; his eyes were darker than before and his skin now looked sallow and blotchy, especially after each weekend of overindulgent consumption.

Between the restaurant and any hobbies or friends I could hang out with, I avoided the flat wherever possible, aware that my presence even in my bedroom could in some way invite Robbie or his cohorts to approach me. I hoped that they would continue to largely ignore me if I kept as low a profile as possible and responded cheerily but briefly when conversations started. Luckily two of his more psychotic friends were doing languages as part of their courses, so were abroad for a good part of this year.

It was a cholerically foggy afternoon when I was sitting in a café half-way along Great Western Road when I noticed Tess, sitting with possibly the most handsome man in Glasgow. She hadn't noticed me, so I wondered how practical it was to leave the café unnoticed, or whether this could be construed as unfriendly. Given that I didn't particularly care about the appearance, I packed up my laptop and gazed ardently at my iPhone as I walked out of the café.

'Adam!' My heart sank as Tess called me. Looking as surprised as my debunked and pathetic attempt at escape would permit, I turned and looked round. Tess walked over and gave me a hug, then introduced me to her friend, a man of rugby dimensions who reminded me that I was still distinctly a beta male, at best, in his company. He shook my hand strongly, a crushing blokey handshake which, despite my attempt to replicate, no doubt primarily served to confirm to us both that I was not the man with the upper hand in this situation. It was hardly required as he stood about 5 inches taller than me and easily had 2 stone more muscle; which will no doubt happen when one person spends their life playing competitive sport and the other reading books and lying on sofas.

Brian (!) was, however, a genuinely nice fellow, as transpired from our chat. Tess and he were, they told me in jointly positive and honestly sickening terms, doing the same course at Strathclyde University, about three miles away and had moved into a flat together just after they met each other in Fresher's week. Tess family had all moved back to Inverness in the summer and it was goodbye Australia and hello chilly Scotland for good apparently. I told them my own situation and Tess had said she had heard I'd flown the nest and asked after my parents.

After about ten minutes of small talk, I excused myself on the premise of a tutorial, which I didn't actually have, so we said our goodbyes and vaguely agreed to catch up sometime. I left the café and mentally noted that I should never go back there, pleased that I had also been vague on where I was staying and the course I was doing. Part of me still wanted to spend time with her, but a larger part of me did not want to get on the wrong side of the hulk sitting across from her at the table. I set off for the flat with vows of keeping my head down, prominent in my mind.

Another few weeks had passed, my routine continuing although I did expand my ability to stay away from the flat by pursuing more activities, rather atypically for me, I joined the uni gym and then the local boxing club. Partly this was due to my feeling of inadequacy after meeting Tess and Brian and partly after examining myself in a mirror, which rather gave me an impetus to improve once I forced myself to accept that I appeared to be getting thinner, pastier and weaker than I was in my mid-teens, something which I had hoped would take care of itself. I spent some time at the gym most days with two of my friends from my course, and managed to - week after week - elicit some positive responses from my muscles and in time, make me look more like a traditional man rather than a mushy student. I kept at the boxing too, throughout the rest of my second year, moving onto sparring with similarly developing, although wirier opponents but mainly just training under the guidance of the helpful if slightly punchy trainer, Ally Moran, who set me a series of monthly targets designed to shake me up, which although I groaned at their sight, accepted that they were both required and actually enjoyable as I improved. I did not share my involvement in this pastime with anyone else I hung out with, preferring to let them assume I was working at the restaurant more, and in Robbie's case, I could have told him I was his imaginary friend and he'd have believed me.

So, I continued to submit my coursework and pass exams well and gain a reputation with my tutors as someone who might actually have some ability to make a living out of putting ink down, albeit generally using my Macbook. I had some articles published in student rags, a couple of commentary essays in national yoof magazines and even a serious article accepted by a national independent agency, The Insider. They were good enough to accept me as an unpaid intern that summer, giving me a real boost to my CV before my third year and only destroying most of my bank balance to achieve it. It was a generally interesting experience, however, I mainly pottered about with one of their older hacks, doing London based stories and buying him pints in return for his wisdom, much of which was bollocks. He was retiring in the autumn so approached me as his last opportunity to pass on the accumulated tips and strategies for success in the world of poorly paid jobbing journalism. Of the hundreds of short advice bullets he fired at me, one of the few I remembered was 'don't work for the fucking Daily Mail or I'll come out of retirement and kick your fucking head in.' I assured him that I didn't see my fledgling career fluttering to that particular swamp, so we became good friends despite our forty-year-plus age gap and the fact that he insisted on calling me Jock.

I left London in the last week of August to start my third year a few weeks later, returning to the flat just after Robbie got back from Ibiza again, looking increasingly like the wrong version of Dorian Gray; the fresh-faced one no doubt happily framed in the attic. I re-assumed my job at the restaurant and threw myself completely into the gym and boxing before classes started back properly, as I needed money badly after London and the gym and boxing were the cheapest ways to spend my free time. By Christmas I had gained about a stone in weight and had a surprisingly late growth spurt, leaving me over six foot tall and now sparring with Light Middleweight guys who delighted in their initial superiority over me. On the plus side, I didn't have a glass jaw, so could take a few punches which made me a popular sparring partner with them from the start. I knew they were taking it easy with me at the beginning of my move up to this weight, but I did gradually through the year get quicker at the punch and better at defending myself, so managed to achieve a decent level rather than the duff beginner I was all those months before. I had then won a couple of amateur bouts, thanks to my gym work of the past sixteen months adding a level of muscle I didn't have previously. Moran was also a great coach and he enjoyed my exponential development; I could punch well over 250psi as standard with my right, testing up to 875 on the fairground-type equipment we had rented for a few days at the club; my hand speed was also getting miles better, along with my defence and ability to pick targets, the same ones which I'd been missing almost completely when I started. All this helped me to look less like the skinny youth who left Mharisaig and now a passable adult male, externally at least.

I had finished a genuinely rough spar one afternoon, my face guard not cutting it against one of the best middleweights in the cub; this was just after we started back from the Christmas break, when I walked upstairs to the flat to find Robbie being marched out by some new friends he'd made at Police Scotland. On determining my status as cohabitee, they rather unfairly gathered me up too and I spent that evening and overnight in the less than comfortable cells in Pitt Street before release, no apology necessary and all that, first thing the next morning. I didn't know what was happening with Robbie, but I suspected that he may now have a major problem. However my immediate challenge was that I might have to find a new flat; I needed to find out if the police had left it at least accessible and perhaps with less marijuana smell, which to be honest I had gotten quite used too. I took the underground back to Hillhead and walked downhill towards the flat to see if I could indeed still get access after they finished shovelling Robbie's stash into bin bags. Not for the first time, I was glad I always made sure that the Yale lock on my bedroom door was kept secure and locked, Robbie was in no way to be trusted not to hide his gear under my floorboards.

Before I went up to the flat, I went into a sandwich shop to get some coffee and a roll. I looked at myself in the mirror, hair lank and with one or two raised scuffs on my cheeks after the sparring. My clothes were also stained and dirty after the gym/sparring/overnight at Her Majesty's, adding to an overall funk which drew glances from some vague acquaintances looking at me as I waited for the Americano. It also took me a while to comprehend that two of the concerned faces gazing at me belonged to Michelle and Tess, a sight which quite took me by surprise, if by surprise I meant nearly making me faint and go weak at the knees.

They walked over with genuine concern, rather unnecessarily taking me by the arm over to a seat at their small table at the far wall of the café. The barista brought me my food and drink, as I looked at them with utter confusion, possibly mixed with embarrassment.

'What's going on?' I croaked, looking from one to the other.

They glanced at each other. Tess admitted 'It was all over social media last night about you and Robbie getting arrested. We decided to meet near your flat to see if we could find out what the hell you were up to and see if we could do anything.'

Seeing my utter confusion, Michelle quickly explained that after she had started at Strathclyde too, they had struck up a mutual friendship begat by their annoyance at my good self, their enmity as ex-girlfriends overcome by their mutual antipathy. I nodded without full comprehension, drinking my coffee, eating my roll and trying to think my way through this new debacle.

'So, how much bother are you in?' Michelle asked.

'None.' I told her wearily. 'Robbie is in deep shit, which I'm not surprised about, he's been completely off the rails since last year. I keep out of it, keep myself busy and let him and his pals get on with what they do. The cops just lifted me with Robbie because I had a room there. They told me this morning that they found nothing in my room, I told them the situation, they gave me a row for not reporting Mr Big and we parted without charges being brought. End of.'

Tess looked dubious. 'So who did that to your face?'

'Unrelated incident' I told them. I inhaled the last bite of my roll and then sank my coffee.

'Look, I'm sorry about everything and it's nice of you to come round. Weird, definitely, but it's nice that you care. I'm OK though, I just need to see if I can get into the flat and get cleaned up.'

They told me that they'd come up and see if everything was OK, which I was torn between being glad about and wishing they would leave me alone. I was used to being a semi-loner to some extent in Glasgow however, after my night of little sleep in the cells and the stress of the situation, I was slightly glad of any support, albeit from this most unexpected company.

We went around the corner and up to the flat, finding the main door undamaged, locked properly and generally intact. It looked like Robbie had just answered the door rather than the police using force to get in, not surprising as he had never shown any sign of aggression, although a couple of his friends looked more than capable of coercing payments from defaulters. His bedroom door had a new metal bar and lock unevenly fitted and blue tape strung across like a saltire, quite the nationalist symbol left for a proud Glasgow dealer. My room door had been left locked although it was obvious that inside had been well searched, as had the kitchen and living room. My MacBook was still in my rucksack thankfully and although it was mixed up, my stuff appeared all there. The other room was open but the last guy who stayed there, of several who seemed to use it as a doss, had gone on a language exchange to Spain or Chile or something, so wouldn't have left anything lying about, the lucky bastard. I left Tess and Michelle in the living room and had my shower, changing into jeans and t-shirt before joining them. They spent the next hour updating me on all things new with them, Mharisaig, my old friends there and partners new for them. They agreed to let anyone who asked and indeed those who didn't, know that I had no involvement in the arrest and were absolutely a good citizen of the leafy West End. Seemingly assured, they hugged me goodbye left me their numbers, agreeing to meet up the following Friday for a drink, which I really could have done without, but couldn't get out of without appearing rude.

As they walked out of the flat, Robbie's dad was walking in. He looked knackered and surprised to see me, but I invited him in and tried to explain what had happened, without saying flat out that

Robbie was a junkie drug dealer and I was the innocent party here. He seemed to take it in, even apologised for bringing me into the situation but told me that no matter what, he was selling the flat. Well, I thought, hasn't the last 24 hours been just fucking super.

Robbie was expected to get out on bail later that day, so his dad told me that he'd be back at home with them for a few days until they could discuss this and they would then let me know what was going to happen. I reasoned with him to take his time and not to sell the flat until after the exams and hoped that he wouldn't be too hasty on this one. Flats sell quickly here, but with the usual legal stuff, I hoped it would take two or three months to get things finalised, which would take me just about to the end of my third and probably last year anyway. If I needed to, I could try and get a cheap room further away for a month or so, but it was doable since tutorials would be finished by then. Robbie's dad took a forlorn look at the police tape on the door, gave me an unexpected man-hug and left, before I could see the tears on his face.

The flat had gone on the market three weeks after Robbie's arrest for possessing and supplying drugs, during which time he had come back with his dad to clear out his room and take everything except the TV and the kitchen equipment. He had actually looked better than he had for a while, although this was mainly due to the awful condition he was in pre-arrest. We had a coffee and a chat while his dad was around at the Estate Agent to discuss the marketing or whatever they do. Robbie was surprisingly just seeing this as a minor blip on his road to fortune, blaming the situation on his own over-use of product and a resultant loss of focus on the whole chain of anonymity. I really couldn't give a fuck at that point whether Robbie made a fortune or ended up dead under a bridge, but my desire to have some leeway with the date for selling the flat meant that for the first time since I ducked out of his plans for me, I tried to appear interested and supportive. His dad came back and they both told me they'd let me know the situation with viewings, asked me to keep the place tidy and said their goodbyes until then. At least I had the place to myself albeit I assumed with the interruptions of potential buyers. Two weeks after that, they had an open day to view the flat, so other than that I was in a blissful state of seclusion before being chucked out onto the street.

At the same time as this, I had been reluctantly impelled by Tess and Michelle to become an adjunct to their group of friends from Strathclyde University who mainly hung out at Pollockshields and Shawlands on the South Side. They were actually a good bunch, liked a drink and a laugh and had welcomed me into their fold easily. I also liked the distance between me and their flats as it meant that no-one would drop over to see me unexpectedly and everything had to be arranged, giving me an arms-length group to drink with while retaining my temporary and blissful solitude to enable me to watch TV on a sofa, a pleasure I had greatly underappreciated until now. Tess and Michelle seemed reassured that I wasn't going to get involved in the undercurrents of Glasgow crime, as if, so they often left me in the bloke element of their group, who were a better laugh than I had expected. It also opened my eyes as to whom Robbie was involved with, they only knew him slightly but the names they mentioned as supplying him were the same names which hit the Scottish newspapers intermittently. He'd do well to escape that lot whether he wanted to or not, was the general opinion.

Thankfully, the flat sold to buyers who didn't want access urgently, so it was after the Easter break when I packed the rucksacks and left my room. I'd sub-rented a room a mile or so away in a fairly modern building, not as handy but affordable and still within walking distance to the restaurant and university. I spent the last few weeks on my course there, genuinely putting effort and time into my dissertation, studying and boxing, in that order; after my finals were complete, it was back to Mharisaig for the end of spring and to await my results.

I'd sent a few applications out to the usual big organisations, each of whom seemed to have let their Human Resources teams go absolutely nuts in the pursuit of high-quality staffers. I was lost in a mire of online tests, telephone interviews and the prospect, if successful, of moving onto another mid-Dante's level of checks and group meetings to see what stars emerged, when I received a job offer back from The Insider, where I'd spent the last summer. The pay was hardly enough to even get a room in London and eat, but it was better than wandering aimlessly around Mharisaig or trying to succeed in a Dragon's Den of thrusting 'young executives', most of whom were probably earmarked for a job anyway if their daddies were friends with the Director and all that;

I accepted the post without hesitation and embarked on the research to find out where best to stay; then, realising that I couldn't afford any of them, where to stay cheaply where I wouldn't live in fear of my life.

The house was a lonely place to go back to; my parents now ensconced in sunnier climes, having settled on a flat a few miles inland of a coastal town, their dream sans son, in place finally. I thought about selling up here, with their permission, but I knew that my early career could be peripatetic, so having a base – paid for and still maintained financially from a distance by my parents on my behalf, was a better plan. Since I was soon to be off to London, I tried to keep the place respectable despite a couple of house parties instigated by Niall, who was by then working in a hotel a few miles away, funding his sought-after car and a life of debauchery, or so he tried to lead me to believe. A few others were back from college and university too, but not Michelle who had elected to spend her holiday months back in Glasgow working in a call centre as summer cover, earning to keep her student loan down. She had broken up with her boyfriend and I'd thought about calling her to meet up, in my moments of loneliness; but my new life in London beckoned and I knew she'd tell me to fuck off anyway, having the wisdom of experience with me to look back on.

So, with a couple of weeks in Mharisaig to kill, I hung about with Niall, driving to a few parties in his clapped out Corsa; My university growth spurt meant that my frame no longer favoured small cars, so I was a bit cramped when we were out and about. He drove, like many of the lads around here, like a man racing to hospital for a life-saving operation, even when going he was just going for a newspaper; in short, it was terrifying and while I appreciated getting a free lift, it was not without this drawback. He'd already crashed into the back of a van, the home-made repair of which was still visible on the bonnet of the Corsa; the suspension was not going well either after an attempt to rally through a field just before I'd got back, so I encouraged him to slow down whenever I considered my life to be endangered.

At the end of the second week back, a crowd of us were sitting in a friend's house, along with a few bags full of beer cans and enjoying the absence of his holidaying parents, who had unsuccessfully forbidden him to have anyone over in their vacation week in Majorca. We were going to another party afterwards and this was just phase one, getting nicely drunk before the main event.

'So, what's the plan for London?' asked Jim Brown, who according to Niall started every drinking session fast and ended up carried home on most occasions. I looked at him, his face speckled with the remnants of adolescent acne scarring 'Got to get a room somewhere down there, start this job and see where it takes me, I guess.'

'So, you'll be loaded then, no need for us?' I didn't really like where Jim was going here, sounded a bit too aggressive and not the usual bantering tone we favoured. 'Nah, just enough to live on - it's just a foot in the door; no idea where it'll take me.' I knew that Jim had fucked up his exams at school years ago but wasn't sure what he'd been up to so, I asked.

'Fuck all' he spat, getting straight into my face with unexpected fury 'can't get anything up here, still at home with my mam while you, ya cunt are having a great time away.' I didn't like being called that one bit and grabbed Jim by the throat, pushing him up and onto the wall across from the bed where he had sat. Niall and the others grabbed my arms and pulled me back from him, but not before I'd involuntarily head-butted Jim, bursting his nose and covering his t-shirt instantly with bright, shocking blood.

'Fuck sake Adam, whit was that for?' Niall pushed me away. I was still raging at Jim, so they ushered him out towards the toilet to clean him up and put a distance between us. It was out of character for me, but I wasn't a kid anymore, even if they wanted to behave like we all were; I suppose the last few years, my separation from Mharisaig, my time in the gym and the boxing had left me with less tolerance and the means to react when provoked, which the unlucky Jim had certainly done. I sat back down and Niall across from me, looking perplexed and telling me to calm down; he looked like he knew fine well that Jim had annoyed me but hadn't expected me to go off like that.

Jim came back in a few minutes later, pieces of toilet paper stuck inside his nostrils and looking bleary. 'Sorry Adam, I didnae mean to call you that.' I looked up at him and the tension dissipated 'Aye, I'm sorry too Jim, I shouldn't have done that either.' I stood up and shook his hand; he looked at me and then left, off home after a bad evening but sober for once; then I was back sitting across from Niall, somebody put some music on and the night re-started; the incident not serious enough to deflect the partially inebriated group from their revels.

'They told him to apologise to you' Niall told me a while later 'He was out of order, the arsehole. It wasn't your job that bothered him anyway.'

I was confused now – I'd be surprised if I'd spoken more than fifteen minutes with Jim in my whole life and certainly not in the past year or so.

'He fancied Michelle, way back. She told him that she was too busy at school for boys; then she meets you ten minutes later and all that goes in the bin. Then you fuck off to Glasgow with hardly any warning and she's broken-hearted and even then Jim can't get any interest from her, try though he sure did.' I nod, although I'd no idea about this previously. 'So, you were the object of his – dissatisfaction.'

'That, and he's an ugly bastard', said Niall, with a wide grin.

Chapter Seventeen

The Third House

John Allanton pulled out through the main estate gates and through the village, south and east, his two companions left to stay again with Galloglas, ostensibly to help him but as they all knew, to retain a monitoring presence and keep Galloglas in his place. They were to sit in the anteroom, taking note of arrivals and departures and generally letting Galloglas know that, as a result of his behaviour, that Sir Mathieson was placing him under close orders until further discussions could be undertaken to clarify the situation. The catalyst for this was Galloglas profoundly inexplicable attention-seeking for the estate, followed closely by a burgeoning feeling of Sir Mathieson and his son's part that the spending on the estate may well be greater than previously agreed.

Allanton junior drove the Range Rover along the village road and past the pub, followed five minutes later by the Nissan van, both now more than half emptied of product and onto their next destination, some ways back towards Lairg. It took longer than usual, delayed firstly behind a slow-moving caravan and then a sheep-filled truck, both passed after they reach a straight part of the road. Allanton knew the risk here, even in the midst of a great nothingness, of crashing a car containing a significant amount of something approaching 97% pure Cocaine Hydrochloride. Eventually, he swung a left and is waved through by a watchman at a manual gate, behind which sits a former manse where he'd dropped his father the day before. As at Inverannan, he drove the car into a garage to the side and motioned the three men standing there to unload the car, walked outside and across the driveway into the bleak house, to meet his redoubtable father.

Sir Mathieson greeted him with a handshake and they sat with their coffees until joined five minutes later by another man, lean and young-looking, Alf White. Sir Mathieson appointed him two years before as his representative in the wider distribution chain; managing and monitoring the overall effectiveness of the operation at the city level and reporting back any issues which required action. Today, they must discuss any recent problems, with the exception of Galloglas who was being handled by the Allantons

126

directly. White had been an accountant, a skill valued by Sir Mathieson but which he had not used in management until this appointment, on a recommendation from a niece who was aware of White's capabilities and his prior involvement in narcotics. Not quite trusted yet, Sir Mathieson was pleased by some of his enhancements in profits although suspicious of the complexity he had introduced to the process, preferring the lean business model in most cases.

'So, can you tell me how well things are doing across our enterprises?' smiled Sir Mathieson to White. He gestured White to sit across from him on a sabre-legged chair, which sat on a plastic sheet which covered an expensive-looking and very old in appearance, Persian rug. He opened a laptop, put in a pen drive to allow them access to his encrypted files and turned it towards them. It showed an exemplary picture of the quantity and value of the powder from leaving them and into the chain of distributors, until the point where they did not care what happened, the product cut to as low as 15%, by then small-scale and off their radar once their payments were achieved. He was concise, nervous even in their presence, usually spending his time in London and visiting the other cities between a fortnightly and monthly cycle depending on need. John Allanton quite liked White; he had been productive, respectful and much less of a discombobulator than that arsehole Galloglas. It was a pity he had to kill him, really.

White finished his presentation, looking up at the two men for some feedback or approval, especially from the older man. 'Excellent. Do you want some more coffee?' asked John Allanton as he rose with his cup and walked to the door, where a tray of tea, coffee and biscuits sat on a table. 'No thanks, I'm fine', White replied politely.

Sir Mathieson looked at him with a slight smile. 'I do have a question, relating to sales in the London area.' Alf looked puzzled. 'I'm pleased with the increase in overall turnover, however, I do have an issue with the variation between what your figures are and what I'm hearing you're charging for the product; a difference of around £1.3 million over the past two years, give or take. In this case, take is probably the word, young man.' He nodded almost imperceptibly to his son, who, having estimated the blood splatter possibilities, shot White through the rear left side of the head, kindly ensuring that his father's tweed suit would remain unmarked as Whites skull took the force of the .40mm bullet. His head flopped to the side, then his body, bereft of life, fell in the same direction and onto the plastic floor covering, placed there in preparation; for in a military operation, preparation is everything.

The manual work immediately began being carried out by three of his trusted former regiment men, brought in specifically for the purpose of White's post-mortem disposal; the Allanton men sat meantime in the kitchen, discussing the forward planning and listening to the sounds of a removal and deep-clean being completed in the drawing room. It was always a challenge when someone useful leaves the business; however, this was made easier here by White's long-term disenfranchisement from his immediate family, the result of youthful heroin abuse and theft in this instance. Disposal of his accommodation was already underway, owned as it was by a subset of one of the property businesses which they used as the main semi-legitimate cover for their activities pan-global; no calls were required for this, as all had been set in motion in the days before; an interim promotion had been made to fill the vacuum and this relevant link in the chain updated at 1100hours, just 60 minutes after Alf White's head exploded on the end of a bullet in a drawing room of the manse, in the midst of the glorious Highlands.

The kitchen door opened sometime later; thumbs-up from the bulky ex-soldier returned with thanks from his old officer, Sir Mathieson. They went back up to the drawing room, fresh as a spring morning now and only a slight dampness alongside the antiseptic odour to suggest that Alf White had ended his days there so recently. Neither man had a preference for White's permanent replacement, although both were fairly sure that their interim man was not really a candidate, his lack of genuine intelligence being a drawback; his capacity for violence only suited the business up to a point, after that there was less aggression required, with value given to the attributes of obedience and calmness under pressure. With the rogue behaviour of Galloglas, Sir Mathieson had been forced to review his long-standing tenets for promotion, perhaps it was time for the experience he had in the business to be supplemented by a breed of younger men who he could trust and control, rather than promote solely on the ability to menace, or those who pushed themselves forward from their own ambition. Yes, he thought, beware the ambitious man – that was my downfall with Galloglas and White, both different but too keen to obtain a position of power. Contrary to the great philosopher's quote, power never corrupted Sir Mathieson completely, driven as he was by the need for continuity; as long as one forgets the moral and legal arguments against his life's work.

The two men left the house, the garage now vacated by the couriers and only the Range Rover remaining. White had left in a body-bag in the rear of the Nissan van; his last duty for the organisation, to feed the pigs with on a nearby farm owned by the organisation after a brief visit to some industrial grinding equipment which would render him, literally, fit for animal consumption.

The two men drove, as they did every fortnight or so, across the country to Dornoch, for a relaxing afternoon game of golf and to pick up some excellent local malt whisky to sustain them on the long evenings in the west highlands. The weather was fine and they both played a fair game, returning to Inverannan after a delightful dinner in the town. It was always a long distance to go, but both men enjoyed the break and felt it necessary to have some time away together from the remoteness of their west highland house. John Allanton drove back, leaving the restaurant at just after 2230 hours and driving fast along the near-empty roads to Inverannan for an overnight, ready for an early start and their breakfast meeting with Galloglas, their next, and perhaps more problematic challenge. They knew that the situation was compounded by the recent visit by the journalist to Sir Mathieson's home and, in whatever connection may exist, the invitation of his two colleagues to Inverannan. They decided to sleep on their decisions, tired after the golf, dinner, the long drive but buoyed by the removal of Alf White, who Sir Mathieson joked, would now be the supper for a few dozen of his finest highland Gloucester Old Spot pigs.

Chapter Eighteen

The Bar at Night

We walk back to the pub in the fading light, wondering between us if Simon was back in London and what had happened, unaware that he was much closer than that and the bereavement was more likely to be his own than an unknown relative.

The pub has actually calmed down a little from earlier and we are able to order food without queuing. Sitting halfway along the room, we are stuck listening to the loud conversations of those hardy few who had stayed there since lunch and are now at the point in the evening where their volume control had dissipated along with their self-control. Emma rolls her eyes at me, after hearing a particularly loud blether from a group in their early 20's about how wonderful their shinty skills were. I explain shinty to her as best I could. 'It's a kind of feral hockey where the guys come down off the farms to play and then get mortally drunk to relieve the pain afterwards. And no, I haven't played it as I'm not mad.'

I glance occasionally at the groups in the bar, some couples and what looks like field workers, their hi-vis jackets in a pile at the far end of the room. Emma asks me about university and how I got on at the last year.

'Bit of an odd time to be honest' I tell her 'I had to get another room for the last while, unforeseen circumstances which I should really have foreseen. Everything other than that was fine; exams no problem and the coursework all sorted so, just need to make my fame and fortune now with The Insider.' I make a face and Emma smiles. 'Maybe you're in the wrong place, for the fortune anyway. So, where do you see your career going?'

I look at the table and shake my head. 'I'm not sure really. I don't think I have a plan as such, I just wanted to be away from Mharisaig at first, then I was in Glasgow but I don't think I felt anything but a transient there, so moving to London isn't a problem. I guess like everyone else I can't afford to stay there forever but maybe a couple of years getting some experience and then see what happens? What about you?' I wanted to change the focus to Emma, since my inherent uncertainty about my journalistic calling meant that I inwardly baulked at the thought of considering a high-flying career which required the commensurate ability on my part.

'No plan either really. I like London though, a lot going on all the time and these assignments are great to see around Europe.'

'Even here?' I ask, looking at Emma with faux disbelief. She laughs, 'Even here; the company makes it!' I nod, acknowledging that she's taking the piss, in a nice way.

We finish our bar food, now getting a bit repetitive on the "chips with everything" front and I order another pint for each of us at the bar. While I'm at the bar, one of the workers comes over and sits down beside Emma, his alcohol and testosterone levels having reached the point where any chance of hitting on an attractive female must be taken. I return to hear Emma telling him politely but rather directly that she is here with her friend for a quiet drink and that he should go back to his chums. She has to repeat this three times, each time cutting off his rural attempts at chat-up lines, after which he rather humiliatingly wanders back his friend's hoots of laughter. I'm not sure what to do here; however, Emma seems more than equipped to handle a gauche labourer without too much conflict, so I figure out that my best option is to remain aloof and tell her well-done on how she handles suitors. She is unfazed and I realise that it's an unfortunate hazard of her gender when in any public place, particularly when alcohol and idiots are present. I make a mental note to never, ever, approach a woman in a bar as I don't think my ego would survive and I couldn't possibly put myself in the same category as guys like that.

We look up as a group of women enter the bar, to a barrage of helloes from the workers, who seem to know them. It's some of the office staff from Inverannan, who sit at the table farthest away from the lads who are at the table at the bar. It looks to me that the young men work at the estate and have finished their work early to focus on the continued destruction of their livers. We have another drink at Emma's request – I think she's going to tell me that it's time to go, but then I understand what she intends.

'Wait a while, these guys are three sheets and the ladies seem to have had a couple of drinks while they were getting ready. We might be able to have a chat with them if they recognise us.' She's right, the first person who gets up to go the bar with their order does see us and stops for a chat.

'Is this the start of a girl's night out?' Emma asks with a smile. She greets us warmly, asks us how we're enjoying it here and Emma tells her that we love it, people are so nice. We tell her we'll catch up soon and she leaves us to go and order, the lads giving her some attempted banter which she braves without any trouble whatsoever.

The evening unfolds to be quite a good laugh, some of the office staff come over for a chat, mainly with Emma and she answers their questions about her job, where she's been and so on, with greater raconteur skills than I could ever muster. She gets some anecdotes going and pretty soon they have shifted along to join us, the drink flowing and me trying to avoid getting washed in alcohol along with it. The lads make a couple of sorties to join us, but these young ladies are made of stern stuff and tell them in no short terms to fuck right off and leave them alone, which seems to dampen their increasingly drunken mood somewhat. I move onto bottles of light lager when I feel myself getting slightly out of control, made nervous by the presence of the estate lads and interested by some of the gossip which we're being told by the ladies. They don't work with the two secretaries at all and don't know what they do either, but they work for someone called Allanton who seems to be a friend or partner of Galloglas. They tell us that Allanton has a son who visits too and they seem to have a collective fancy for him, the mention of which causes much hilarity and a few suggestions of which of them would jump on him first. I hadn't previously been exposed to this level of female crudity, which easily matched and surpassed anything me and my friends had ever come out with. Emma had been matching the ladies drink-for-drink, presumably to help the gossip flow and had nudged me to take some recordings, which I do by leaving my phone on the table beside my drink, occasionally saving the file while they asked me what I was doing with a mobile with no reception. I tell them it's' down to habit and wishful thinking and, lost in their laughter at me, they think no more about it.

I wondered if there was such a thing as closing time in this pub and, thanks to my restrictions on my beer intake, realise that including the barman, I'm easily the most sober person in the room. Eventually, he rings the bell, which seems to be the signal for everyone to rush to the bar to stock up. Half an hour later, the gossip has turned to matters personal and I'm wishing that we could get the hell out of here; at least two of the women have started to leer at me and I've got a poor track record with temptation. The bell goes again and the hee-hawing drunken contents of the room start to pour themselves out to the car park. A couple of other groups head off straight away and the lads manage with some difficulty and minor shoving and pushing to get their work jackets on and follow us out; the barman wobbly too but having practised this before, ushers them outside with relatively good humour and farewells. I wonder how they are getting home, but a land rover with what looks like a patient father turns up and picks up two of the women who stay a distance away, them also giving two of the lads a lift. It looks like the rest stay a walking distance away, as there seems no attempt at driving the one or two cars left there. One of the women starts arguing with the remaining lads and I have a sinking feeling when I see her throwing a slap in his direction. It's broken up by the other lads but I stand to the side, watching.

One of them comes up to Emma, the one from before and starts to call her "stuck up". I walk over, not sure whether Emma will just turn and walk away to the B&B, but she's a fair bit drunk too and gives him a mouthful back. He's losing the battle of wits, so turns to me and says 'what the fuck are you looking at?' a traditional Scottish habit of starting a fight. He walks towards me with a slight stagger to the right and throws a punch with his right hand, which I move under and hit him with a smack in his face around the eye and then a right hand into his stomach, which sends him to the ground, vomiting and retching. If I'd hoped that this was the end of it, I was wrong as the other three came drunkenly but quickly at me. I moved back from the first one and then quickly forward, catching him on the tip of his nose with a punch which came right from the legs up, throwing him down and stopping the other two in their tracks. The alcohol-fuelled adrenalin gets the better of the first one though and he comes at me with a flail of arms and hands, which I avoid and hit him on the ear and in the mouth, putting him down near the first one as I move into some space to let me move more easily. The last fellow moves towards me and I hit him three times, before he turns and runs like hell along the path in the direction of the loch. I had become unaware of the shrieking noises, the retching and the stench of the vomit of the first bloke as I focused on applying my hard-earned pugilistic skills in their first non-gymnasium bout. Surprised at the effectiveness of my work, I stand still while the lads pick themselves up and with a humiliated air, head down to the left-hand side of the village, calling insults back once they were twenty metres or so away. There is a slightly unreal air to the car park now, then a shriek of laughter comes over the ladies and we head back into the bar, the barman telling us to get in and be quiet.

I get another drink and go to the toilets to get cold water on my knuckles, which are sore as hell; their first bare-knuckle experience after being wrapped and gloved for every other session. The barman gives me a clean towel to wrap them in, joining me in the toilet to check I was OK and apologising.

'Where did you learn to do that? I thought you were a journalist.' He puts off the cold tap for me, my right hand now throbbing badly.

'I was in a boxing club in Glasgow. Those lads there were just drunk. I should just have walked away.' I tell him, wary that he might warn of repercussions.

'Well don't worry about it, they'll realise they were in the wrong when they wake up. You might even get an apology if they see you, they're aye doing stuff like that, I've had them rowing and then rolling about on the floor umpteen times; there are no any hard feelings as long as it's a fair one. Which it wasn't even, there being more of them than the one of you.'

I nod agreement with the logic of the inebriated barman; there was indeed only one of me in the fracas. We walk out and back into the now deserted bar, I pick up my half-finished bottle of beer I'd left earlier, drain it and go outside to see where Emma and the others have gone. They are all indeed gone except Gillian, who sat beside me earlier. The bar door closes and locks behind me us she links arms with me and tells me to come home with her for a drink, which I agree to gladly, with a kiss as we walk entwined to perhaps a better end to the day.

What I don't see as I walk away with Gillian is a car parked just out of obvious sight, partially hidden by some waning trees. There are two men in the car, one being Sir Mathieson Allanton and the other, his son, John. They hid with a discreet view of the car park some time ago to see what the commotion was, coincidentally passing on their way to their overnight at Inverannan House and only stopping to watch the Estate workforce at play.

However, after intuiting who we were, they now glance at each other with a mutual uncertainty over my legitimacy as a journalist. Once I am out of sight, John Allanton starts the car and the two men return to Inverannan House, the situation perhaps now even less clear to them than before.

☐

Chapter Nineteen

Simons Escape

Back in a freezing garage some ten miles north-east as the crow flies, Simon was oozing back into existence despite his multiple injuries, inflicted by the inheritors of Galloglas role as Sir Mathieson Allantons' muscular minions. Simons face, bloated by the impacts of fists the previous evening, was now impeding his vision considerably after a night of swelling, worsened by lying on the tarpaulin-covered wooden pallet. He was, despite being befuddled by his injuries, acutely aware that he'd shat himself and was in danger of dying a very smelly man indeed. He rose crustily from his bed of wood and plastic, dragging his bruised carcass towards the one, cobweb-covered window of the garage. He couldn't see anything except the track outside but knew he wasn't far from the house he'd stayed in so comfortably just the previous night. Simon understood that his plan for taking a part of the coke supply of London was now long gone, but for now, his inherent human desire for survival was preventing any thoughts of self-pity. He lurched over to the main garage doors, which were securely padlocked from the outside and of no help to him at all. Then, he noticed a glimpse of a door to the rear, stacked behind a pile of tyres and boxes, which he started to push to the side, yelping as his ribs jabbed him with pain. He had to kneel down to push and pull the tyres away individually, but despite the racking agony of moving his arms and torso, he cleared the way to the long-closed door. He tried the round metal handle, which turned, but still, the door would not push open. He turned the handle as far as he could, then leant against it, hearing the click of the rusty mechanism release as he did, but still, the door couldn't open to let him out. He dropped back to the ground and, at eye level, tried to see what was inhibiting it. Years of uncut grass and weeds had grown thickly at the base of the door, stopping it from moving. Simon slid his hand out and grabbed at it, pulling as much out from the roots as he could, clump after clump, only resting to let his aching hands and side recover enough each time. Eventually, after two failed attempts to stand back up and push it open, he finally had torn enough up undergrowth to enable his exit, squeezing his fractured ribs through the small gap and thanking the lord that he was such a narrow man. He pulled himself out and turned back towards the house, keeping to the scrub and trees at the side, not the track lest he was spotted and returned to the garage, or worse. He peered around a dense shrub towards the building and was elated to see his hire car still there, although he had no keys on him. Even better, there were no other cars, neither four-wheel drive cars of his hosts in sight, although Simon obviously did not know if he had minutes or hours before they returned. He had to get into the house and get his keys, his jacket, get clean and get out of these clothes, although even the 'get clean' might not be the least essential of those priorities at this point.

Simon found a way to go back and across the track at a point where he couldn't be seen from the house; then back towards it past an LPG tank and round the outside of the building and to the rear, where the kitchen was and he may be able to get inside without detection. Gingerly, he tripped his way along the side and peered in through the window to a thankfully desolate kitchen. He wondered if the servant would still be in the house, but figuring that there was probably no-one else to drive those cars, that their absence suggested that the house was unoccupied. He turned the handle of the blessedly unlocked door and entered the house, moving slowly along the corridor to avoid noise and upwards on the stairs to his room. He picked up a metal torch from the stand at the back door and stopped before each doorway, glancing in and holding it ready to strike if he was confronted. After a few minutes of gradually creeping towards his room, he was finally sure that no-one was home. His room appeared untouched, his bag and clothes still there. Simon decided that he had to clean up, despite the risks and put on the shower, inching his revolting trousers off and throwing them to the side. He had to change the shower heat to cold as his body was still shivering at the low temperature from his incarceration in the garage overnight and he let the water and a whole bottle of shampoo help to return him to a condition which would let him get away and back to civilisation. Quicker now, he dried and dressed, finding some Paracetamol in his bag and taking all four which were left in the packet, shoved his laptop and clothes into his rucksack, leaving those which were left in the bathroom as a parting gift. He limped back downstairs, hunting his bag for his keys as he went. Unfortunately for Simon, those keys were currently in the possession of John Allanton, as he sipped coffee with his redoubtable father, ensconced at Inverannan. Simon flopped down on the second bottom step of the stairs and wearily re-packed his rucksack, his outline plan to flee in the Golf now somewhat obstructed by the lack of keys. Simon knew that cars could be hot-wired, but not how to do this. He also knew there were no other cars to steal and he knew that there was very little traffic here, so stopping a car for a lift would be difficult and more likely to fall back into the hands of Peter, or whatever, and those two brutes if he headed back along the road. He wearily looked at the printed sheet from his rucksack, showing his ill-fated drive here and seeking an escape route which didn't mean too much risk. There were such few roads, just tracks, but he did realise that he recognised the village name, there in the very bottom left-hand corner of his map, a small river leading him most of the way from here to there, in what looked a distance he could walk. It was Inverannan, the location of the assignment he'd dismissed, where hopefully Emma and the other guy still were, and safety. Simon smiled a cracked smile and knew that this was his best way out.

Simon went into the kitchen and, using some kitchen roll, blocked the sink. He put on the taps and left them overflowing as he raided the fridge for food and took two bottles of water, drinking as he looked around. He put on the gas on the Aga, both hobs and oven, leaving its door open and hissing as powerfully as its prestige brand would suggest. He left, closing the rear door and seeing the river not far away, joined it on the closest bank on its journey to the south-west, buoyed by his work at the house and his pain now slightly helped by the Paracetamol.

Chapter Twenty

Simon Goes to Inverannan

Simon, whose mannerisms and inherent foolishness had indeed contributed to his own recent excruciating experiences, now set himself to trek to Inverannan, unwittingly and blithely back towards his tormentors. The terrain had proven challenging for his footwear, which was now chillingly sodden from each step in the brackish peaty heather and grass. The painkillers initial effect had also worn through as the morning cold ebbed, his occasional misstep causing his diaphragm to shift and drive a jagged torment into his cracked ribs, which needed a few moments of recuperation. Regardless, without a better option, he continued along the side of the small burn which would lead him to his colleagues. Simon wondered how the hell this all went so wrong, what happened to Miles and how this would all affect him personally. He vowed to give up his friends, those shits, to sell the flat and move to somewhere cheaper, pay off the credit cards and start anew. He'd apply for jobs away from The Insider, Christ, even away from London altogether. He'd enjoy telling them where to stuff their jobs, after all the crap, all the disciplinary actions they'd taken towards him just for stuff everyone probably did. Well, not the thing with the woman, that had just been a mixture of too much coke and stuff, but he even said sorry. The Written Warning was still on his record, so, Simon forced himself to confront his resignation from the Insider, which might best be done quickly before they got a chance to sack him, as that would possibly fuck up his subsequent employment chances.

He began to wonder about Miles. Was he, as that brute Allanton told him, taking the piss out of Simon? It certainly looked like it, now Simon had the chance to think about what had happened to him. If Allanton or some underling wasn't the voice on the other end of the line, was it someone Miles had got to do it? He had thought at the time that he could hear something in the background, like the person was in a pub or something, people laughing in the background. At the time, he'd just that it was the pub explanation, but it could have been anywhere, even in Miles' house or a pub with his city pals pissing themselves at Simon, the fool. Tears of self-pity ran down Simon's face as he trod painfully by the side of the stream, legs half-drained now thanks to his lack of fitness and the boggy, cloying soil, making is uneven walk take one hell of a lot longer than he hoped. Simon hoped that he could reach Inverannan by nightfall when the dangers of breaking his ankle in the pitted moorland would become an even greater risk than now. Recovered from his self-indulgent lachrymosity, even feeling a bit better on having thought his way through to a lifestyle change and having had a bit of a cry, Simon put up with the occasionally acute pains and concentrated on just putting one foot down after the other, step by careful step.

Simon kept a steady, slow pace for most of the remainder of the next four miles or so it took before he could see a welcome flow of peat smoke from a remote property, surrounded by dry stone walls. As he approached, he hoped to see it as the first house of Inverannan Village and the next step to his escape back to civilisation. Alas, the house was in a solitary position in what now looked like a short distance from a range of hills. Simon dropped to his knees, deflated and exhausted, at the rather disappointing realisation hit him that his Google directions map he printed did not include land features such as 1,700 feet of heather-flecked mountains. This also explained why the river turned sharp southwards on his map and unsurprisingly, the road didn't go directly there either. He was starting to feel the same depression from earlier, along with the exhaustion-fed tears rise again when he realised someone was looking at him from the wall around the cottage. He rose, hoping to god that the inhabitant wasn't a drug-dealer or psychopath, the only two types he'd met since leaving Inverness. Simon was also enthused by the realisation that there was a nice new, red car sitting in front of the white cottage, which would ideally be offered to him as a lift to Inverannan.

The owner of the cottage, Malcolm MacLeod, looked warily at what he initially thought was a lost rambler in need of guidance but now increasingly looked like a victim of some heinous crime. Simon had almost got used to his aches and facial bulges; however, he did, in fact, present quite a hammered looking visage as he approached the cottage with a rictus smile beaming from his melon-sized face, black with bruising and with a sore looking cut, possibly from a finger ring, across his right cheek. Malcolm's dog, a jolly-natured cockapoo called Fergus, moved from his usual hyperactive welcome to a rarely heard bark of concern as this intruder now loomed hideously towards his beloved owner.

'Shello' said Simon, unaware until now that his speech was impeded by twenty or so punches and a series of water-based tortures. 'Gneetooget to ivverananannn. Will you dwive me?' Simon gurgled slowly through his mask of bruises and expanded purplish skin. Realising now that he couldn't speak properly and that the man was staring at him with what appeared to be a complete lack of comprehension; he pulled the now-muddy map from his pocket and pointed to his intended destination. 'Gere. Ingerangannn' he tried to emphasise, which made it even more incoherent and somehow introduced a rather rude, demanding tone. Simon felt around his numb mouth with his tongue, remembering that he seemed to also have lost a tooth or two, which couldn't be helping his enunciation skills. Mr MacLeod, helpful by nature, pointed along a track from his house. 'It's about seven miles along there and you should take a right after a mile or so. There's a signpost there, that'll keep you right.' He glanced at Simon's shoes and trousers, appearing to be more suitable for a day at an office rather than a moorland hike through the highlands. Simon was also coated in black peat mud and also seemed to have some kind of psychological impairment, on top of what seemed likely to Malcolm, to be a direct result of a badly lost fist fight. Malcolm and his wife had been, in the past, happy to give a lift in their car to hitchhikers, to those who had mistimed a hill walk or just those who were tired and in need of their altruism. One two instances he'd helped to clean up walkers who had fallen in mud and given them spare clothes. His wife had administered first aid to one who had twisted his ankle while out there and they had even driven him and his companion the long miles to the doctor in Scourie, with no more reward sought than a polite thanks and the knowledge that they had done their duty to a fellow human.

In this case, though, Malcolm decided, this idiot can walk. He said a polite goodbye and gathering up his rather lovely little dog, walked away and inside leaving Simon's disappointed, puffy face gazing at him as he went. Simon wondered if he could steal the car but having had all the bruising he ever wanted, realised that another conflict was unlikely to turn out well either. Shoving his cursed map back into his rucksack, he trudged off again, at least this time on a road of sorts, towards the fading light and eventually

Inverannan Village. It was another two hours before Simon saw the next set of house lights after he walked alongside the road in the relative silence of September, a total of four cars passing him after he reached the main sealed road, thankfully none of which was a Range Rover full of his tormentors. One of the vehicles looked from a distance like their car, so he hid in the undergrowth until it passed, heart rushing inside his bruised rib cage until it passed, a different type and colour of vehicle altogether. His shoes were all but destroyed by then, especially after tripping a couple of times, the front sole now flapping open as he limped along the single track, undulating as it wove downwards past the foothills and towards the lower ground where he finally saw the distant lights of a few houses in the breaks between the trees and hillocks. Simon was completely exhausted and could barely put one foot forward at that point, wishing that he could just stop, lie down and die peacefully. However, he kept heading despairingly towards the village, the dusk dropping into darkness like the last insult to his many injuries of the past day.

It was full-on dark and time had become irrelevant to him, when Simon stumbled onto an ancient moss-encroached caravan in the roadside grounds of what looked like an abandoned farmstead, opened the door and crept inside. It seemed to him to be a farm workers digs or something, old cigarettes and crushed beer cans on the table and an air of disarray, a few blankets were strewn in each of the two tiny rooms at the right-hand side. Simon sat at the table and drank the last of his bottled water, the pain surging again into the cuts inside his gums and damaged tooth cavities. Exhaustion hit him suddenly and he fainted to the side, even his fractured ribs incapable of preventing his collapse.

Several hours later and for the second morning in a row, Simon wakened in agony, with no immediate clue as to his whereabouts. He sat up, whimpering at the pain in his head and torso, his hair sticking up vertically after a night stuck in the same filthy cushions of the old caravan. His hands felt over the surface of his face as he tried to assess the damage caused by those thugs back at the Allanton house. He burned with impotent thoughts of revenge but these were followed by a realisation that he had no real means of revenge and his priority was to get to Emma and the other guy, get their help, get home; get away from this horrible, mean place. He stood, dizzy like a new lamb and limping along the narrow caravan, found a narrow door which revealed a small, fetid toilet. He took off the filthy shoes, trousers and jacket, leaving them on the floor and going into the toilet. After he'd finished, he washed with a wafer-thin piece of soap in the microscopic sink in the kitchen section and wondered if anyone had left clean clothes around. A quick search of the bedroom provided only a large pair of swimming shorts, not clean but not bad either, and an XXL checked shirt which to all appearances, was devoid of any critical human outpourings. He put these rather oddly combined garments on and looked under the beds for any shoes; however, this was not as successful. He picked up his own ruined shoes and examined the left sole, which was hardly attached any more. He found some string in a cupboard and a pair of scissors, which enabled him to lash the sole back onto his shoes like Ahab to the whale. Pleased with his repair, Simon opened the door and sucked in the morning cold with not a little pain in his lungs. The visage was pleasant enough, steam rising from the neglected field as the sunlight played across the near-icy field. He put on his jacket and picked up his rucksack, lurching back through the gate and along the tree-lined road towards the village of Inverannan.

Another ten minutes brought Simon to the first houses of the village, which seemed quite spread out and perhaps harder to find two journalists in that he thought. He kept on until he came to what appeared to be a Bed and Breakfast with one or two cars outside and a view down to a lake or whatever they called these things here. He sat on the front step to let his ribs recover and to re-tie the string around his shoe, somewhat difficult now that some on the sole side had frayed. He heard the door open behind him and realised with relief, there was a rather perplexed Emma standing, wearing what looked like running clothes and trainers, frowning down at him without any sign of recognition.

'Heggo Ebba' Simon slavered with an attempt at a grin, again having forgotten that his vocal facilities were both severely inhibited and that he hadn't uttered a word since yesterday. 'Jesus Christ! Simon?' she came down the steps and looked at him from the front, to better see the damage which had made him more like an air-inflated version of his normal self. Emma knew as soon as she looked at Simon that her concerns over his bizarre recent behaviour were well founded and that whatever he'd been up to, it had turned out badly. She took him by the arm, inside the house and up to her room, then past Adams room without knocking, until she had dealt with the immediacy of this issue.

Simon's shorts and oversize shirt, along with the pallid hue of his skin and foul, lingering smell suggested that the first thing she needed to do was get him cleaned up and figure out what the hell was going on. He sat on the bed, head forward and arms folded protecting what appeared to a pain in his ribs. She knew that she needed to get him a warm shower and get some clothes on him. Since he was so slim, her clothes would fit, so while Simon sat in a haze, she looked out a pair of track pants, a clean t-shirt and some sports socks. She removed the tatters of his shoes and threw them into the bathroom; they were a size or so bigger than Emma's so no help there. She thought that Adam's shoes would probably be another few sizes bigger again from memory so something else would be needed before they could take him anywhere except for an ambulance. Not knowing yet what had happened, Emma couldn't decide whether to call the cops from the landline, Billie or wait for Simon to tell them what was going on. At this point, she thought that Adam's input would be helpful and went to knock on his door. It took an age, but finally, a bewildered Adam came to the door, still in last night's clothes.

Chapter Twenty One

The Morning Meeting

Having risen early at their rooms in the hotel wing of Inverannan House for their 0730 hours meeting, Sir Mathieson Allanton and his son had breakfasted and were now listening to George Galloglas explaining his understanding of the current predicament. They sat in his office, which itself inherently annoyed the younger Allanton, as he knew that Galloglas had employed an interior designer, at huge expense, to make this and other prominent rooms appear that they had been in this condition for decades and to ensure that the contents were suitably tasteful and recognisable, specifically the paintings which he took time to examine every time he came here for a meeting. He knew that Galloglas was fundamentally a sub-intellectual brute with aspirations of being a highland laird, trying to pretend that he wasn't funded by the narcotics he helped distribute and no doubt desperate to rise through the ranks of civil society as he himself had so successfully done at the coat-tails of his father, the originator and the real intellect behind the success and expansion of his own illegal ventures. They had bought Inverannan House and one other property in this area, not by any means all of the land hereabouts but a substantial strip of land, from near the coast, to the one which Sir Mathieson had owned previously as a semi-retirement escape and occasional family bolthole. Many enemies had been made throughout his father's long, sometimes vicious and partly self-serving military career; so many that there could be no thought of his spending much time without either a bodyguard or staying somewhere like this, so remote that personal security was much more achievable. His battalion batman, Benny McGowan was still with him and acted as cook and as a rather geriatric security man when his two main bodyguards were not available. He was there too, of course, the good son, ready to take over the family business when told, despite potential competition from some very capable relatives in their other Real Estate organisations. They had parked some of their UK property work for the meantime, although John still kept an overview of the London-based office, moving money into it and buying and selling regularly with accounts in Bermuda, Switzerland and a host of shell companies safely hiding the cleaned money from the vagaries of taxation. After causing such misery to society, Sir Mathieson Allanton certainly wasn't going to contribute to the national health, social services and police which were left to deal with his detritus.

John Allanton looked at Galloglas with some intent and more hostility than he meant to display. Galloglas loved the sound of his own voice and, as John had thought many times before, it would only take a bullet to make the noise stop, in an ideal world, fired by him. Galloglas had been explaining why his interpretation of hiding in plain sight included advertising a drug transfer location in a range of glossy magazines across Europe. Sir Mathieson listened without speaking during his monologue, as was often the case when he was trying to collate all the information before reacting appropriately and in a considered manner, a manner which had proven fatal to many who had crossed him since his business began. John wondered if Galloglas thought that he was indispensable to his father, who had been loyal to him before, no doubt, although this series of blunders could be considered far worse any previous misdemeanours.

'So' Galloglas finally cutting to the chase after blethering for over ten minutes, 'my point is that we can move money through here as well as the property portfolio. By building this up, to become a valuable and legitimate going concern, we can sell it down the line and move the money on. By my estimates, we could turn this into 8, maybe 10 million pounds worth of business, ready to sell after it becomes a globally known, high-end brand. That's why this publicity is vital to the expansion, we'll get the hunting and fishing side of things promoted in high-end magazines across Europe and in Russia and welcome them in, I'm confident the turnover will be far higher than anything we could get elsewhere, so every penny spent here will make at least double what we clean and at the end, it's as legitimate as anything we do across the business. He sat back, smiling at his own cleverness and waiting for the applause, which didn't come. Sir Mathieson was thinking of an appropriate way to handle this situation, all the time aware that he had previously had a number of opportunities to offload his old employee or to rein him in before this potentially catastrophic blunder had come to its almost painful conclusion. He stood and looked out of the window, down to a gardener a few hundred yards away, spreading feed on the far sign of the lawn in preparation for the coming winter.

'How much have you spent already?' he enquired directly but without turning.

Galloglas opened his laptop and powered it up. Allanton Senior glanced at him with a look as deep and dangerous as the crevasses which cut into the mountains he could see in the distance.

'Never mind that shite. How much have you spent?' More direct now, his old military strength still there for the most part. Galloglas, for the first time since he arrived at the Estate, was feeling like he was back as a subordinate to the former officer who stood before him. He closed the laptop and looked at Sir Mathieson, drew in a breath and, in the style of a post-mission report, reeled off a list of capital costs, starting with the harbour and ending, oddly, with the advance paid to The Insider for the benefits of its article, ably provided by Adam and Emma. He told them a total estimate of spending and looked to the immobile figure of Allanton for his response, as yet unclear but from John's perspective, unlikely to include many congratulations. Personally, John thought, I'd shoot the fucker right here and now and get him to the pigs in time for their lunch. His father, however, was inwardly calculating what Galloglas had cost the business already and whether it was best to take the route that his son was envisaging, or stay on board and give Galloglas time to make good on his pipe dream here at Inverannan. In the end, after his initial consideration, Allanton decided that he did not, as he'd hoped, have the full and requisite facts needed to assess whether to get his son or one of his able henchmen to liquidate this overdrawn chancer or whether to continue to permit him to throw money at a potentially problematic financial hole in the highlands. God help me, Sir Mathieson thought, I share the blame, putting him in place here when he was clearly more suited to sitting outside, waiting to be told who to knife next.

'George, you will continue with this venture for the moment; however, focus the distribution of the magazine carrying this article solely outside the UK and primarily in the locations where you expect the most potential customers and buyers to come from. Saudi, Russia, that sort of thing. Get me a detailed copy of your income and expenditure, I'll read it later.' Allanton senior waited for Galloglas to move, which he didn't, then he turned and looked at him. 'Now' he finished. Galloglas rose and for once temporarily silent, headed to the office with his laptop to ask them to print the spreadsheets, which unfortunately he knew would not impress his paymaster.

After he left, John Allanton joined his father at the window, admiring the view but intent on using the time to make his views known.

'He's a liability, plain and simple, dad. It looks like he's been up to something too, how the hell did he have enough to pay for all this, it's like he's got a never-ending pot of cash here?' He glanced quickly at his father, whose face looked wearier than usual in the harsh grey morning light.

'I know. We'll see what he's done here and have a chat later. We need to discuss these journalists, see what our options may be if they find out anything.' Moments later, Galloglas entered, handing a copy of the information to both Sir Mathieson and John Allanton. He started again to reassure them, at some length, that the spending may seem excessive but would all be recouped perhaps even four-fold when the estate was established as a going concern and then sold. John's tolerance for Galloglas was now nearing his previous day's level with Simon as he settled down to another ten minutes of blether from his father's erstwhile comrade-in-arms, the redoubtable Galloglas.

After he had eventually exhausted this last point, Galloglas looked pleased with himself, pouring out another coffee for the Allantons. Sir Mathieson took his drink and recapped the known situation with the journalists and last night's incident. He then turned and addressed his son, asking for his thoughts on the problem with the journalists. Galloglas was about to interrupt, however, Sir Mathieson raised a hand to wordlessly silence him. John Allanton pondered for a moment and then spoke in a deliberate, slightly softer voice than normal. 'The one who came to our place, he's not a threat as a journalist, or he wasn't until I had him worked on. Now, Christ knows what's best. We can threaten him and send him on his way or we could return his hire car to Inverness on the QT and throw him into a deep hole for a walker to find next spring. Either suit, but I'm veering towards the latter given that he can potentially find out who we are. These two, from what you told me yesterday, you say he's not much of a journalist but he made short work of a few of your guys last night, even if they were drunk - it's something to think about.' He took a drink of his coffee and resumed his mental analysis of the options available.

Sir Mathieson joined them and they sat in the circle of chairs by the side of the window, Galloglas wishing he had his whiteboard to help picture the scenarios, just like in the old days. He tried to work out what the journalists' angle could be, other than what he asked them to do, but nothing made complete sense. Atypically, he stayed quiet and let the Allantons talk for now, as they recounted the incident in more details at the car park of the bar – involving Galloglas staff.

Sir Mathieson summed up his son's description; 'From what I saw last night, the young lad knows how to deal with combatants. He's too young to have been in the military for any length of time, so either he's freelance muscle or he's just got a hobby which he's particularly good at.' He looked at Galloglas with an expression of very little patience and asked 'So, putting aside the gross and unfathomable mistake you made in inviting journalists here for this article, do you consider from your dealings with them that they may have any knowledge of our activities?'

Galloglas was about to launch another defence of his publicity strategy but was silenced solely by a flat-hand gesture from Sir Mathieson, then a move-along gesture to get him to answer the question. He spoke quickly and with a certain rabbiting quality 'no, not at all. I mean the boy questioned the finances and looked at our figures for a while, but he did not, at any time suggest an awareness of anything "off the books". I'd have talked him round if he did.'

'Of that, I have no doubt' said John Allanton, simmering with resentment at Galloglas' idiocy.

The three men discussed the options available in dealing with the three journalists; Galloglas was adamant that there was minimal risk in the two journalists for Inverannan; John Allanton thought otherwise. Eventually, they broadly agreed that all three could require severe pressure to ensure that facts pertaining to the project remained unpublicised and confidential.

Sir Mathieson had been in command of many, many military scenarios similar to this and knew the thought-processes and options better than most men alive. There was, he knew, a question of ideology which underpins these decisions. He knew that, sometimes, it was appropriate to take a draconian approach to operations, an option which often depends on the location of the problem and the proximity of the rule of law. This makes the decision making process far simpler, however, the world is a more connected place now than ever and negative publicity can also be a whip which lashes one afterwards, after you think all is complete, neatly handled. Sir Mathieson was not, despite his track record, a man who naturally fell into the role of despot or brute. Rather, he was a thinker, a man who would have done well in the East India Company, he always thought, when opportunities were readily available for an intelligent man with the means to back his decisions with military force, or the threat thereof.

'We must act while continuing to gather intelligence' said Sir Mathieson, summing up their discussions as befitted his role as both leader and customarily the smartest man in the room. 'John, get everything else you can on these two individuals and have the information from their employer on my desk by 1100 hours. Get the hire car from your man back to Inverness with no trail; George, make sure the other two journalists to come back here for your invite at 1200 hours, make some excuse why it's so late.' He thought for a moment. 'John - get our two friends to wait at the road outside the village with a description of the journalists' car and registration plate. If they bolt, tell them to run them off the road and get them back here, car back into the garage and so forth ASAP. Reconvene at 1100 here. I'll work in here until then.' With that, he dismissed them and took over Galloglas office, consigning him to the anteroom, quickly vacated by the two secretaries as they left on their mission to guard the only road south out of the village.

After briefly giving the two men their instructions and the car details provided by Galloglas, John Allanton set out for the garages, telling two of the more capable Estate men to head for the other property and with instructions to take Simon's hire car back to Inverness, drop the keys through the door of the place unseen and drive back in an anonymous vehicle. After they left, he went back to the anteroom where Galloglas was on the phone and used the second line to call and leave a voice message, to make sure that McGowan had fed Simon and made sure he hadn't died.

McGowan was increasingly unreliable; the impact of early old age, long-term alcohol abuse and the resultant multiple bar fights during his egregiously violent military career had cumulatively taken their toll on his memory and, increasingly, continence when drunk. His father still had use of and trusted McGowan; however, John was less convinced over who looked after whom now. He thought about sending another two of the men to check on McGowan, but this was the busy day and they were stretched as it was, taking the vans down south and back. He looked out of the bay window over to the estate gardens and noticed their beauty; the pleasance of their surroundings funded by the business and lorded over by Galloglas.

He turned to Galloglas and wondered if it would cause his father distress if he killed him now and disposed of him, asking forgiveness rather than permission. He still had the pistol and silencer in his car, under the seat, a tempting thought which brought a smile to his face. Galloglas looked up and noticed him, smiling back as comrades do.

Sir Mathieson was also busy at work in the office, taking on some more of the higher-level, strategic tasks on board. His son had given him the details of the owners of The Insider, so his dependable operatives in London were immediately information-gathering on them and their financial positions, as well as any other useful details and their potential to accept communication. He knew that he still had favours to call in from the corridors of power, but these were best used only when absolutely needed, a finite resource to be held until deployment essential. He also knew that, despite all the many and varied means of communication available to journalists, they still worked for someone and, one would assume, had family members who could be used as part of a negotiation. His considerations had left him with the thought that, certainly at this time in the UK, it was harder to hide a dead journalist than threaten three live ones, even young ones who may have principles, if indeed they did. Even better though, was to do what all great leaders do in their campaigns – assimilate, merge, join, take the best of and stand beside former enemies in the achievement of riches not yet won but to be shared. He pondered on how to play the meeting with the journalists, whether to leave it to Galloglas or join in himself; settling on Galloglas first and see whether he could diffuse the situation through his now-developed skill of talking constantly until he wore everyone down. This was an unexpected metamorphosis in Galloglas, his truculent menace of the old days replaced by an ambitious salesman with less wit than he gave himself credit for; this lack of sense and poor judgement, thought Sir Mathieson, now manifested itself in the burgeoning Inverannan and the commensurate risk he introduced to the business. He saw the way his son looked at Galloglas and wondered at what point he'd be faced with another black body bag and an apologetic son; this, he thought, would not necessarily be the worst option and could indeed have the benefit of introducing his son as a successor not to be taken lightly.

He made another two calls, one to Alf White's replacement to keep him up to speed and to allocate some tasks to him, busying with his network of contacts live and operational across the UK. The other call, to his nephew in Italy, was to inform him of the situation and prepare to activate the alternative routing arrangements which their Continuity Plan set out. The military vein ran strong in the business, always had; always will, as long as an Allanton ran the show. He enjoyed working with his colleagues on the continent, particularly Italy; their planning, experience and professionalism was beyond reproach, as well as their ability to retain almost 95% of the product through their part of the supply chain, using a combination of bribery, expertly hidden storage and an ability to hold whole communities in their thrall, open for all to see but none to stand against. Cultural advantages, he thought, with a tinge of envy, but you know, it makes his part of the business all the more admirable and perhaps hardest to manage. The rise of the competitors was a constant bane in this line of business; however, he was always ready to use precise and final force in those occasions to ensure that a reputation was retained, certainly in the circles that thought it was an achievable or even a possible ambition, to take on his organisation. He'd been dented, many times, but each had been dealt with either immediately or soon afterwards by his capable emissaries and their ever efficient clearing methods. In one recent case, all eight foreign nationals from a new venture had been terminated and removed with no evidence left on any of the sites and not a mention in any media, a case study for mass murder, if a forum for such a thing existed. His men were still the best of breed, now unfettered by the mores and restrictions of formal military regulations; a reserve army of hardened men and intelligence experts topping their pensions up with contract work when required. The product they extracted from that particular mission paid for their work more than four-fold, never mind the benefit of wiping the competitors from the face of the city and sending a message out that the company was still there, with all others taking what sectors they were allowed, at their permitted scale. Anything over that level, youthful exuberance aside, would be dealt with harshly. If a new challenger were open to the opportunity of wealth without power, they were sometimes integrated into the supply chain, perhaps having shed their protective officers to a greater degree, as part of the deal. It never surprised him now, how often lifelong friends permitted their subordinates to be terminated in the face of a generous offer of a more comfortable and indeed, continuing, existence.

He sat back after his calls were complete and as was his custom, pondered if any left-field actions were possible and how he would resolve them. It was possible that the journalists had already shared their concerns with their superiors at The Insider; this would require handling through the means he had already set in motion. They could have attempted to glean information from the staff at Inverannan, which may be why they were socialising with the rowdy locals last night. He opened the door and asked Galloglas to come in, leaving his son there tapping at a laptop.

'Find out exactly what happened last night at the bar. Ask the boys out there first, then validate with the office staff. Do it quickly and report back.' He waved him out, Galloglas not speaking and realising again that today, he was not the master of Inverannan Estate.

Galloglas left, his face reddened by the curt manner he'd been handled when given his orders, like an underling who doesn't matter. He felt like taking them down right now, taking over and blaming it on a competitor, or an accident or just a hostile takeover. He'd have had done it last year too, when John Allanton had tried to muscle him after an argument over this project, the young shit. Nepotism, that's all that's got him to the top, thought Galloglas for the hundredth time, his dad looking out for him, showing him the ropes and ready to step in as boss when it should be him, Galloglas, forty years of fighting, learning, ambition held in check, watching the officers give orders and him and others doing the nasty end of it, the knives, the guns, the bodies, plenty of them, all dealt with for them. He knew that if John Allanton took over the business he'd be on notice; those two uncommunicative bastards from Special Forces ready to do him in, he knew how it all worked, knew that when you were in their sights you were fucked, good and proper and for all time.

Fuming with impotent anger at his employer, he strode to the rear of the garages and told the chargehand to get out of the small office and send the men in to him; the chargehand knew exactly who he referred to and nodded, leaving in a hurry and off to gather them in from their fence building for what seemed to be a severe arse kicking from the boss. The men were a mile or so away and contactable over the radio, so drove back in ten minutes in their Land Rover, their faces grey from a hangover and the shock of being summoned suddenly by the sometimes-ferocious Galloglas.

He watched them shuffle in, their stench of work and their wet jackets steaming in the heat of the room. Galloglas assessed their injuries, which appeared minor; black eyes and scuffs, as he expected. 'So, what happened last night? Did you start it and if so, why?' he leaned back and waited for the juvenile nonsense to start.

The first one, McIntyre, who had started the fight, raised his bruised face to Galloglas. 'Aye, it was us. We were drinking and they two sat with the lassies. We tried a bit o'banter but they were taking the piss, so it was ye ken, winding us up.' He was as red in the face but clearly wanted to tell all. 'I flung a punch at him, but he leathered me, to be honest, then thae got a hiding tae.'

'I can see that. Apart from giving you pathetic articles a beating, what else happened? Were they asking you anything?'

'No us, but the lassies might tell ye different.' His face looked near to tears at the pressure of Galloglas stare.

Galloglas stood and walked to them, more menacing in an instant. They stepped back in fear of his barely-controlled anger; his voice now changed back the one he used all those years ago, a sergeant terrifying his cadets. 'Get back to work. If I hear of you fighting again, you're sacked. OK? In fact, if I ever hear of you putting a foot wrong, you will have me to deal with personally – understand?'

In unison, 'Yes sir', they turned and escaped from their uncomfortable dressing down, their stomachs clenched and each silently swearing never to get back in a room with that man, ever again.

Galloglas left after telling the chargehand to keep a daily watch on them and that he too, was responsible for his men. The chargehand decided, wisely, to nod and accept the responsibility rather than to argue with him and take an extended version of what the lads had just endured. Galloglas left and strode back to the main building, stopping to look over where the transport vans left the garage, following as they did an irregular schedule prescribed to avoid the attention of a fleet of vehicles leaving a small village at the same time, one of many details which Galloglas had to grudgingly admit that Sir Mathieson brought to the business. He walked back to the main building and stood outside the tall, black door which leads to the offices and staff kitchen. Taking a deep breath, he re-assumed his more charming demeanour which he used for white-collar workers, which made him feel more paternal to the predominantly female house staff as opposed to more brutish approach given to his men. It was always this way with Galloglas; he could change personality as easily as changing a hat. One wag back in his regiment even called him "smiling tree monkey" back in his early days as a sergeant, his men under him looking up to an arse and those above looking down to a smile. He walked in and briefly met in a side room with the ever-professional Office Manager, who had not been at the pub last night and had been told nothing of it. She seemed shocked and left to ask in the open forum, exactly whom had been there. She then brought the six staff involved into the room, each looking far less hungover than their male counterparts. They took chairs from a stack and sat across the table from their manager and Galloglas.

'Now' said Galloglas with a smile, 'I have no problem with you all having a good time at the pub after work, but I'm concerned that there was an incident at the end of the night and I wanted to make sure that you were all right. You weren't hurt in this incident, were you?'

'No, not at all' said Gillian 'we were going home when the lads started, but it was really nothing.'

'I understand our two visitors were there at that point and that young Macintyre threw a punch at him?'

One of the younger women spoke up, 'Yes, it was Adam that they started on. McIntyre was drunk though, just trying to act hard.'

'So what was it about? Were the journalists asking questions?' Galloglas fished for any clues.

'No, not really; we had been talking about what it's like working here and stuff, a few stories but it was just chat - honest.'

Galloglas thought about a different line of questioning and decided that being direct was the best way here. 'Did they ask you anything specific about the estate?'

Gillian stressed 'No, we were just having a laugh, really. It was a good night until then.'

Galloglas spoke gently but reassuringly 'I've spoken with the boys and they know that they are on a final warning about their behaviour, so I'm sorry you were caught up in that. Please be assured that I value you all very much as colleagues and I value your loyalty to the estate at all times.' He looked at each of them for a moment in turn as he spoke, emphasising the word loyalty and leaving them in no doubt that their confidentiality, explained at detail in their induction, was to be remembered.

'Please remember that - particularly when dealing with journalists, you must always be cautious; even in this case when they are here for a promotional article. We value our business here and the income it produces, so we must all be vigilant, so I would ask you to refrain from further discussions on the subject of the estate. I will handle this aspect of the communication, along with any other officers I nominate.' He nodded at Eilidh then thanked them for coming in and speaking to him.

They stacked the chairs as they left, silently and glad to be out. Galloglas had a feeling that the two journalists had been fishing for information, but maybe that is an occupational hazard for them; he wished now that he hadn't started this publicity drive and considered cancelling it, but how else was he to kick-start the business here and its' journey to legitimacy?

Chapter Twenty Two

The Walk of Shame

I wake up and check my watch; it's 5am and Gillian is sleeping, on her side and with her back to me. Easing out from under the covers, I get dressed in the narrow space beside the bed, my clothes crumpled but at least all there, in a trail from the bedroom door to the bed, so I retrace my steps, picking them up and putting them on as quietly as I can. I don't know who else lives in the house, so best get the hell out before anyone sees me and/or asks me what's going on. Before I close the door, I pull a scrap of paper from my jacket pocket and write my number, an x and my name, in case she doesn't remember, which I inwardly acknowledge may be a bit unfair on her. She looks stunning as she sleeps there, the light of morning not wakening her after, perhaps, a little too much to drink.

After going down the stairs as silently as a hungover ninja, I head out the front door, which is I think the way we came in the previous night, kissing passionately as soon as we rolled in. Walking outside, I genuinely have no idea whether to turn left or right, so decide on the former and walk in the morning chill towards what I think should be the road to the loch and the pub. Thankfully, I'm proven correct by a view of the water through a rise in the road and after a good ten-minute walk, I'm standing back at the fork in the road and the pub car park, with just one car still there. I wonder if the barman drove home last night; I suppose there wouldn't be much else on the roads at that time - if he did he was probably putting himself at more risk than anyone else. In my dad's day, I knew that almost all the adults drove home from parties or the pub with a good drink in them, but nowadays everyone's more aware that it's a genuinely bad idea to increase the odds of killing yourself and some other poor sod just because you can't be arsed walking a couple of miles home.

Turning away from the loch, I trudge determinedly to the B&B, which thank god is open, so I get in, up the stairs and into my room as noiselessly as possible. Clothes still on, I wrap the duvet around me and fall into sleep borne of alcohol and exhaustion, replete with a warm feeling of satiety and blessedly ignorant of the trials ahead.

I'm in the deepest sleep possible when I hear a repetitive knocking noise. I'm not sure if it's inside my head or somewhere else; waking, I realise that it's someone chapping the door, not loudly but sure as hell not giving up. I wonder if it's Mrs MacEachen and I've slept in, but my watch confirms that it's just after 8.45 and, as we don't have any interviews planned until later, I assume it's Emma checking on me, or telling me I'm about to miss breakfast. Standing up with a newly found swirl in my head, the alcohol moving into its' next stage, I open the door to see a very concerned Emma, who pushes past me and sits on the bed. She looks pale and worried, so I ask 'what's up?'

She looks at me with the beginnings of tears. 'It's Simon. He's in my room and he's been beaten up, really badly.' I can't figure this out. Simon should be in London, so I ask 'why – what's he doing here?'

'I don't know. Just put him in there out of the way, but he needs medical attention, his heads all swollen and he's not making sense; he might have a concussion or something.' I wonder if he's turned back from whatever he was doing and met those guys from the pub, out for vengeance, but this doesn't seem likely.

'OK, let's find out; then we'll ask where the nearest doctor is and take him there.' She nods and we go into her room, where a rather tragic looking Simon is sitting on the bed. He looks up at me with a hellish visage, teeth missing and the inside of his mouth red with blood; he's had a kicking, that's for sure, I think to myself. He's also wearing a pair of shorts and a shirt which looks like a lumberjack died in it. Looking down, I see that his feet are also covered in cuts and bleeding blisters, marking the carpet.

'Simon, what the hell are you doing here - what happened to you?'

He puts his head down 'Isha long shtory.' Incongruous as it seems, I suppress the urge to piss myself laughing at his predicament. Emma is genuinely concerned so I push down the feeling and try not to think about anything funny until I've gotten through my immature reaction.

Emma leans over and tells him 'we need to get you to hospital.' Simon thinks for a moment and looks up.

'No, I can't. Shfine.'

158

My amusement now temporarily curbed, I feel a surge of impatience and hiss at him 'What the fuck happened to you then. Last time we saw you, you had a personal problem and were heading to Inverness station to get a train back south. A couple of days later, we've done your work for you; then here you are, not in London and with a face like a fucking bruised melon. So, fucking tell us what you have been up to, OK.' I realise as soon as I finish speaking that I may have been a tad harsh with him and that Emma is looking at me with wide-eyed disapproval. Simon sobs and starts to babble a load of bizarre shit, half of which I can't make out and the other half, which I do hear correctly, I can't believe. We question him on the bits we can't make out as he sits, tears dripping onto his bare thighs and the occasional snort to inhale through what looks like a broken nose, pushed rightwards from the centre.

'Is this a joke?' I ask him. 'Did you walk straight into a drug trafficker's house and show them your Press ID before trying to do a deal with them?' I feel the hilarity thing rising again.

'Yesh' he tells me sadly. I walk into the bathroom and stand with both hands on the wash hand basin rim, shoulders heaving with silent mirth, tears running down my face. A few deep breaths and a slosh of icy water on my face, it looks like I've been crying, which Emma may mistake for empathetic sobbing rather than the cracking up with laughter which it was; I definitely need to try and be less immature in these situations, I think to myself.

When I go back into the bedroom, Simon is sobbing and Emma has his arm around him. My amusement now assuaged, I can perhaps be of more practical help, so I tell him that we're going to take him to hospital. 'NO!' he crackles at me; then starts coughing at the pain in his ribs, racked by what must be a couple of fractured bones there, I know how sore that can be so I'm momentarily sympathetic.

He looks at me with somewhat haemorrhaged eyes and speaks slowly 'No, jusht want to get away. Thish place is dangeroush. No hoshpital.' He looks distraught and Emma lowers him onto the bed, on his left side. He groans at the pain but lies there, like a foetal ruin of Monday's Simon. I gesture Emma to come with me and we head into my room to try and figure out what to do.

'Well we need to call the police, that's' for sure.' She emphasises.

'Look, we need to think this through. One thing that is for sure is that Simon is in deep shit if we call the cops. Trying to get a drug deal going with god knows who up here – what the fuck was he thinking? I know of some guys who do this and believe me, he's lucky to get out even in that state, these guys don't fuck about when it comes to protecting their business.' Emma looked uncertain now, trying to understand the reality of what Simon had done. 'So what do we do?'

I don't know either, to be honest, so after a quick mulling over, I offer what I think is the safest option. 'We finish up in Inverannan, get a coffee with Galloglas and that's our job just about done. We leave him here until then, tell Mrs MacEachen that you have photographic stuff in your room so not to go in; we'll get back as quick as we can and off to Inverness – when we get back to Inverness or Glasgow or London, whatever, Simon can get to A&E and tell them he got mugged, then he's safe and away from whoever done that to him. Once they find out he's done a runner, these guys might well be looking for him and he's not exactly inconspicuous in that state.' Emma looks rather unconvinced but nods anyway. She heads off to check on the semi-comatose Simon and we agree to get our breakfast, act as if nothing has happened and call the estate to try and get the Galloglas visit over asap, letting us start our trip back to civilisation.

So, after much mulling over what the hell was going on, we head down to the dining room, saying our good mornings and apologies for being late to our host; it looks like we are the only guests there at this point. Emma manages to stuff some of our breakfasts into a napkin in her bag when Mrs MacEachen isn't in the room, she plans to take these up to her room and leave them beside Simon, who we'd left to sleep in her room covering his feet with a towel and pulling the duvet over his injured body.

As we're just finishing breakfast, the landline rings and Mrs MacEachen comes into the dining room to tell me. It's Eilidh from the Inverannan office, passing on a message about an invite to conclude our work with Galloglas as soon as we can get there; he's now unavailable later so it has been brought forward. Fuck it, I think to myself, what's going on here; that's the call I was about to make to her. Still, if we get out of here sharpish, get Simon sorted and back to the comparative sanity of London, I'll be happier, so I tell her it's not a problem, we'll be there as soon as we can.

There's a pause on the line and Eilidh says, with a slight concern in her voice 'I heard you were in a bit of a fight at the bar last night. It's just the lads doing what they do, there's not a brain between them.' I assume that the others in the office had told her, but I didn't really want to get involved further; the only matter concerning me was whether they would try and get back at me for their humiliation before I leave – I couldn't be sure that my boxing skills would be as effective when faced with sober men.

'Aye, they just had a few too many, definitely. I should have just backed off; I hope they don't have any hard feelings?'

'They won't have. Mr Galloglas seems to have given them a stern warning about it, so they'll be keeping their heads down, that's for sure. He's not a man to mince his words with the men, or so I've been told. Anyway, see you shortly, bye Adam.'

'Bye' I say to the dialling tone, my head lost in thought. I wonder about calling Billie and telling her about Simon, but decide it's best to keep quiet and let him explain to her when he gets back. He'll probably get sacked, I think, so that's another bonus for everyone at The Insider. I shout thanks to Mrs MacEachen and head upstairs with Emma to talk about the meeting and to figure out what do when we get there. We go into our respective rooms to shower and change; then Emma comes into mine to dry her hair without waking Simon. While she's quickly working on some make-up, Emma asks where I got to after the bar and the fight; her memory is blurry so she wants to piece together the end of the night.

'So, when did you get back?' she asks me, straight.

'I sat with the barman for a while; he gave me a cold towel for my hand, so you were all gone when I got out. You must have crashed out when you got in?' She looks at me askance.

'Well, no. When we realised you weren't following us, we got worried about you, so we walked back to find you, but you weren't there. Nor was Gillian, if I'm remembering her name correctly.' I scratched my head, a pain from my knuckles reminding me of the other part of last night.

'Yeah, well, you know', was all I could think of to tell her; Emma shakes her head slightly at me. 'To be honest, I don't think my casual relationships are really the main issue here. We've got a

161

pummelled colleague in there and unknown assailants at large, probably looking for him as we speak.' Emma nods in agreement.

'Let's get the interview over as quickly as we can, get him and us out of here.' She agrees.

To remind the landlady of what we'd told her, we lock the room and put the Do Not Disturb message on the handle; other than that, she'll be in for a nasty shock if she goes in and sees Simon's bloaty head, I think to myself. We gather up our bags, head to the door, paying Mrs MacEachen but arranging to leave our rooms until we get back and check out properly after Emma's pretend photography has finished in her room.

We drive out of the village back towards Inverannan House; I think to myself that, perhaps as it's rather like Mharisaig, I have grown a certain affinity for this place. Simon aside, it's been fine here, I've escaped a fight relatively unscathed, apart from a scratch on the side of my face from a flailing hand which I hadn't realised until I shaved in the shower. I've almost finished my first article proper, as well as meeting a rather attractive new friend who I was trying to figure out what to say to if/when I meet her back at Inverannan House. I wonder if she's told her colleagues, or if they would just figure it out as Emma did – it doesn't exactly require great detection skills to figure out that the two missing members of the party may have gone home together after a ton of booze.

Chapter Twenty Three

The Allantons Intervene

After the meeting, John Allanton sat at the desk in the anteroom of Inverannan House, starting on the necessary calls which the current debacle required. He knew that this wasn't as big a deal as say, a team of Albanians muscling in on the distribution of the products, but in that type of scenario, the anonymity of the business was almost completely secure with all the protagonists unlikely to seek either the police or publicity. What Galloglas had done, was to bring a different type of danger to the organisation and not only that, to the lives of his family who carried his name and that, that would not be tolerated. He decided to convince his father to deconstruct this project and with it, Galloglas, as soon as the pressing matter of the journalists was forced to a conclusion, with minimal or no risk remaining. Suppressing his desire to shoot Galloglas in the face, he turned from him and went downstairs to the toilet to freshen up before putting these further suggestions to his father in private. Before going back upstairs, he heard his name shouted and saw Ranald Mair, one of the Estate men, standing in the corridor, his face as usual as impassive as an Easter Island statue, albeit one which drank a bottle of cheap whisky every day.

'Could I have a moment of your time sir?' he bellowed.

John Allanton nodded, gesturing him to go for a walk outside somewhere unoccupied where his high-volume vocal talents could be masked by the trees and the sounds of the estate. 'What's eating you Ranald?'

Ranald stopped as the stood a hundred or so metres from the House and into a copse of yew trees beside the path. 'I was coming in this morning and see something. Yon caravan at Ellie's field, there was a laddie coming out of there, half-naked by the looks of it and with no business being there. He'd had a right doing, face all purple and walking on sair feet. I wondered about it, and then I heard the lads had got into a rammy outside the pub last night, but it wisnae one of them, or the laddie that was here for the interview with him upstairs.'

Allanton had no idea who this could be; then a feeling of dread came over him. 'That bastard got out.' He whispered to himself, turning and then stopping. 'Where was he going when you saw him?'

'To the village, ye ken, he sat doon at MacEachen's stairs last time I seen him.' Ranald watched as the younger man sprinted back to the house, feeling that it must be something important to make him do that, but it would it would have been nice if he'd said thanks. He wandered back to the garages to see what else needed doing now that all the cars were away.

Allanton raced up the stairs, through the anteroom past Galloglas and into the office. 'That journalist we had at the house, he's here, possibly at the B&B with the other two. We need to get him.' Sir Mathieson, momentarily surprised by the outburst, looked up and said to him 'it appears then, that we may indeed have a concerted effort on their part.' His son looked at him, then the door opened and Galloglas came in, asking what was going on.

Sir Mathieson looked at his two men and shook his head. 'Sit down.'

He looked up at the clock, it had just turned 0915 hours and his operation, never mind the information he needed was far from complete. 'Can we assume that this young man either walked here or found some other means of transportation yesterday and perhaps overnight? If so, given the restricted communication options available, the pressing requirement would appear to be to prevent them from calling anyone from the landline in the B&B or other in the village, or indeed leaving with urgency. George, arrange for a call to him immediately meeting; have your office manager do this, this will let them imagine that all is genuine.

He thought for a moment, how best to gather his targets in. 'John, if you could fetch our two colleagues back from their roadside duties, ask them to return to the village and ensure that our two journalists leave alone from the B&B towards here. Stay with them. Do not indicate your presence to the journalists. Once they leave, arrange for the other one to be transferred here, to the garage preferably, unseen. Enquire of Mrs MacEachen if anyone of them has made a call this morning?'

Sir Mathieson thought through the possibilities quickly. 'Perhaps divert her attention, John, while they extract your journalist. Quieter the better, please, we're amongst friends, but in plain sight, remember.'

John Allanton nodded to his father and both men left to carry out their orders, their plan ahead of schedule thanks to Simon. John cursed himself for not containing the problem, neither getting any useful information from Simon nor terminating him; his father would know that the job was botched because of him, making him seem more like the bungling Galloglas than he liked to imagine, dear god.

He got into his Range Rover and sped along, past the B&B where the journalist's car sat; on another mile and the two men were sitting, recently arrived in their vehicle in a lay-by. They listened to the update silently and followed him back to the village, where they waited some way off from the B&B, unnoticed but in a position where John could be seen. Ten minutes later, they received a thumbs-up from him; presumably, the first part of the operation had been triggered by the two journalists departing for the Estate. Moments later, both their vehicles were parked outside the B&B, John Allanton going inside first and the others outside the door, waiting for a signal.

'Good morning.' He smiled a charming smile to Mrs MacEachen, who slightly recognised the man as being connected to the Estate. 'Hello, how may I help you?' she replied.

'I'm holding a rather large party at the Estate in the near future and wondered, given the number of guests, whether you would have availability?' She opened her bookings folder and confirmed that the weekend he suggested was fine for the four rooms she offered.

'They have children with them, would they be able to have extra mattresses perhaps in the rooms for them?' he quizzed.

'Yes,' she smiled 'I have lovely wee folding beds we use for just these occasions. I might need to get more though if there's a need.' His charm and the prospect of a full house were working as well as he'd hoped.

John glanced past her. 'Is there a garden here for them to have a bit of a play?'

'There is – come and I'll show you' she beamed, leading him through the kitchen door, which he slammed behind him. 'Sorry' he apologised 'I'm more of an outdoors man. Don't know my own strength.' She smiled, knowing the very type of man and they walked into the garden for a round of questions from John Allanton, then a tale of his party and the fabulous guests he hoped to bring along. Mrs MacEachen was entranced by Allanton, who if he'd been a few years older, would be just her type, for sure.

The two men entered the B&B silently, got to the first floor and saw four doors, two of which were ajar; shouldering in the closest one with comparative quiet, they found Simon fast asleep under the duvet. One lifted him with ease, however, the movement wakened him, his eyes bleary but immediately terrified; a clinical punch from the other sent Simon back to the blessed relief of unconsciousness, letting them carry him downstairs, out and into the boot of their four-wheel drive unseen. They sounded the horn as they pulled away, allowing their colleague to finish his blethering about fictitious parties, which he found fairly easy to recount, using a combination of his oldest daughter's recent birthday party and the celebration they had, a year or so ago, enjoyed for his wife's 30th birthday. With assurances to be back in touch, Allanton politely extracted himself from the B&B, back to the remainder of the operation at Inverannan.

Chapter Twenty Four

The Reckoning

As we arrive at Inverannan House, there's little activity around, just one gardener working at the lawn and a couple of four-wheel drives parked beside the main building, joined by another which drives past us rapidly and towards a large garage fifty metres or so away, as we stand looking over at the lawn. 'Maybe that's the paying guests just starting' I say to Emma as we get our bags from the boot; Eilidh walks from the door to greet us, smiling as always and asking us to follow her to the main entrance, rather than the lowly staff door we'd used before.

'Mr Galloglas is in the downstairs library this morning, he's been busy with meetings and will be again later, so thanks for coming up early.'

'No problem at all.' I tell her. 'We were glad of your call, we can get back on our way once we're finished here; it's a fair journey back to London.' Emma tells her the detail of the various legs of our trip back, which makes it sound all the worse to me; we chat for a few minutes outside and I wonder if she's bringing me in the front door so that we won't see the office team, if Gillian is embarrassed, but maybe I'm over-thinking that. Eilidh opens the main door, part-glazed and very grand, opening into a baroque hallway, replete with a suit of armour, for god's sake and walls decorated to the tall ceiling with every type of animal head, sword, pike and shield imaginable. She opened a heavy, wooden door and there inside, was our subject, Galloglas, standing and looking at me with a harder gaze than I think necessary, his fists clenched at his side.

'Come in, have a seat' he tells us, breaking his stare and falling back into whatever persona he seemed to think we require. I shake his powerful hand again, this time ready with my own to meet the pressure from our first meeting; he looks at me, sensing that I'm deliberately matching his grip.

Emma shakes his hand too, unlike mine's Galloglas is gentle to her; this is a waste of time, I think to myself, lets' get this done and try not to get in any deeper, not after Simon. I can't be bothered at this point to ask anything about budgets or dodgy funding or even what he's doing in this backwater.

Then, as he's politely pouring us our coffee, in a room filled with what looks like more expensive artworks, the penny drops for me; why else would this guy be trying to set up a harbour, a strip of private land and a place where there's not a police presence for eighty miles, at least. What I don't know yet, is what the hell he wants us here? I can't for a minute imagine, whatever he's moving through here, would he want publicity? I calm myself, feeling a tingling in my face and neck at the thought of the danger we could be in and I decide to play nice and roll over, do this article whatever way this clown wants, get out of this as soon as I can. Emma must sense something is wrong with me, she leans forward to look into my eyes, but I shake my head to dissuade her from speaking to me.

I panic again, realising that Galloglas, or some of his cronies, were probably responsible for Simon's pulping and incarceration; fuck me, if they know he's in the B&B, they might think we're involved with him. I can feel my stomach tightening with stress, my heart rate increasing. I try to control myself, get a grip, and tell myself I've made a leap of imagination here, its odds-against that being the case. Fuck, I think, as he hands me a coffee and a chocolate biscuit. Fuck.

He sits across from me with his back to the bay windows facing the lawn in a similar chair, high backed Chesterfield, leather; it always makes me think of a gentleman's club when I see these. I'm internally babbling and I know I need to calm down, act naturally or I might let him know I'm rattled. I sip the hot coffee and start to control my emotions.

'I hear you had a little unfortunate incident with some of my young employees last night' he smiles, a snakelike smirk. 'I've given them a warning talk. I was very disappointed in their behaviour.' The faint smile fades. 'As I told them, I'm the only one allowed to do the punching on my estate.' He laughs; a hollow laugh which both I and Emma tried to humour.

'I do apologise on their behalf' he went on 'that's partly why I wanted to see you as soon as possible this morning, as soon as I heard. I don't want you to leave with any negative thoughts whatsoever about my business here; quite the opposite, I need you to be fully committed to producing a piece of work which will help both publicise and enthuse the readers to visit, enjoy and perhaps even invest in Inverannan in the future. We are building a great estate here, the biggest venture in the far north of Scotland since the Sutherlands in the 19th century, history in the making, if you will.' He stands and turns, gazing out in the same direction as our chairs, facing directly out of the tall sash box windows towards the lawn.

'So, tell me, both of you, what are your impressions of the estate?' he is fishing for information here and I am sure that Emma knows that too. I hope she speaks, as my mouth seems stuck.

Emma does indeed help here, thankfully. 'It's fabulous what you are doing here. We have some great, terrific content already and perhaps if you could give us a quote or two about the future of the estate, we could drop that into the last paragraph, entice some customers to look at your website and visit. It's such a lovely location and with all the activities on offer, I think you're going to be popular.' She finishes immaculately with a smile at him as he turns for a moment, beaming at him with faux enthusiasm. I nod, hopefully, that will prompt him into a monologue and then we can get the hell out.

My hope for leaving without incident is dented significantly by the sight of Simon, hands tied behind him but legs pumping like pistons, running across the lawn, pursued moments later by two burly black-clad figures.

'Fuck' say both Galloglas and me, simultaneously.

I stand up beside Galloglas, watching Simon hurdle the wall into what looked like a fair drop. 'What the fuck are you up to?' I just have to ask Galloglas, face to face now. He grabs me by the shoulders, but I twist away from him to see a horrified Emma, unsure of what to do; he starts towards me and throws a punch, but I hit out at him a few times, surprising him but hardly in danger of putting the solid character down so easily. I back off towards the open door but he rushes me and we crash through it; I see others there but I need to keep an eye on Galloglas. He throws his arms around me and he's tough as hell, I can't get away from his powerful grip, but I push with my legs and get him levered, onto the wooden walls to and fro until the back of his head hits the timbered wall and he lets go. I step back to get away from both him and some broken glass, we must have smashed a bottle or something; he comes forward with his arms wide, leaving gaps for

169

me to punch into, which I do with all the force I can muster. Still, the fucker won't go down, goes back for a moment then comes at me again; he looks groggier after I catch him on the chin with a left; so, hoping he's not suckering me in, I launch a right straight from my legs. I hit him bang in the middle of his face and down he goes, probably for some time if the pain in my already damaged knuckles is anything to go by; I turn my attention to the others, the two from the lawn who chased Simon, a tall younger fellow and an older man, both of whom seems completed unfazed by the mayhem wreaked around them. This is weird, I think to myself, as I find myself shaking hands with the dark-haired bloke, who seems genuinely pleased with me, introduces himself even. Accepting the invitation of the older man, I join them in the library, as the two chunky thugs are sent to see what happened to Simon.

I sit in the library, feeling like my hands are broken, particularly my right after its impromptu visit to Galloglas' face; it's an unreal situation and I have no idea who these men are, they certainly aren't the police so my best guess is that they are colleagues or rivals of Galloglas. There are no more introductions but it appears that the older man is in charge and, as the other one pours him a coffee, he looks at me with oddly piercing eyes.

'So' he says, turning to Emma, 'I do apologise for all this nonsense, most of which is due to your host outside.' Emma goes as if to speak, but holds silent, waiting for him to finish.

He resumes 'I am, as of this moment a former colleague of George; he made an error of judgement in commissioning the article which you were sent here to write. I have been in touch with the proprietors of The Insider and reimbursed them, rather generously, for your work here and the trouble we have put you to. As per the agreement, albeit entered into by Mr Galloglas but hereafter assumed by me, I have this right and the right to subsequent anonymity, which if breached will result in legal proceedings.' I can't believe what I'm hearing; he can't possibly get away with this nonsense. I exhale involuntarily and he turns to me.

Although Galloglas was, especially when we first met, an intimidating figure – this old guy was another league higher; I just about flinch at his stare when he turns to me and I realise that I'd be better listening to him, for now.

'You are correct to be suspicious of this approach; I can't expect you to remain silent solely on the basis that your article will no longer be published. However, I do have a proposal for you both, as individuals, which I'd prefer to do separately, given the sensitive nature. John, will you accompany – Emma – to the office upstairs, I'll be there shortly. Please have no concerns, I am not the erm, type of person whom you have dealt with before, nodding to the door and Galloglas.

I look to Emma and although she seems like a barely-contained bag of nerves, she goes out with John Allanton, past the still recumbent Galloglas and upstairs to, I assume the front way of accessing the office we'd used for our interviews with him. A hand is held out and I shake it. 'Sir Mathieson Allanton, late of the British Army; I feel I need to provide you with some context here, perhaps you will understand the situation more clearly.' I nod agreement.

He goes on with his curiously old-fashioned, clipped tones. 'We are part of a larger organisation which has many strands across the globe; I am in semi-retirement at the moment and plan for my son', with perfect timing as John rejoins us; 'to assume the lead role within a month or so. This particular project you were unfortunately invited to write an article upon may, depending on your decision, be closed down permanently and the staff disbanded. It is merely one of many dozens of supply chain points across the globe and therefore both disposable and replaceable; as you may imagine there are plans already ignited to carry out this action, however, they are at the present still reversible.' He paused to sip his coffee.

I need to speak, as I'm completely lost here, shouldn't they be tying me and Emma up beside Simon? Not that I want that to happen, but for god's sake what do they want from me? I try to sound calm.

'So, why are we speaking here?'

He smiles paternally at me. 'I can see potential in you, Adam. From what I perceive, you saw straight through Galloglas and his rather optimistic business plan and I assume you had already concluded where his capital investment emanated from?' I nod, although I hadn't really figured that out exactly until ten minutes ago.

Sir Mathieson continued. 'I have also witnessed you twice dealing with aggressors in a calm and highly proficient manner, despite appearing in both instances to be unlikely to emerge victorious; this is most impressive and I can assume from this that you have a certain capacity for at least defensive aggression, my preferred type these days. What I need to know from you, before we proceed, is whether this aptitude for violence is matched by a...moral fluidity.' I think he's asking me to join the business, oh shit oh shit oh shit. I don't know if he can see my panic, but I try to stay as externally relaxed despite being inwardly immobilised.

'We have – shall I say – vacancies at present for men of talent and youth. I can be honest with you; many of my counterparts are no longer in the age category where they can continue to support my son for a great deal longer. I have carried out some preliminary, albeit incomplete investigation into your personal situation.' I can't believe this, but his son hands him a folder with my name on it.

'You were arrested but released without charge as a result of a narcotics investigation in Glasgow. From this, I can assume that you were operating on a small scale but smart enough not to get caught, which is wise indeed. Here in Inverannan, for example, I am showing my son the risk of proximity to product which he will never repeat in this profession after today.'

I look at John Allanton, who nods at me thoughtfully and I assume the older man has had him moving some of the gear about to let him know how risky it is. Fuck me, I think, what am I doing here? I can't run away, so I need to play along. I wish I had recorded this conversation, cursing myself inwardly.

'So, are you willing to listen to an offer of employment?' he asks me directly. I can't wrap my head around this yet but nod and I hear myself saying 'yes, but what do you want me to do?'

He asks me 'will you wait here for a short while? I will discuss matters with my son and resume our conversation soon.' He beckons John and they leave, I see them looking at the unconscious Galloglas before the door closes. I am baffled; what the hell does he want me for? I guess if I join them, then I won't be able to publicise that they are drug traffickers or smugglers, or whatever they are. I am in way above my head here, I'm just three months out of university and I've been offered a job doing god knows what for some scary ex-army drug baron. Fuck me.

Outside the window, I see four men carrying a stretcher with, I assume, Simon attached to it; as they pass across the lawn I see that his face isn't covered with the blanket which I hope means he isn't dead. They take him into the garage across from the house and hopefully they're calling a doctor; he was in bad enough shape before he jumped over that wall to god knows what. I try to figure out what to do, maybe guess what they're saying to Emma, if anything; she won't accept a job from a drug dealer, that's for sure; maybe they are just kidding us on, going to kill us once we aren't alert or once they get us somewhere else. I look round the room, it doesn't look like there's anything to defend myself with in here; outside though, there's plenty of knives and stuff, so I decide to nip out there and get something which I can slip down the back of my jeans in case I need it.

I open the door and see that Galloglas isn't there anymore; they must have had him taken away, hopefully for good. I look around the walls for something small enough to secrete about my person, but most of these things are either long or would cut the back of my arse off; then I see a glass case with what looks like a set of sgian-dubh knives, not the ornamental crap but the real solid ones. I try to open the case when I'm hit on the back by something solid, painful and wielded by Galloglas.

Suddenly, I'm looking up at him, the glass case I was holding crashed and broken around me and I'm struggling to breathe after he hit me; he's holding a three-foot-long shillelagh, a wooden club thing I saw on the wall as we walked in and by Christ, it hurt. He's grinning at me maniacally and I start to try and edge backwards when he comes at me again, skimming the edge of my left shoulder as I scamper away from him. I jump up, trying to ignore the pain in my back as he swings again but I weave backwards and he hits thin air; I slide on the broken glass and he's on me again, but I get up and block the strike with my left arm and punch him with a short right hand, making him grunt.

He punches me in the ribs, still holding my left arm up with his stick, again and again until I twist myself towards him and use my weight to pull us both to the ground. He's stronger than me, so I'm losing and my back is lying on broken glass, which is agony; I try to get up, but he's pulled himself onto me punching me but not hitting me cleanly as I try to use my arms to defend my head. He reaches back to pick up his shillelagh, looking to stand up and give me a dose of it again, but I grab onto him with my left hand, dripping with blood but held firm in the nape of the buttons on the front of his shirt. I feel glass on the floor with my right hand, then

173

the handle of a sgian-dubh; it's slippery, but I feel the worn leather into my grasp, blade forward and plunge it, hard as I could into the side of his head. It goes in deep, my adrenalin giving me the strength to thump it into his left temple as he turned back with the shillelagh; I push him over and off me, his body instantly sagging as his life ends. I push myself up from the bed of broken glass and take my shirt off, it has shards embedded in it and they come out of my skin as I pull it from myself, excruciatingly. I feel that I'm going to faint, but I go into the library and over to the drinks table, pouring a tumbler of whisky and drinking most of it in one go. Then Sir Mathieson Allanton and his son are standing in the doorway; the younger man is grinning widely as his father turns to him and says 'I think we have our man.' With that, I sit on the sofa, caring not a fuck how much of my blood stains the delightful antique.

☐

Chapter Twenty Five

Simon Falls Down a Hill

Simon wondered if he'd imagined the awakening, brief but painful, by his two tormentors; he knew that he wasn't dead; there was too much pain and motion for that easy release. He was in the pitch dark of some sort of enclosed space, a car boot he thought, lying uncomfortably on a hard foam surface with lots of individual storage gaps; the journey was short, moments even, though he couldn't remember how he got in there. The boot opened and light blinded him, even inside what looked like a garage, but not the one back at the house, this was bigger and other men were there, watching. They pulled him up, roughly bent him forwards onto the boot floor and put plastic ties back on his sore wrists, the swine. One of the men who had watched came over to see what was happening, it sounded like he didn't like the situation; his two captors turned, telling him in no uncertain terms to mind his own business, giving Simon the opportunity to run for the door, shoeless and desperate.

He suppressed the various pains in his body and head as he surged out the door and along a grassed area, barely noticing the stately home to his left; he could see two cars in the driveway ahead and thought that he could reach them, see if someone would help, but mainly he knew he had to run for his life. The men were pursuing him, but he was fleeing for his life and they were sixty years old, easy, bulky and immobile; he veered past an astonished workman who tried to grab him and thinking the house unachievable, Simon jumped over a small stone wall, unexpectedly freefalling and then crashing down a steep ravine for some forty or so metres downwards, spinning through wood and sticks until his head struck the stump of a sawn tree, courtesy of George Galloglas recent removal of all non-native pine from that part of the estate. The two chasing men, regaining their breath after a rare run, looked down the steep slope at Simon's inert carcass, deciding with unspoken agreement that someone else would be going for him.

Upstairs, Sir Mathieson Allanton had watched the two journalists arrive, accompanied into the main entrance by the Office Manager Eilidh for their meeting in the library with

Galloglas, away from where the office which he had taken over; then he watched his two men drive in, and park in the workshop, hopefully with the other journalist in the rear, ideally incapacitated; he noticed his son arrive and park the Range Rover just to the side of the main entrance and all seemed to be going to plan. He wondered why no-one had closed the workshop door, the attendant appearing to have gone inside. Then, a scrawny half-naked man with no shoes had sped out, over the gravel and the lawn, pursued by his men; the figure had vaulted a small stone wall at the edge of the parterre and disappeared without a trace, leaving his pursuers looking down after him. Sir Mathieson knew the hillside to be extremely steep there, more so following the removal of all the pine trees; he also now knew that although his men were strong and able fighters, he would have to consider using younger men, if any matters required fitness of that sort. What was worse, however, was that the entire incident was almost certainly witnessed by the other journalists.

Sir Mathieson opened the door and walked downstairs to the front entrance hall, where his son stood, hands on his head. The two men were returning slowly to explain their mistake when the library door opened and Galloglas came through, grappling with the other male journalist; Galloglas seemed to have received the worst of the exchange, his face reddened and marked. They grappled past him and his son, crashing into the table at the foot of the stairs, sending a decanter and some glasses smashing to the floor as they fell. The two secretaries stood beside the Allantons to view the tussle, along with the girl; the former soldier wrestled with the younger man; a few moments later, the journalist broke free from his grasp, getting up and moving into a boxing position. Galloglas launched himself at him, but a series of heavy thunking blows forced him back; the older man was now visibly dazed and trying to defend himself unsuccessfully from the astonishingly quick punches. The younger man took an opportunity to go through him cleanly and struck him perfectly in the centre of his face, dropping him unconscious to the glass-strewn floor. Unaccountably, John Allanton began to clap, then stopped, realising that at least theoretically, Galloglas was on "his side".

Sir Mathieson looked at the debacle in front of him and told them 'please, can we take a moment to calm down and return to the library.' He turned to the two, slightly sheepish looking thugs and said 'Can you fetch some men from the workshop and retrieve their friend; hopefully, he isn't too badly hurt. Bring him into the garage and assuming he requires medical attention, call Dr Gibb on this number.' He handed them a card from his wallet, then walked past the confused Adam and into the library, the better to calm matters down and seek a resolution to this odd problem. Adam had lowered his fists and looked at John Allanton, who looked a real challenge if he had to fight him; instead, Allanton put forward his hand in friendship, with a smile and the introduction of his name. They shook hands and Adam told him his, Allanton replying, 'Pleased to meet you Adam; that was very fine indeed. I enjoyed that.'

The library door closed, the recumbent Galloglas for the moment, forgotten.

Chapter Twenty-Six

The Offer

It's an hour or so later and I'm getting fixed up by a geriatric medic by the name of Gibb; he doesn't have much of a bedside manner and has a proclivity for dousing wounds in what he tells me is an antiseptic solution but feels like acid. He's tweezered at least eight chunks of glass from my back and put loads of little white strips all over me, watched by a frazzled looking Emma. The Allantons were with us for a while but seem to be off handling the Galloglas situation on my behalf, or possibly theirs, or maybe both. All the mess had all been cleared up by them Emma had been brought back down, but I confirmed straight away to her what John Allanton had told her about my second fight with Galloglas; I think she wondered if they were bullshitting her for some ulterior motive, but so far they had been more than fine with us, considering the situation they were in. Doctor Gibb offers me some opioids for the pain, but in the circumstances, I tell him no. I'll keep a clear head despite the temptation to numb my senses of the multiple injuries, better to see what else today is going to throw at me.

'What did they say to you?' I ask her wearily while Gibb is rummaging in his bag for more white strips. She looks at me with tearful eyes. 'I'm just going to go back; they won't do anything else to Simon if I do. They've had Billie told to expect me back on Monday and the article's been cancelled, but I don't know what she'll make of this. I've not to tell anyone about this.' She is holding back something; that I can see.

'They are bastards.' She whispers. 'They mentioned my parents and sister, you know, just in the conversation; then they told me that they have deposited fifty thousand pounds into my bank account, just to ensure that my services, as they put it didn't go unrewarded. 'Bastards', she repeats, softly. I think to myself, they are not such bastards that you turned their fifty grand down; so much for your journalistic principles. She's just taken hush money to turn a blind eye to high-stakes drug dealing, Simon's torture and the minor problem that I have just stuck a dagger into the head of the businessman we were here to interview.

178

I have no words for her, so I shrug and let Doctor Gibb put whatever is left of his hellish cures on my punctured back; it must be about noon now and I ask Gibb how Simon was doing, although to be honest, it's for Emma's benefit; I couldn't give two fucks whether he lived or died at this point.

'Fine, under the circumstances, no lasting damage except the need for some dental work; this is not however within my purview.' Emma looks relieved. She asks him 'will he be able to come back with me to Inverness?'

He peers over to her 'If there is an urgent requirement to travel, there is no reason why not; however given the fact we have no access to x-ray equipment, I'd recommend keeping him here for a day or so, but it's unlikely that any serious problems would be encountered by moving him, carefully of course.' Emma nods and seems to be wondering whether to leave him here, I can't blame her for that. The door opens and John Allanton comes in. 'Emma, may I speak with you?' She stands and leaves, closing the door behind her. Gibb finishes and I stand, grimacing at the movement of my broken skin and the tension of the strips across the cuts. He closes his bag and with a curt goodbye and after I refuse his second offer of morphine for the pain, leaves me to the solitude of the library; my shirt has been taken away, so I'm starting to get cold and I see a tartan blanket on the back of one of the chairs, which I wrap around me and look out to the lawn. I hear a car starting up and pulling away and I know its Emma, leaving in the hire car without a goodbye. My shoulders sag as I'm here alone now waiting for god knows what to happen; they can't mean to kill me surely, if they are letting Emma go, unless she's been paid to forget about me too; that doesn't make sense so I decide to just keep going along with it, as if any other choices were open.

John Allanton comes in, my bag from the car with him which he hands to me. We look at each other and he smiles. 'I've imagined doing what you did, many times.' I don't understand what he means; then I get it, he is talking about killing Galloglas. 'You did me a great favour doing that, father was perhaps coming round but I don't know if loyalty would get the better of him with Galloglas. He's been a complete liability since we got here but now, we'll deal with the estate and keep going for the foreseeable.' Again, I find myself not giving a fuck about the estate or his father's faith in that murderous lunatic I spent part of the morning grappling with.

'Here, put some clothes on; we need to speak, upstairs when you are ready. Lunch too, if you've an appetite.' I most certainly have, despite recently having stabbed someone to death and sustained copious injuries in the process. I start to get changed and he helpfully guides my arms into the sleeves of the shirt before leaving me to follow him once ready; I walk into the hall, which is sparkling clean and no sign of a drop of blood or glass. The table is gone and there's a gap on the wall where the sgian-dubh case was; other than that, it is business as usual. There's a small bathroom under the stairs, just five paces from where Galloglas breathed his last, so I go I and wash my face and hands, already wiped by Gibbs but to try and get the antiseptic stench away. I take the stairs slowly to make sure the skin on my back isn't moved, which is causing me to regret my decision to turn down the offer of painkillers. Not sure where I'm going, I wander along the mahogany-lined corridor until I see the door to the ante-room; I go in and see the two secretaries, who, for the first time, nod at me, one of them with a grin. I nod back at them and knock on the office door, entering on John Allantons' invitation.

They are waiting in the room and a tray of sandwiches sits on Galloglas beautiful desk; Sir Mathieson beckons me to join them and we start on the food, his son pouring coffees while we eat. I don't know how the hell I can be hungry after what I've done this morning, but hey, I am, so I dig in.

Sir Mathieson smiles at me. 'I was always hungry after a barney. We used to head straight to the mess, soon as we'd sorted what we had to do and cleaned up; drink too, the best one you ever get is after a scrape. Some chaps couldn't you know; weren't suited to it, thought too much about it. That's one of the things that separate them from us, the ability to keep going.' He takes a bite of sandwich and keeps chatting like we're talking about a game of golf, for god's sake.

'I mean, correct me if I'm wrong – you aren't particularly concerned about Galloglas, or Simon, or even Emma?' I realise that he's more or less correct. I have little, or more exactly, no emotions towards any of them; none. He looks into my eyes; smiles at me, intuiting that he's read me correctly, better than I knew myself. I still don't know where he's going but I don't seem in any immediate danger, although that could still change.

He goes on. 'It's not a bad thing, quite the opposite; some would call it a lack of empathy or consideration, and it may well be that, but it does potentially equip you to participate in our line of business. Tell me, Adam, are you an ambitious man?' I'm acutely aware that both of the Allantons are staring at me, serious now.

I'm not sure what they want from me, so I reckon that I'll just be honest, if he can read me as well he seems to, there's no point otherwise. 'No.' I tell him. 'That's not to say I don't want to do well. We never had any money when I was growing up, so I suppose I don't want to spend my life being poor; I guess that's why I moved to London, you know a job, get on the ladder.' I am babbling I suppose, but there's truth in my words, whether I've thought much about it before or not. 'I don't think I'm cut out to be a journalist either; this is my first assignment and I've no desire for another one, so I guess I'm out of work.'

'Well then' said Sir Mathieson, 'there are some things I'd like to discuss with you.'

Chapter Twenty Seven

Simon's Recovery

The last few hours were a haze for Simon; he'd wakened up in that B&B staring into the eyes of one of those fuckers from the house then nothing. He'd then wakened again up in the back of their car, presumably, yet again with those plastic clip ties around his arms, then he saw his chance to run, knowing that to stay would be a very, bad thing. He took his chance when they thought he was knackered, running away, not sure where but away, towards someone who might help.

His escape ended with the realisation that the low stone wall concealed not a path, but a straight drop and then a steep incline spattered with tree stumps. He didn't remember anything else but the feeling of pain as the fall impacted his already pummelled frame and then, again, darkness. Then, a doctor or something gave him a check over, light shone in his eyes and a stab in the arm, a needle and off again he went.

Simon woke in a bedroom, on a bed and still achingly alive; he had pyjamas on, covering a number of plasters and bandages, splints on two of his fingers and his arm attached to an intravenous drip. This suggested to him that some time may have passed since his flight over the wall and now; how long, he had no way of knowing except that he had some more beard growth on his chin, albeit wispier than before. He lay back; his head thumping like the insides had been broken into pieces and put back together in the wrong shape. He looked around the room, just a normal bedroom, not a hospital; the curtains were closed and he couldn't get out of bed; there was a pipe coming out of his cock which was painful too, but there was no way he was pulling that out.

He tried to call but his voice just made a gargling croak, so he managed to get some water into a glass from a jug beside the bed; spilling a fair bit but got some in without making the glass fall. He slurped at the water, the relief of the liquid on his parched throat spoiled by the pain of the cold on the gaps where his teeth so recently resided. As the pain receded, he croaked for help, hearing the movement of a chair outside the door. Simon whined audibly as the door was opened by McGowan, who shared Simon's medical feature of having bandages on his head and one of his hands.

He looked at Simon and without acknowledgement, closed the door as he left to fetch his master; minutes later, a grey-haired gentleman stood looking at Simon, not a friendly look either.

'So, you're the troublemaker. Trouble indeed seems to follow you from place to place; you've given me no end of bother.' Sir Mathieson stood at the foot of his bed, looking circumspectly at the recumbent Simon.

'Shorry' was all that Simon could offer back, searching the older man's face for a clue as to whether he intended further harm to him. He hoped that the sign that they'd kept him alive thus far was an indication that they were not planning to kill him.

'Sorry indeed, young man. You almost killed my batman there; got himself singed badly when he got back and you'd left the gas on. We'll have the builders in for a few days to fix the kitchen and the windows, but no matter, it'll be sorted in due course. Don't know what you were thinking but our fault for letting you out, I suppose. Lessons learned.' His clipped, polite tones disconcerted Simon, who had no idea what was going on. He was also, perhaps for good reason, even more scared of this elderly gentleman than even those he'd met before.

'We are left with something of a quandary with you, however. We haven't had a chance to speak to you, not properly; I'd like to do that once you're feeling better. Is that alright?' Simon nodded, his tears dripping down his nose and onto the bed.

'Well, let's hope your recovery continues and if all is well, you can look forward to returning home. Goodbye, for now, Simon.' Simon nodded, filling his catheter warmly and involuntarily.

It was another three days before Simon was removed from the room; a nurse, who had visited intermittently since he had woken, had removed his various protuberances and pronounced him fit to be moved. Unsteady at first, he soon managed to walk, albeit hunched forwards against the pain of his spinal and rib injuries; heavily laden with whatever opiates he'd been given, the worst of his agonies were blunted, at least in the physical sense. Mentally, Simon was all over the place; his plan for entering the narcotics business long forgotten, his self-esteem diminished and his energy depleted, he was more or less content to be washed along with whatever plans they had for him. Thoughts of escape were gone too, his trek across the moors to Inverannan unrepeatable in his condition.

Simon was also deeply unsettled by what they intended to do with him; although he didn't know who they were, he supposed that they still could perceive him a threat to their anonymity, knowing as he did their location and faces. He thought about what to say when they spoke to him again, how he would assure them of his silence and that they'd never, ever hear from him again if set free. He wept more than once at the memory of his naivety, walking into their lair with a Press ID, asking for a few kilos of coke to sell on, without as much a down-payment; what a fool he was and how he'd suffered for it.

Still, he was alive and being cared for, instead of being buried in some remote field in the highlands of Scotland. They wouldn't do all this just to do away with him, he knew; rather, he was trying to figure out what their motivation was, what they wanted of him now. He wondered what Billie at The Insider knew, he hadn't called for perhaps a fortnight and maybe she would be trying to find him; maybe Emma and the Scottish guy had managed to call the Police and they were looking for him, right now. Or, he thought more likely; Emma and he had given up on Simon and went back to London, leaving him in the hands of these scoundrels. Nothing made much sense to Simon about this, so when the nurse took the catheter out and the IV drip afterwards, he knew that he'd soon be having the discussion which would determine his future.

It was a few hours after she had left, taking all the medical kit with her; the scorched McGowan brought him food, as usual, the tray beside him with no chat and the distinct feeling that he harboured a major grudge at Simon for his stunt with the gas leak. He didn't know that Sir Mathieson had specifically told McGowan not to kill Simon for what he had done, despite McGowan's initial remonstrations to the contrary. McGowan was still considering this, as the explosion had blown him off his feet, could have killed him if he'd been any closer; the burns had taken some of the hair from his head and he doubted the scars on his hands would ever heal. Several people had died at McGowan's hands for less, far less; it would be his pleasure to add Simon to the list, perhaps even the last name he'd add, now that he was old and back in the UK. However, military obedience ran deep with him and he did not want to initiate a falling-out with his officer over a wee shite like

Simon Conner. Still, there's more than one way to skin a rabbit, as he was fond of saying.

When the door opened eventually, Simon was again faced with the elder Allanton; he stood across from him, seemingly interrupting a busy schedule doing god knows what to settle Simon's future.

'How are you Simon?' he began brusquely.

'Fine, thanksh; I jusht want to go home now, pleashe.' Cards on the table straight away thought Sir Mathieson. Simon's facial injuries had improved, the swelling brought down by the passing of time and the ministrations of the private nurse, a wife of one of the transportation men who could be relied upon in exchange for a considerable remuneration. Simon had cost Sir Mathieson quite a lot of money over the past week with the doctor, nurse, builders and tips to the Inverannan men to keep quiet, although that particular reward was also for their support in the invisible extraction of Galloglas' carcass.

Sir Mathieson had wondered whether to submit to his son and McGowan on this one; however the strategy of containment appeared best for the other two and, given the impact it would have otherwise placed on those successful resolutions, he thought it best to allow Simon to continue his existence. Despite the expense, he knew it was the right thing to do, particularly as the subject, Simon, appeared to have no criminal background if one excludes his stupidity as such.

He embarked on the explanation of his proposal. 'Simon, I wish to discuss the forthcoming period of time. I have a proposal for you, which I believe may be considered reparation for your – injuries - and represent a generous payment, for which all you have to do is to never disclose anything relating to our business here; nor shall you discuss what transpired here or attempt to identify either myself or any of my colleagues. You will not discuss this with anyone at your employer, other than to tell them that you had a mountaineering accident or some similar explanation for your current disablement. Is that clear?'

Simon nodded, not fully taking in the exact words of Sir Mathieson, but rather the general theme; no mention of the drug business here or anything about these awful people; as if he would.

'In addition, we will monitor you indefinitely, including your online activity; we have this situation in place and will extend it to include your workplace and home, although to warn you, I will consider any leaking of information, regardless of specific evidence, to have emanated from you.'

This didn't seem fair to Simon but he was hardly in a place to argue terms, so again he nodded.

'You have no close relatives it appears so our typical methods of leverage are solely focused on you. You must understand that whatever tribulations you have suffered recently will be as nothing compared to what we will do to you if you cross us, believe this.'

Sir Mathieson then relaxed a shade and bestowed a small smile upon Simon; he opened his hands before he spoke, to better appear honest and that he could be trusted. 'Simon, we will place a large amount of money – twenty thousand pounds – into your account. We will also clear the quite astonishing levels of credit card debt you have somehow accrued; this, in addition to your continued existence, shall be the last interaction we have with you. Do we have a concord?' He held out his hand, which Simon shook, even though the splint on his fingers prevented a firm grip.

'Very well; we will travel back to London tomorrow, in separate vehicles of course. We have business there, however, I have no doubt you would prefer the comfort of a car rather than public transport.'

'Shanks' said Simon.

☐

Chapter Twenty Eight

Simon's Homecoming

The next morning, early, Simon thanked the silent McGowan for bringing him breakfast, poached eggs and toast; he ate quickly and dressed slowly, taking a while to manoeuvre the clothes he'd been given onto his fragile frame and leaving his shirt buttons undone over the baggy t-shirt. His bag was in his room from when he wakened, all there including his laptop and phone; he looked out of the window, but didn't recognise the driveway; it certainly wasn't the house he'd stayed at before. Who cares, thought Simon, I'll be in London soon, for once with money and maybe try to forget all about this, as you do after some trauma – like soldiers get, he thought.

McGowan rattled his door and motioned him with a jerk of his thumb to follow him; Simon gathered up his jacket and bag, taking a look to make sure he'd got everything and followed the sturdy fellow downstairs, both limping for different reasons. The two awful men who'd tortured him were in the front of the black Range Rover; Simon stopped for a moment, thinking it a trap, but they could have killed him anytime without the need for the rigmarole of medical care and release, he hoped.

McGowan took his jacket and bag from him, placing them in the boot; Simon got into the back of the car without a word and then gradually began to calm his thumping heart as the vehicle headed out through a barrier and left, heading in what he hoped was the direction of London

He didn't know how long it would take, but at least he was going home. Eventually, they reached the central belt, passing Stirling and Glasgow. He wondered if the two men were going to share the long drive and travel through the day and into the evening to their destination; they did, although he could barely tell them apart, thinking of them as twins of evil. He fell asleep a couple of times, the painkillers he'd been given now wearing off but the physical damage making him weak and tired, like a hangover that wouldn't go away.

Past signs for Liverpool then Birmingham, getting along the interminable distance from the very north of Scotland to the wonderful London, thought Simon; he'd never go back, Watford would be as far north as he'd ever travel in that direction. He'd tell Billie that he wanted to stay in London unless there were jobs in Dorset maybe, or over to Brighton, he quite liked it there.

The urban sprawl was beside them now; he looked out at Brent Cross as they hit the outskirts of his home city as darkness spread over and the lights were everywhere, the gleaming wonderful fantastic city full of people and policemen and everything Simon just wanted to be in the middle of. He felt happy now, even his mouth didn't bother him so much; he'd get painkillers from the chemist and sleep for a few days at home. They took a while to get through the traffic, didn't seem to like driving in London, the guy swore and Simon felt like telling him to soak it up, London is wonderful; but he didn't.

They stopped outside Simon's flat, a last silent message that they knew everything about him; it didn't matter to Simon. He checked himself from giving them a caustic, cutting comment as he stepped out of the car, firstly as he didn't want to antagonise them and secondly as he couldn't think of one. Retrieving his jacket and bag, he stood watching as the four-wheel drive pulled away as soon as he'd closed the boot. He stretched his back and put on his jacket; his keys were in the rucksack and he opened the communal door, which opened to the stairs to his second-floor apartment.

Simon limped upstairs, the inertia of the twelve-hour trip making him stiffer than he was when he left and the need to piss almost crippling him.

He reached into his jacket to get his keys, finding them and a small plastic bag, secured at the middle with sellotape; Putting it back in his pocket, Simon went inside to the toilet and relieved himself, although it stung badly as the result of his catheter. After cleaning his hands and washing his face, he went back into the lounge, putting the heating on as he went; he took the bag of powder out of his jacket and examined it. Coke, if he wasn't mistaken; he opened the bag and took a few particles on the nail of his pinkie finger to try. The instant numbness told him it was good stuff; it had been a long, miserable time since he'd last had some, so he decided to end the evening with the clarity of thought and the much-needed energy that the Charlie would give him.

Drizzling some of the fine powder onto the glass coffee table, he carefully took one of his now-cleared credit cards from his wallet and chopped it into the most perfect line. He had a lovely decorative pewter straw he kept on the table for just this purpose and picked it up, looking inside to make sure it was clean and clear. Putting it into his favoured nostril, Simon sucked the coke in one determined draught, the hit immediate as his sinuses took the swooshing impact. He sat back on the sofa, the coke filling him with the confidence and life that had been so absent these past days. His mind suddenly went to Miles, his friend who had tricked him as they sat there, on that very sofa; he'd set all this in motion and Simon felt he'd have killed him, if he'd not died already.

Simons nose tickled, then bled; he felt his neck twitching. His head jerked back and he felt like he was going to be sick; foam came up from his throat, choking him while his body convulsed. He fell back onto the sofa, his body going into fit after fit, Simon trying to breathe but air wouldn't come in. His throat closed completely and with it, Simon's life ended.

Back in the house near Inverannan, Benny McGowan sat in a chair at the side of an old iron range; he had finished putting the cream from the doctor on his burns and was sitting down to finish a bottle of malt whisky that his employer had left him. He wondered if that wee shite had sniffed his coke yet, one of the purest grades they had ever imported; he'd maybe have a few minutes to enjoy his hit before the strychnine took. He'd told Sir Mathieson's accountant fella not to bother putting any money into Simon's account, or clearing his cards; a waste of money all round and not deserved anyway. McGowan knew Simon's type; one night, sometime, he'd get full of drink or drugs and tell people about them, of that he was sure. Sir Mathieson was a good judge of character, generally, but on the occasions when his judgement was wrong over the years, Benny was the very fellow to fix things for him. He raised his glass to the glowing coals and sipped the malt, a rare smile playing on his lips.

☐

Chapter Twenty Nine

Mharisaig

I've been back in Mharisaig for nearly two weeks, my cuts mostly healed and my face back to whatever standard it had been at previously. Apart from a couple of nights in the pub with various redoubtable locals, I've spent the time in solitude, mostly, hacking the garden of my cottage back in preparation for the coming winter and to give me a decent start if, or when I am back in the spring of next year.

The break has done me good, I feel; my recognition that I'm a little bit different had developed into an understanding and even some research on my behalf. A couple of evenings online revealed that my thought patterns were not so unusual, either in the world of criminality or the world of business; maybe ideal for a life in criminal business, then.

The day before I plan to leave is one of those rare highland days when the world glows red with the light of autumn and the ochre tinge of the leaves covers roads and grass alike with fading loveliness. I decide to go for a run, the better to try and reconnect with fitness and enjoy the feeling of running, fast and pure; my trainers are the worse for wear, but I figure I'll use them until they fall apart and buy new ones in Glasgow or London when I leave. So, I'm out and onto the road, stretching and forcing my joints to move and avoid a strain; I head off, turning right and into the village; I'm enjoying the feeling of the fresh air on my face, my hair needing cut is flowing as I run past the first street, where an Alsatian barks from behind a gate, startled by my appearance and doing his guard-dog duties.

Five minutes later, I turn left onto the dirt track towards the ruined cottage, which as Niall told me, is even worse than I remember; the walls have come down a little and everything burnable is charred or gone. I look inside, there are rusty beer cans in a corner and bottles of cheap, fortified wine; I couldn't ever drink that stuff, it was too nasty even for my palate back then. I look back at the track and there's someone jogging towards me, a woman dressed in dark running Lycra; she gets nearer and I see that it's Anna, my friend from long ago.

190

'Bloody hell, what's all this?' she smiles. 'I heard you were back to haunt Mharisaig, but you only believe in ghosts when you see one yourself.'

I grin back at her. 'Yeah, yeah, I know. I've been called "The Lost Boy", "The Seldom Seen Kid" and a few more rude ones since I got back, so being called a ghost isn't the worst. How are you, you look great?'

'All good, heading off next week back to uni, I'm at Abertay in case you had forgotten', which I had; if I'd ever known.

'Cool. How is it there?'

'It's fine, the course is more hard work than I wanted but I'm too far into my student loan to chuck it now.' I nod my understanding, not mentioning that I didn't take a loan, it tends to annoy people when I tell them. Even a psychopath has feelings, I think to myself.

'Fancy a drink later?' I hear myself saying; apparently, my mouth has become disconnected from my brain again.

She looks at me, hesitates and nods. 'Yeah, all right; meet you in the pub at eight?' I smile back at her and she runs off, to the right and along a sheep track that winds back to the village, about a mile round.

I start running again, driving myself forward in an extended sprint until I am half a mile away, panting with the effort and wondering why the hell I'd asked Anna for a drink. I had a bus to catch on Friday morning and god knows what lay ahead, so socialising or adding complications wasn't really part of the plan. I jog back the way I came, vowing just to have a couple of beers and go home early; let's see how that works out, the devil on my shoulder tells me.

After showering and getting into a tracksuit, I do one of the last things on my to-do list, ready for leaving. I throw all the clothes that don't fit me any more into a black bin bag; a tattered load of shite that I'd be embarrassed to take to a charity shop. All the underpants and socks go too, giving me a laugh as I find the Marvel Avengers boxers which I had to avoid wearing to school on days where we had PE.

That complete, my remaining wardrobe consists of one pair of jeans, two t-shirts and a cardigan which was my dad's, before middle-aged spread took its' final toll and it became a hand-me-down. I have the rest of my stuff in London, so as long as I left

191

one set of clothes here, I'd be fine. My old shoes didn't fit either, so they go from the cupboard into the black bin bag too; my adolescent gear takes just under ten minutes to dispose of. I wander into my parent's bedroom, for the first time since I got back. It was chillier than the rest of the house and I realise that they've left the window open slightly, perhaps to let the room air; there's a brown funerary layer of dead midges on the window sill, which I wipe into a bag using a rag from the upstairs toilet cupboard. From here, I can look out the front to the still-untidy front garden, small but as unkempt with trailing jagged weeds and dandelions. Fuck it, I did the back garden but this one can wait for next year, I think. I close the window and leave the room, no emotion at all.

I set down to the laptop and write my piece on Forster; I'd arranged to get this to Billie and been putting it off, although the deadline wasn't near she wanted it complete and submitted. I had done a module on project management at university, so after sending the file to Billie, I spend an hour or so browsing through sample spreadsheets, drawn to the simpler versions which suited my linear mind. I'll maybe use this myself, I think to myself, wondering how the Allantons organised their business; the risk of someone finding a document and using it as part of a prosecution may be an issue but still, I guess they have to manage things, after all.

The rest of the day I just chill out, eating the last of the food, no point leaving anything to rot in the fridge, although I do childishly ponder on leaving a meat pie there to see what it would be like when I got back. I fall asleep until about 7pm and after a shower, I'm ready for the pub; I walk down there, knowing that Niall and others will be there already so maybe Anna will just join the group and it won't look like we're there on a date or anything. I find it difficult to judge these things; maybe it's just a drink, so I'll see how it develops and don't assume she's interested in me.

It's just gone 8pm when I open the bar door and as expected, Niall and four or five others are there too, I presume the two young women sitting beside them are girlfriends and this is confirmed when I'm introduced. I get a bottle of sour faux-German beer and settle beside them and soon the banter gets going. Ruaridh has got back from an eventful stag-do in Magaluf with his pals from college, so I wince at the stories and laugh at others. The bar is pretty full by 9pm when Anna comes in, looking absolutely beautiful and perhaps here's finding that I do have some emotions left after all. I rise and give her a hug, taking her to the bar for a drink and bloody hell, I'm acting like it is a date; I didn't mean to do this, meant to play it cool and distant, but here I am and I'm not.

We sit back down after I eject one of the guys from my seat he casually attempted to pinch while I was at the bar. Anna tells of her delay, her family a constant source of chaotic complexity, all cousins and broken down cars and dramas and I can't take my eyes off of her. The night rolls through another few hours of laughing and talking and drinking, then we're in my house and Anna is, really beautiful.

I wake early but she's gone; must have left when I fell asleep, I guess. There's a note on the mirror, tucked under the wooden frame at the top. She tells me she's sorry to leave me like this but her mum cracks up if she's not back; there's a mobile number and an x so I guess we're cool.

After my shower, I stuff the laptop in my bag and check I've not left any electrical stuff on; my head is fine, I don't have a hangover and I suppose this is down to me eating the entire contents of the fridge before I had a drink. The morning sun-warmed mist rises in the village like wraiths, their arms reaching from the fields and gathering the houses in an eerie embrace; it's that strange time of day in Scotland when the icy chill of night metamorphoses into a warm morning, the day to come like a last offering of autumn heat.

Back at the bus stop, the journey starts with the bus back to Fort William; I change there and take the next one all the way to Glasgow, Buchanan Street station vibrant with the flowing hordes of the city. I lunch in a café near Merchant City and buy some trainers in Greaves Sports on the way back to Argyle Street Station, where my train for London awaits.

It's a quick journey down, getting there for the end of the rush hour; I jump on the tube connection and soon I'm back in my shared flat with some M&S sandwiches for my dinner. One of the flatmates says hi as I walk past the kitchen, so I walk back and we have a quick chat; I can't remember his name, but it doesn't matter. He gets me a couple of letters which came for me, one hand delivered, no stamp.

I head up to my room, crash out for an hour after the journey, all day travelling – sitting down all the time but still tiring. The letters are just bank stuff, except the hand-delivered one; it's from Sir Mathieson, or MA as the signature indicates. I'd texted John to confirm my return when I was in the café in Glasgow, so I guess this was dropped off after that. He wants me to meet him at an address in the south bank on Monday at 9am; seems I'm starting a job with them after all.

☐

EPILOGUE

It's been fourteen months since I got back from the Inverannan assignment; it's been an interesting experience, working for John. His father announced his retirement in a meeting the afternoon I started work with them, as we sat at a long polished metal table in a boardroom of an angularly spectacular building overlooking the south bank of the Thames.

My interview, although I could hardly it call it that, was brief and to the point; I was to support a recently promoted interim representative called Thomas Birton aka Masby, now responsible for monitoring and coordinating the supply chain across the UK, mainly the high-population cities. It didn't sound too complicated, perhaps their military thing kept it simple. They worked in cell structures, with only one person other than the Allantons knowing the full picture, that person being Birton and soon his assistant, me. I couldn't believe at the time that they were putting me, a soon-to-be former journalist, in this position but they did just that. They also reminded me of the impact of any betrayal and after that, told me the financial rewards, which started with a flat between Knightsbridge and Hyde Park; I must have looked like bewildered, I remember John whispering to me 'it's a nice one; used to be my London crash pad.'

After that, we'd had lunch and I'd been introduced to Masby; the meeting they were having immediately after that was with some of the Allanton family, so I kicked my heels in a waiting room for an hour with Masby. They brought us back in after that and Sir Mathieson told us that he was retiring and that John would take the reins, everything else continuing as normal.

He spoke directly to Masby. 'You, Thomas, are now in a key role in the business. Do not let me down.' His eyes dark as coal, the older man still a force even as he stepped out of the role he'd held for so long.

Masby assured him that he was the man for the job; he looked like it too, another ex-military guy but one who had gone straight into narcotics before joining Allanton. We'd shook hands and left them to the rest of their day, which looked like they were spending it with the rest of the more prominent figures in the business, as yet unseen by me.

I was handed an attaché case by the receptionist which I didn't open yet; I and Masby went into a meeting room where he briefed me fairly enthusiastically on his thoughts on the direction of the job. Fuck me, I thought, he's a Galloglas in the making, this one. We got on fine though, starting work together the next day, in the afternoon after I resigned from The Insider; Billie spoke to me after I called to let them know, annoyed that I was bailing out but then more understanding after I told her that I'd made a mistake, journalism wasn't for me. She tried to ask me again about Inverannan, but I just told her that everything had gone well, they seemed to be in the middle of replacing Galloglas so the story was pointless and we all got paid, so no harm done.

The only other time I spoke with Billie was when she called me to tell me the arrangements for Simon's funeral, his body having been found by one of his friends after a number of days lying on the sofa; the assumption by the Police was that the coke had been cut by someone who didn't know what they'd been doing, too much strychnine put in or put in by mistake, these guys aren't trained chemists and the cops see this stuff cut with everything from talcum powder to arsenic and all points between. I spoke to Emma after that, the last chat we'd have, agreeing that the chapter was over; at least for her.

I told John Allanton in person just after I heard that Simon had died; he nodded and shrugged, showing me that he already knew. I still don't know exactly what happened but, in their place, I'd have done the same. John told me a few weeks later that Galloglas body had been found in the south side of Belize City; apparently murdered some time before by persons unknown, the victim of a robbery while there on holiday. It was on the Belize news, briefly and not in the UK at all.

The attaché case they gave me at Reception after our first meeting contained a set of keys and some paperwork with an address for the apartment, along with some cash and an offer of employment in a property business. I'd left the old flat that night, there being no point in staying; the new apartment was impressive, part of the Allanton Property portfolio and two streets down from Hyde Park. I enjoy living here and although I am away much of time, I do my best to return here at night, even if it's very late. It's secure, has a 24-hour presence at the door and lets me walk to the theatres and restaurants, my circle of friends restricted but generally able to find company when I need it.

I enjoyed working with Masby for a month or just over, until I shot him dead in a house just outside Manchester; John agreed with me that his ambitions were too similar to Galloglas to even countenance proceeding with his frankly hare-brained schemes. In preparation, I had assessed the loyalty of his acolytes, most of who either disliked him intensely or tolerated him while he worked as their superior. Tellingly, he had a predilection for domestic abuse which neither I nor John could forgive; the two men who he did count as friends were despatched at the same time as Masby, in a separate location. We replicated something akin to the Allantons' highland disposal method, so useful for Masby's predecessor, so John told me. The management team in each location now seems tightly controlled and on a more professional footing; I visit them less frequently than my predecessors but am more forensic when I do. White had done the accounting side of things well, however, this was a skill I couldn't be arsed learning, so each city chief is solely responsible for the numbers now, in a standard format and checked by me. I've made them dress like the businessmen they are too, those at the top anyway, each with their cover businesses now more like legitimate organisations; engineering firms instead of taxi companies, that sort of thing.

The business is doing well, I feel I have a talent for reading people's honesty, perhaps the result of my journalistic training; John stays at home for most of the time now and we have introduced a new level of management for the transportation of product, neither of us willing to risk being in the presence of the incriminating merchandise, after all. His father's insistence that John transfer the high-volume product at Inverannan was one of his last lessons to him; if the net closes, don't be standing right in it. John is a genius at the property business too, having bought a series of high-cost apartments across London over the past few years and having them renovated to hyper-specification, selling to whatever oligarch wants to give us their tens of millions, the money nice and clean and back to somewhere pleasantly tax-light. That bubble is bursting a little now but John sold when the prices were at their highest, and I watch him and learn, after all.

Anna has been down here a couple of times too, at first surprised at my high-flying situation but then understanding that since the property business is so lucrative, why would I waste my time in investigative journalism. We go out on the town when she visits and you know, maybe I need to close that one down too. Prying eyes and all that, best avoided.

Printed in Great Britain
by Amazon